Between Oceans

Crooks, Creeps, and Crazies on the Isthmus

Roan St. John

The locations, characters, and events portrayed in this book are fictitious and solely the creation of the author's imagination. Any similarity to real persons, living or dead, is purely coincidental and not intended by the author.

To protect the privacy of certain individuals, names and identifying details or information have been changed.

ISBN-9798489804738

Printed in the United States of America

The path to Paradise begins in hell.
Dante Alighieri

Lies and hypocrisy are part of daily living in Paradise. With a few exceptions, Paradise is the same as any other place.
"Expats in Wonderland"

]

The Isthmus

On that narrow strip of land known as the Isthmus of Panama lies a flyspeck of a country called Malpaís. Sandwiched like a piece of dried bologna between Guatemala, Honduras, and El Salvador, it was roughly the size of Delaware, but with half the population. Its terrain was so inhospitable that none of the bordering countries would claim it. Even migrating animals from South America veered away, depriving Malpaís of prey for food and reducing its inhabitants to a diet of *camotes* and whatever could be harvested from the sea.

According to legend, Malpaís was settled by survivors of a shipwreck washed ashore when their vessel, on its way to Costa Rica, was destroyed in a hurricane. To endure such hostile territory, they developed unique survival skills, including an instinctive distrust of outsiders. Quite content to be isolated, this tiny country was ignored by Central America (and the rest of the world) for three hundred years. Its insignificance is best exemplified by the blank area in the shape of Malpaís on the IMF map, giving it the inimitable distinction of being the only Latin American country not indebted to them or the World Bank. It also had no Army, Navy, Air Force, Coast Guard, or Marines. Some even joked that it had no latitude or longitude. On top of that, it was virtually inaccessible. There was one small port, but all the roads in the neighboring countries ended at the borders. Who in their right mind would invade this place?

And then the inevitable happened.

A motley group of out-on-parole internet scammers, Ponzi schemers, and failed emu ranchers from Florida formed a land development company. Their grandiose concept, hatched during a stint in a federal prison for bilking gullible investors out of twenty million dollars, was to buy dirt-cheap land in a place nobody had heard of and market it as the last undiscovered Paradise. Their glitzy ad campaigns targeted those who missed land booms in Hawaii, Malibu, the Maya Riviera, and Costa Rica. Poor Malpaís, tragically trapped somewhere in the Middle Ages, was suddenly catapulted into the twenty-first century. And with the completion of its first airport in 2000, it was finally possible to lure investors to the pristine beaches and the verdant valleys that lay between its perfect volcanoes. It was not surprising that a "diverse" assortment of characters took the bait: expats enchanted by the concept of owning a piece of Paradise and the usual crooks, creeps, and crazies looking for virgin territories to exploit. We all know what happens to Paradise then. That's right. You can kiss it *adios*. This is a tale of how that happened.

Chapter 1

It was the kind of day that made Maya nostalgic for the Green Season in Malpaís. She particularly missed how clouds of steam rose from the blistering concrete after a brief shower filling the air with the scent of petrichor. Alas, there was no rain in the forecast for Aix-en-Provence for the next week, only more of this oppressive heat.

She parked her car across the street from Boulangerie Fleur and that's when she saw him lurking in the shade of the same plane tree as the previous Monday. Perhaps, if she hadn't been distracted by the news that her best friend had stage four cancer, she might have paid more attention to him then. Instead, she walked past him after only a cursory glance. Today, however, he stood in the dappled sunbeams riddling through the boughs, creating an alluring image that was hard to ignore. He had an air of refinement with his limber stance, dark hair, prominent cheekbones, and dangerously cold eyes the color of amber which he squinted in her direction before looking down at his phone. The *boulangerie*, located on a narrow, dead-end street made it unlikely he would be there by accident two Mondays in a row. And that's why his presence unsettled her.

During the three years she lived in Aix, she had not seen him in any of the bars or restaurants frequented by expats. Perchance he had come to see the lavender fields in bloom; it was the height of the season after all. Problem was, he didn't look the type to be tromping along dusty paths in a perfectly starched white shirt, gray slacks, and Gucci loafers with no socks. She branded him Ivy League and snobbish because of the arrogant smile on his face. Even if she was wrong about those things, his appearance didn't augur well, and she was relieved to see he was gone when she exited the *boulangerie*.

She drove up the hill to her farm, ruminating the entire way about how long he had been following her. Or had her normally over-active imagination gone off the rails? As she aimed the remote control at her iron gate, she noticed a sliver of white protruding from the wrought iron latch. She stepped out of the car, plucked the card, and knew instantly it belonged to the stalker outside the *boulangerie*. William Balthazar Hastings. *Yep, that would be him – a snooty name to match his snooty attitude.* Scribbled on the back of the fine linen stock was a Washington, D.C. phone number. *Here we go*, she thought to herself. Tossing the card onto the passenger's seat, she accelerated up the driveway to the house and pulled into the *porte-cochère* where she was greeted by her gardener Louis.

Holding a large bouquet of freshly cut lavender, he

said, "*Alors*, you had a caller after you left for town. By the time I got to the gate, he disappeared."

"Yes, I know, Louis. He left a card. Have you ever seen him before?"

"No, *pas du tout*," he shrugged, shaking his head back and forth.

"I'm having dinner in the village tonight, so please make sure to replace the burned-out light at the entrance.

"*Bien sûr*."

Her new life in Aix had been one of obscurity since moving to Inspector Vernier's farm. The first year was spent in solitude trying to put the events in Malpaís behind her. As her sorrow-soaked memories began to fade, she developed a routine, dull and repetitive, that consisted of going to town once a week for supplies, and the monthly dinner with other writers. Otherwise, her time was spent cloistered in her house writing or tending the lavender fields. It had been a peaceful respite from her turbulent marriage to Lucien Desmarais and its violent end.

This month's meeting of women writers was held at Le Môme, renown for the best local cuisine in Aix. Maya and one other woman lived here year-round, while the other four were summer residents. It was a welcome break from their monotonous routines as well as an opportunity to complain how writing wasn't the easy task everyone thought. More importantly, there was local gossip, on which both the village and expats thrived. They were seated at the outdoor patio at six p.m. and by ten they were well fed, slightly tipsy, and ready for bed. The streets were still bustling as Maya strolled towards her car three blocks away. It was a balmy night in Provence, the air redolent of basil, lavender, and lemon. She was a few meters from her old Citroën when she saw the silhouette of a man in a dimly lit doorway. *Him, again*! He looked up from his phone with the same smirk on his face he had this morning. She quickened her pace, keys held strategically to fend off a possible attack, and tried to get into the car before he approached.

"Ah! There you are," he said exuberantly, slipping the phone into his pocket.

"Don't come any closer. I have a panic button to summon the *gendarmes.*"

He thrust his empty hands in the air and took a few steps forward until he was bathed in the light cast from the streetlamp.

"You were outside the *boulangerie* last Monday and today, and you left the calling card in my gate."

"Guilty as charged," he laughed.

"Why?"

"I want to talk to you. You're a hard person to reach. Elusive. No social media. And you never answer your phone."

"What is it you want?"

Looking at his watch, he said, "It's not that late. Let's have a drink and I'll explain why I'm here. That bistro across the street is still open."

Maya glanced toward the restaurant and saw it bustling with patrons. She hesitated a few seconds, assessing him. *He looks harmless, but then so did Lucien Desmarais and Ted Bundy.* Finally, she conceded, "Okay, Skippy. One drink."

The *maître d'* escorted them to a table at the back of the

restaurant. In perfect French, William Balthazar Hastings ordered two glasses of Calvados.

"What makes you think I want Calvados?"

"Ah, well," he grinned, picking at a piece of non-existent lint on his shirt, "you ladies wolfed down enough food for ten people and quaffed three bottles of wine. A Calvados would be a good digestive. Now let me introduce myself. Properly."

"Don't bother. I know your name. Who are you is the big question." Maya leaned back in the wicker chair and crossed her arms over her chest. "Start talking."

William sighed, running his fingers through his hair. "They warned me about you," he said with resignation.

"Who?"

"My employer. Said getting you to cooperate would be a Sisyphean task, on par with herding cats."

Maya laughed. "Okay, William Balthazar Hastings, get to the point."

"You can call me Will. First, take a sip of that Calvados."

Maya raised the snifter to her lips. "That is tasty. Too much of this and I could go before a firing squad with a smile."

"Good. It'll make my job easier."

"And what is your job, Will?"

"To convince you to perform a service to my company."

She looked at him disdainfully. "Don't be coy. You mean *the* Company."

Will sat up straight, his golden eyes wide in surprise. "As a matter of fact, yes."

"Look, I quite like my peaceful, boring life on La Petite Ferme, and have less than zero interest getting entangled with a bunch of spooks."

Will cleared his throat, set his drink on the coaster, and rested his arms on the table. "Are you always on the attack? Couldn't you let down your defenses for five minutes? I'm no threat to you, but it's my misfortune to have been assigned the grim task of laying out our proposal. Maybe, I should have worn chainmail as someone suggested."

"That's almost funny, Will," Maya snorted, resuming her annoyed expression. "Could you please get to the point so I can go home and go to bed?"

Will studied her face. She had aged since the photos in her file were taken, but nonetheless, she was still a beautiful woman. Her shoulder-length auburn hair had glints of gold from the sun, and her green eyes were both intense and inquisitive, even a bit menacing. The few lines fanning out from her eyes added character, especially when she narrowed them, as she was doing now. He'd been warned. This was a woman who could break a man's heart as easily as she broke his balls.

Clearing his throat and finger combing his hair, he was buying time until he figured out how to explain why he was here without her becoming feral. "As you have probably surmised, I have been thoroughly briefed on your previous encounter with the Agency. The late Riggs Haywood filed copious reports, not only about your professional activities but also your relationships with Harry Langdon and Martin Wilson. The details of your cavorting with the leader of the new Nazi party to expose why he wanted his father's portrait were well documented. I think it's safe to say there's not much about you I don't know. In fact, it was Martin who suggested we contact you."

"Ah, yes, Martin. . . the master of stealth, deception, and betrayal. Then I am sure he also told you I don't like being told what to do or when to do it. I have a litany of reasons not to trust you or your employer. Surely, there's someone better suited for whatever *folie* you spooks have on your agenda this go-round."

Will heaved a sigh. "Ah, yes, your recalcitrance is legendary. However, what makes you an invaluable asset to us is your knowledge of Malpaís. As you probably know it went from an undiscovered piece of dirt to being one of the hottest spots in Central America. It was inevitable that an assortment of people would flock there."

She looked at him suspiciously. "And?"

"Since you left three years ago, it's become a hotbed of certain activities, some legal, but most not so much." He swept his hair back from his face and looked at her sternly.

"Let's hear the rest."

"Okay, I'll be perfectly frank. It's become a mess."

Maya looked confused. "I'm not sure how I could be of use to you."

"We need a person to assimilate into the local expat culture and become an information conduit, reporting back to us about anything or anyone that appears suspicious."

"You want me to gather intel on the expat community?" Maya snickered. "A group of people biding time in God's waiting room?

"Uh, yes," he laughed. "That is correct."

"I hate to break it to you, Skippy, but I was never part of the expat crowd. When Lucien was alive, we rarely socialized with them because we had so little in common. The few we did mingle with left when their investments tanked. The one close female friend I had went back to Spain. I knew a few others peripherally, but I haven't heard from any of them since I left. And besides, I'm not eager to go back there. Too many unpleasant memories for me."

"We understand that. But all we're asking is that you spend six months to a year there. You know the country and you still own a house there. Once we have enough information, you'll be free to return to Provence and resume your life here."

Swirling the remaining Calvados around the inside of the snifter, Maya pondered how best to respond. She left Malpaís - escaped would be more precise - because it represented the trauma and privations she had suffered during her marriage. Yes, it was a beautiful and magical place, and she loved the house she built, but she would rather put her face in hot oil than be confronted with memories of her experiences there. After a full minute of silence, she replied, "No! I don't *want* to do it, and I'm not *going* to do it. And that's my final answer."

Will leaned back in his chair and stroked his chin. "Okay, then. Now I must inform you that we have evidence that may motivate you to change your mind."

"Oh, you do, do you? I can't imagine anything changing my mind."

"We shall see," he said, a wicked sheen in his eyes. "Let's start with your late husband. His *liaisons dangereuses* got him killed. The local police couldn't have cared less about this case. One gringo more, one gringo less didn't matter to them. Fortunately, we were able to unearth a few details never part of the official investigation."

Maya furrowed her brow and focused on his eyes with lashes like a fringe of marabou and noticed that they shifted from gold to pale green when he had that smug expression. She didn't like where this was going.

"Several weeks after your husband's disappearance his cell phone was recovered. That allowed us to reconstruct his activities leading up to his disappearance."

Maya sputtered, nearly dropping the glass from her hand. *What the hell*? She bit the inside of her cheek to keep from revealing her shock.

"We also obtained security camera footage documenting his whereabouts the day before he vanished. Plus, the phone's location history proved that his phone was at Finca Azahar when the calls from his presumed captors were received. All the while he was seven miles away in San Pedro."

Everything around her began to spin.

Will pursed his lips and tilted his head. "According to our analyst, the first two calls went unanswered. The third call went to voice mail. Then both the message and call history were scrubbed. One could reasonably conclude that you facilitated his kidnapping whilst you safely escaped to Guatemala. Is that what happened, Maya?"

"You're out of your mind. I'm not listening to any more of this nonsense." Maya sprang up from the table and faced the door.

"I wouldn't do that if I were you. Now *sit down*!"

She froze, turned around, and slowly lowered herself into the chair.

"Let's assume for a second that's how it unfolded. Maybe you saw this as an opportunity. Were you having problems in your marriage? Did you want an easy way out? Unfortunately, it doesn't matter because if you scrubbed that phone, you're an accomplice. To kidnapping. *And* murder. The authorities in Malpaís might not care. However, I'm quite sure the insurance company would like their two million dollars back, with the option of prosecuting you for insurance fraud."

Her stomach clenched in a painful spasm.

"I applaud you, though. It was quite clever and for whatever reasons you did it, it allowed you to buy your little farm and reinvent yourself as a grieving widow without getting your hands dirty. So, you see, Maya, there are far worse consequences than doing a little favor for us."

Maya raised her hands to her face to avoid looking at Will. She took a deep breath, hardly able to believe what he just told her. How did Lucien's phone not wind up in the belly of some hungry crocodile along with him? Even in death, there was no escape from this man. She struggled to quell the impulse to get up and flee.

"I'm sure you find this very overwhelming. I suggest we call it a night and resume our conversation in a day or two." Her stricken face almost made him feel sorry for her. He stood up, pulled some euros from his pocket, laid them on the table, and continued in a conciliatory tone, "You have my number. I can come to your farm or meet you in Aix. Your choice. *Bonne nuit* and drive safely," he said, touching her lightly on her shoulder before leaving the bistro.

Chapter 2

A glaring shaft of Provençal sun aroused Maya to a waking state. The two or three hours of sleep she managed to get were punctuated by nightmares, along with intermittent waves of paranoia and fear, causing her to spend most of the night in a state of torpor as she processed the day's events in a continual loop.

It started out like any other Monday. Coffee on the terrace with Louis, a quick run to the *Poste*, the *charcuterie*, then Boulangerie Fleur, Aix's best kept secret. The first time she saw Will, she assumed he was a tourist seeking relief from the heat under the towering trees that lined both sides of the street. Now, his second appearance had taken on a treacherous importance making Maya wonder for how long had he been following her? Was it just the last week? Longer? She had no way of knowing.

After Lucien's disappearance and until his death was confirmed eight months later, Maya had been extra cautious about who she talked to or interacted with. Her darkest secret was guarded, buried deep within the recesses of her consciousness. She didn't even tell Liz what she had done. After Liz educated her on the danger of narcissists and sociopaths, along with the sordid tales Inspector Vernier told her about Lucien's past, including the suspicious deaths of two of his former lovers, she feared for her life. He stood to benefit handsomely from her demise, or so he thought. A messy divorce was one thing; winding up dead was a whole other scenario. When the call came from one of the criminals to whom he owed money, no words were minced when he threatened to kill Lucien, and his wife if she was there, and feed them both to the crocodiles. Was it really such a terrible thing she did, erasing that message and the call history, and then getting the hell out of Malpaís on the morning flight to Guatemala City? Okay, slipping the car key into her pocket as he gave her a final embrace ensured that he would be home when they arrived; in essence, sealing his fate. Regardless, she never felt a scintilla of guilt for her actions because she did it for her own survival. Relief was all she felt.

Those first months were the hardest but when not one hair of suspicion was raised about Lucien's disappearance, she put the entire experience behind her. When appropriate, her feigned grief was worthy of an Academy Award. The memories of how she wound up in this little country were the hardest to reconcile, but when the insurance company told her DNA tests proved that the partial femur found on the beach belonged to Lucien Desmarais, a tsunami of relief washed over her. The day she received the check, she called Inspector Vernier and made an offer on his farm. Three months later, she arrived in Aix, having left everything she owned in the house in Montaña Fea.

But now, her clandestine world was upended by William Balthazar Hastings coercing her into doing the bidding of the most powerful intelligence agency in the world. The uncertainty of what they knew, when they knew it, and what the consequences would be if she didn't comply, made her teeter on the edge of an abyss that could destroy her carefully constructed life. What choice did she have?

The bakery goods she bought yesterday were still on the counter when she walked into the kitchen but the thought of putting food into her quivering stomach made her gag. With a cup of French press coffee, she strolled to the terrace and gazed at her property acquired with ill-gotten gains. She loved everything about this little farm and would hate to lose it. Especially, after all she had been through, so ignoring Will wasn't an option. He made it abundantly clear that unless she cooperated, the Agency would leak the information to authorities. And then what? She'd lose the farm and maybe wind up in prison? That wasn't going to happen, not *now*, not *ever*. When she finished her coffee, she walked down the stone staircase and strolled between the neat rows of lavender, breathing in the heavily scented air while trying to organize her thoughts. Cooperating with the CIA was a tacit admission of her guilt, but she vowed she would never confess outright to deleting those calls and messages. No matter what.

Chapter 3

Maya languished all morning, but by noon when the air was stifling, she retreated to the coolness of her bedroom and crawled under the covers. When the light began to change towards the end of the day, she took a shower, put on clean clothes, went downstairs to the living room bar, and poured herself a stiff drink. How long could she put this off? Wouldn't it be easier to meet with him and get it over with? She refreshed her drink, picked up Will's card, and walked to the terrace to watch the waning sun dip behind the sprawling field of lavender. When she drained the last drop from her glass, she dialed Will's number. He answered on the second ring. She gasped slightly but in a totally neutral voice that belied the fear gripping her like a vise, announced, "Two p.m. Thursday, my farm. Don't be late." Before he had a chance to respond, she ended the call.

William Balthazar Hastings arrived at the entrance to

La Petite Ferme five minutes early, standing off to the side so he wouldn't be seen, and waited. At exactly one minute before two, he pushed the call button on the stone pillar and a few seconds later the gate languidly swung open beckoning him to walk the gentle incline to the stone farmhouse. Cradled under his arm was a box of chocolate truffles from La Cure Gourmande. Why had he bought them? This wasn't a social call where arriving empty handed was a *faux pas*; he was here to carry out a task he had done many times in places far more forbidding than Aix-en-Provence. Recruiting an asset in a smokey, mud hut reeking of goat urine in Somalia, or sipping green tea and eating brains masala in a decrepit tea shop on a fetid street in Peshawar would be precious highlights of his career, events he would look back on fondly when this broad was done putting him through the meat grinder. *Why me,* was the question that looped in his head. When Will asked Martin why he hadn't volunteered for this task, his response was, "Are you crazy? I know better. And I like my junk."

Will had almost reached the steps to the terrace when Maya walked through the French doors to welcome him. She looked far more at ease than she did the other night and had a healthy glow to her skin, unlike the ghostly pallor that washed over her when he told her about the deleted phone calls. A loose ponytail held her thick hair away from her face as a zephyr scattered a few stray tendrils across her forehead. She was dressed all in white -- baggy linen trousers and a diaphanous cotton shirt through which he could see the outline of a lacy camisole. With the striped canvas espadrilles on her feet, she looked very French and completely in her element. Her posture was relaxed but he detected clenched hands buried deep in the pockets of her pants.

"Right on time," she quipped, then smiled slightly. "Come on in."

He followed her along the terrace and into the living room. "Here," he said, presenting the box of chocolates.

"You didn't have to do that but thank you." She smiled warmly when she saw the name embossed in gold on the box. "Jeanne is here today, so she is making us lunch." Walking across the room to place the box on the sideboard where an assortment of liquor was displayed, she turned her head and asked, "What would you like to drink?"

"Whatever you're having is fine."

"Campari and soda? It's refreshing on a hot day like today."

Will nodded and smiled diffidently. He took the glass from her hand and followed her to the terrace where they sat in overstuffed wicker chairs covered in bright blue and yellow Pierre Deux fabric. Neither said a word until Maya broke the uncomfortable silence. "Let's get to the point here. What exactly is it you want me to do?"

"I see you've reconsidered. . ."

"Oh no, Skippy, I've done no such thing. My journalistic instincts prevailed. After all, I got a *New York Times* bestseller out of the last escapade you guys recruited me for. So, my prime purpose in cooperating this time is to duplicate that experience. Don't read anything else into it."

"Okay, I understand." Will laughed to himself. *Yeah, right. The prospect of going to prison had nothing to do with it. If you say so.*

"Now please explain what it is you want me to do," she said, curling her legs under her and clutching the tall glass in her left hand.

"We've compiled a list of names obtained from U.S. Customs and Border Patrol and the U.S. State Department. These people entered Malpaís in the last two years and have not returned to the U.S." Will reached into his pocket and pulled out a sheet of paper which he unfolded, and said, "Here's the list," then handed it to Maya.

"Why are they on this list?"

"A variety of reasons: past criminal history that includes scams, petty theft, embezzlement, drug dealing, pimping, human trafficking, and a couple of them escaped from a mental hospital. Malpaís is the perfect hunting ground for these kinds of people."

"I would think the U.S. would be happy to get rid of them."

"Oh, we are, but some of those people will get mixed up in more dangerous activities. Just as your deceased husband did."

"What exactly was he involved in?" *I know what Lucien told me but do pathological liars tell the truth about anything?*

"You really don't know?"

"I know what he told me." And from what she could piece together, he led a double life. There was Lucien the emerging artist, husband, *bon vivant* and *raconteur*. His other life was forging art pieces, conning rich women, stealing, extorting, and possibly murder. His beguiling charm and knowledge of how to play the system, allowed him to escape the consequences of his actions. Alas, Malpaís was his undoing. She didn't see the need to mention he tried to extort the bank manager for twenty thousand dollars, and when that failed, coerced

Maya into loaning him the money to pay off drug dealers, who presumably kidnapped and murdered him.

"We believe the people he owed money to were part of a drug cartel trafficking cocaine from Malpaís to Guatemala, destined for the U.S. That U.S. citizen shot by the local police after a routine traffic stop was in possession of a kilo of cocaine, procured from your husband. That kilo was part of a shipment, which was confiscated in a recent bust."

"Yes, he did mention something about that. And one night after dinner, two suspicious characters followed us. Perhaps they were members of that cartel. I never bothered investigating," she lied. She had investigated, at least enough to discover that one of the two had been a member of the Guatemalan death squads. "But let me state this for the record: I will not get mixed up in any criminal activity, or associate with known criminals, or put myself at risk exposing such people. Do you understand? Because if you don't, this conversation is terminated."

"That's perfectly understandable and we're not asking you to do that." *Like hell we aren't.* "We have an entirely different agenda for you. If you haven't been following the news in Malpaís during your absence, then you are probably unaware that the expat population in and around San Pedro grew by five thousand people."

"That can't be good, but I'm still unclear what exactly it is you want me to do."

"We want you to keep your ears open if any of the dozen names on that list are mentioned in a conversation or whether anyone you meet might know them. As much as it's against your nature, we are asking that you attempt to fit in by joining the club, so to speak, and attend whatever social events expats routinely have. Every week, someone will contact you and debrief you on activities you participated in where these individuals might have been present or mentioned in conversation."

Maya studied the list. "So, basically my job is to be on the lookout for this bunch of crooks, creeps, and crazies?"

Will threw his head back and laughed. "Yes. Instead of regarding this as an onerous assignment, for which you will be handsomely compensated I might add, I'm sure you can inject some levity into the whole ordeal."

Maya laid the paper on the chair next to where she was sitting and gaped at Will with an expression that belied her trepidation. "Well, alrighty then. I guess I'm in. At least you're not giving me a new legend or asking me to be a honeytrap like the last time."

Will laughed. "We value your insight, attention to detail, and your ability to move through a variety of social circles. To facilitate this, we've created a cover for you. A magazine for which you will be the senior editor. Our staff writers will generate most of the content, but this will pave the way for your entry into expat circles, legitimize your position, and give you authority to investigate whatever you have an interest in."

"I'm not sure I understand."

"The name of the magazine is *Neotrópica – Living in Malpaís* and we will provide you with credentials."

"What would I be investigating?"

"Local customs, new businesses, activities in the area, personalities, politics, it's wide open. You'd be surprised how many people will want to be included. You could even generate some stories, but most of it will be created by our staff. Once you get back to San Pedro, there will be a packet of information waiting for you – business cards, a dedicated cell phone, and a few odds and ends you may find useful in your surveillance of the expat community where those on the list may be lurking. For someone like you, it won't be difficult at all and as you pointed out, may actually provide you with the material you need to write another best seller."

Maya turned her head to see Jeanne standing in the living room waving her hand. "Ah! Jeanne has alerted me that lunch is ready. Would you like to eat out here or inside?"

"This terrace is lovely. I would enjoy eating here very much."

"You sit tight; I'll get plates and silverware and ask Jeanne to serve us out here."

It was a delightful lunch of chicken Provençal in a creamy sauce with cherry tomatoes and green olives, served with tiny, grilled zucchini, and baby roasted potatoes. Maya brought out a very chilled bottle of *sauvignon blanc* and poured it into cut crystal stemware. Will was relieved that her demeanor had shifted from being combative and stubborn, to being gracious and welcoming. Throughout lunch they talked of trivial matters: the weather in southern France, the abundance of food available at the outdoor markets, the best restaurants in town, the easy weekend side trips to the local villages. She deliberately steered the conversation away from her new assignment until the very end. Finally, she smiled at Will and asked the question that had been on her mind.

"To whom will I be reporting whatever information I

gather on those pesky expats and anyone on the crooks, creeps, and crazies list?"

"You'll report to me," he said, gazing at the wine in his glass.

"You're my handler?"

"It appears that way."

She let out a groan and refilled her glass, passing the bottle across the table to Will. "This should be interesting, but I know nothing about you."

"What is it you want to know?"

"The color of your jockeys or what kind of toothpaste you use aren't of interest to me. Just some basics will do."

"My history is embarrassingly predictable. Yale undergrad, degree in world affairs, master's in Middle Eastern languages from Harvard. I live outside Langley but spend a lot of time in East Hampton. Before that, I lived in New York, London, Paris, Bern, Madrid, Rome, and Buenos Aires."

"And your family?"

"No siblings. My father, who's eighty, lives in Alexandria. My mother died ten years ago."

Maya did some quick calculations and determined Will was probably around fifty.

"Let me guess, your father was also with the agency?"

"I told you it was predictable. He and Riggs Haywood were colleagues at one time. When my dad became station chief in Rome, we moved to Europe."

"You didn't think about pursing a different career path?"

"I grew up with this, so it seemed like the natural progression given my interest in world politics and Middle Eastern languages."

"Married?"

"You, of all people, should know that spooks are lousy marriage material after your relationship with Harry Langdon."

"Yeah," she sighed, "all too well. So, you know about that, too? Ufff."

"Unfortunately, yes. Riggs was not happy about that. There are lots of details in your file."

"I'll bet," she groused, thinking of that video Riggs had of her and Harry making love.

"How soon do you think you could return to San Pedro?"

"If I'm going to be gone six months or more, I have a lot of things to arrange here first. Realistically, I could probably be out of here in three weeks. You mentioned compensation. Would it be crass of me to inquire about that?"

"Not at all." Will leaned to the side and took his wallet from his back pocket, flipped it open, and removed a debit card. "Here you go. Do you want to see the balance?" He picked up his phone, punched in some numbers, waited thirty seconds, and then turned the phone for her to see. "This is two months' advance payment; after that your monthly stipend will be credited on the first of every month."

Maya gasped. "You guys must be desperate for information if you're going to pay me that much."

"I told you, we value your capabilities." Will glanced at his watch. "It's been a most pleasant afternoon, Maya. Lunch was delicious and I enjoyed spending time with you, but I have an evening flight to Paris, so I must get going."

"Okay, William Balthazar Hastings. Thank you again

for the chocolates. Let me escort you to the gate."

They walked down the slope and Maya opened the gate from the inside. "*Á bientôt*," she said, extending her right hand, which Will held for just a second too long.

"We'll be in touch," he smiled, and leaned in to give her a traditional kiss on each cheek before walking to his car. *Wasn't as bad as I anticipated, and I got out of there with my manhood still intact.*

Chapter 4

By the time Maya arrived at Finca Azahar, she was exhausted. It had been two days of travel. First a flight from Nice to New York, where she spent the night, then on to Mexico City, finally arriving in Santa Lucia, Malpaís late in the afternoon. Maya had forgotten how wonderful the warm, humid air felt on her skin and how the sweet-smelling fields and blooming flowers exhilarated her senses.

Magdalena was at the house to greet her when she arrived and was overwhelmed with excitement at seeing Maya again after such a long time.

"It is so good to see you, Doña Maya," she exclaimed, embracing her and planting kisses on each of her cheeks. Maya started to cry.

"And it's good to see you, too, Magda. You look wonderful." Maya surveyed the living room and saw that everything was exactly as she left it. It was sparkling clean, as it always was, and Magda had placed huge *ramas* of tropical flowers in strategic spots around the room. On the counter was a Talavera bowl filled with fruit and next to it a box of pastries from Maya's favorite bakery.

"I went to the *mercado* and bought you some foods for the refri. You'll have plenty to eat for a couple of days."

"How sweet of you. I would like to stay home and adjust to being back. You can resume your normal duties and life will be as it once was."

"*Con mucho gusto.* I will leave you now so you can settle in. If you need anything, you can call me."

After Magda left, Maya stood on the terrace and gazed at the twinkling lights dotting the road in the distance as darkness slammed down like a lid on the valley below. Obviously, there had been some changes to this area since she had been gone. She wondered what it would look like in the bright morning sun and if she would be as in love with this place as she had once been. She went inside, locked the terrace gates, opened the cabinet near the sofa and saw that the liquor was still there. She grabbed a glass from the cupboard, added several ice cubes, and poured herself a generous portion of Absolut. Then she stood there, taking it all in, letting it wash over her. It had been hard to leave here, but after the ordeal with Lucien, she wanted to run away. And never look back.

Glass in hand, she walked to her bedroom and flipped on the bedside lamp. Magda placed a bouquet of roses and lilies next to the bed which was freshly made with her favorite linen sheets. She kicked off her shoes and laid down, staring at the little beaded angels over her head swirling in the current from the open window. There would be so much to process: the years leading up to her decision to move here, the experience of building a house and dealing with Lucien who had no interest in living here even though he eventually conceded and pretended to be happy, while continuing his nefarious activities behind her back. As a result of those activities, he was kidnapped and murdered. Had she even worked through all those complicated emotions? Of course, she hadn't. During the months that he was "missing" she only pretended to grieve because in truth she was relieved to have him out of her life. The mind games, manipulations, gas lighting, threats, and psychological abuse ended the minute she got on that plane to Guatemala City. Once she learned of his history with other women, she felt lucky to have gotten out of this marriage alive. A part of her believed he had gotten what was coming to him. Did that make her heartless and cruel? Maybe. But she never regretted what she did, even if the CIA was now using that knowledge to coerce her into doing their bidding. Her last book, *Between Volcanoes*, had sold well but she hadn't been up to a book tour or even any interviews. Writing it had been a way to purge all her conflicting emotions and reconcile how she had gotten ensnared by the likes of Lucien Desmarais in the first place. It allowed her to stop blaming herself and shift the blame where it solely belonged – on him. He had orchestrated his own demise, as far as she was concerned. All she did was get out of the way.

Being back at Finca Azahar was like time traveling. She returned to a past life the minute she walked into her house. Everything was the same, except that Lucien wasn't here sucking the oxygen out of the environment. Before she left for Provence, she had disposed of his things, and gave his unsold paintings to gallery owner Ramón on consignment. Then she redid his room in muted colors of sage and cream and added new furnishings, a few pieces of art, and a couple of rugs she bought in Guatemala. When she was done, there was nothing inside the house to remind her of him. All of this would take some getting used to, but she had decided on the long flight here that she would make the best of it. As if she had a choice.

Her drink finished, she went to the kitchen to rummage for something to eat. Instead of going through the trouble to heat up some food, she grabbed a banana from the top of the fruit mounded in the large bowl. That's when she saw the brown envelope lying near the coffee maker. Was this the package Will had told her about? She took it to the sofa, peeled off the tape, and emptied the contents onto the cushion next to her. There was a new iPhone, a laminated press pass, a five-page document which she would read tomorrow, a mock-up of the magazine *Neotrópica,* a list of suggested articles, and another copy of the crooks, creeps, and crazies list. It was too much to process, so she shoved everything back in the envelope. Then it hit her. All this contemplative reverie produced a wave of emotion -- joy, sorrow, grief, anger, and despair. She slid to the floor, pulled her knees to her chest, and sobbed. For the last three years she wondered when this would happen. Now it had, and the only way out was to go through it, to feel everything in the depth of her soul, to wail and cry for all she had been through and survived. When she had no more tears left, she shuffled to the bedroom, threw herself across the bed, buried her face in a pillow, and fell asleep.

Chapter 5

It was ten hours of blissful slumber. No nightmares, no night sweats, no feelings of loneliness or despair. Maya awoke completely rejuvenated, leapt out of bed to make coffee, and flung open the terrace doors while she waited. As she took inventory of her property, she saw that the tropical plants had grown immensely in three years and with the cacophony of birdcalls, she felt at peace. Maybe coming back here wasn't such a bad idea after all. The ringing of a phone she didn't recognize jolted her back to reality. She rushed inside, grabbed the brown envelope, and shook its contents onto the table. It was the iPhone. "Hello."

"I see you made it home and had a good night's sleep, I hope."

She knew immediately it was Will by his posh Mid-Atlantic accent.

"And good morning to you, too. I did sleep well. And it felt good."

"Have you had a chance to look over the materials we

sent you?"

"I glanced at everything when I got home but I was too beat to really focus. I'll take another look as soon as I've had coffee. It is going to take me a few days to get back into the go-slow rhythm. The mock-up of *Neotrópica* is very slick. Is this going to be both print and digital?"

"Yes. And your press pass is official. You are now part of the *periodistas* on the isthmus. It will give you the same access as any other journalist. We've already laid groundwork amongst the expat crowd by posting announcements in various Facebook groups and internet fora. The outline will provide you with some suggestions about how to present yourself to the expat community so they will feel comfortable divulging what they've heard or what they know. The rest we are leaving up to you."

"The first thing I have to do is catch up on what has happened here since I left. I'll be as thorough as I can to get a feel for what's been going on and who to contact for a backstory. Wouldn't want to disappoint you spooks since you're compensating me so well."

"That's what we like to hear. I'll be in touch in a few days. Feel free to call me anytime day or night if you have questions or concerns. Now, go have your coffee, and enjoy your day."

Maya shoved the phone and the other materials back in the envelope. It was then that she realized the envelope had no name, no address, no postage, nothing to indicate how it was delivered. She would have to ask Magdalena about that when she came to work. Meanwhile, she fished around the kitchen drawer where she stashed her local SIM card. No sooner had she inserted it when her phone started pinging, indicating a lot of voice messages. Then, it rang, catching Maya off guard. It was from an unknown caller.

"Maya Warwick speaking."

"Welcome back," the female voice warbled in a Texan drawl. "This is Maybelle Stevens. We met a couple of years ago at that expat mixer in San Pedro."

Maya was sure they had never met for the simple fact she had never gone to an expat mixer. *Ever*. "Yes?"

"I read about your new magazine in the expat paper. It sounds fabulous, and I am sure you know, doll, there is so much to write about this place."

"I hope so. How can I help you?"

"Oh, I wanted to be the first one to welcome you back. Things just weren't the same without you here. You were such an integral part of our community and we all missed you so. I also want to invite you to the ladies' luncheon this coming Friday. It will be a good way to meet the newcomers and reacquaint yourself with your old friends."

Maya laughed to herself. She didn't have any friends, old or new, that would be part of this group, but, per Will's instructions, she didn't dare decline the invitation. "Friday sounds good. Where and what time?"

"Café Roma, across the street from Banco Nacional. It has a lovely outdoor patio which we've reserved because there will be about twenty of us. We're so anxious to see you and hear about this fabulous magazine. See you then. Kiss, kiss."

Maya stared at the phone. Why was this woman, whom she didn't know, so excited to get together with her? She'd find out in a few short days. Now it was time to unpack, settle in, spend some time in the hammock, and adjust her mindset to the new mission she was on. She refilled her coffee cup, went to the terrace, and surveyed the beautiful vista that lay before her. The two volcanoes looming in the distance were as majestic as she remembered them, and the space between them was as calm and peaceful as ever. There was so much to put behind her, and at the same time, so much more to look forward to.

Chapter 6

Magdalena arrived promptly at nine a.m., smiling, and singing as she usually did when she came to work. Leaving her shoes outside, she asked permission before she entered.

"*Con permiso*," she said softly, walking into the living room. "*Buenos,* Doña Maya. *Estás bien?*"

"*Sí,* Magda. And I am very happy to be back. Thank you for taking such good care of everything while I was away."

Magda went straight to the kitchen and positioned herself in front of the sink. Maya could see the scowl on her face as she stood there with her hands on her hips.

"I'm sorry for the dishes in the sink. I ate something late last night, but I was so tired afterwards that I went to bed."

"Oh, it is very, very bad to leave dishes in the sink at night," she clucked. "You see, in our culture we believe that hungry spirits come to eat food that remains on plates. This is wisdom that has been passed down for generations. It must be true, or why would they say it? When we hear noises in the kitchen, it is them, and we need to worry if they decide to feed on the souls of those who are sleeping. That is why you must never leave even a crumb because it will invite the spirits into your home. You have seen enough tragedy, and this one can be avoided if you are always careful to wash every dish or plate before you go to bed." Magda began scrubbing those two little plates and a coffee cup as though her life depended on it.

Maya was overwhelmed with contrition. How was she supposed to know of this ancient legend, which she thought was both curious and frightening at the same time. "I promise it will never happen again."

Magda's response was a grunt and a nod of approval.

"Magda, I have a question for you. This envelope that you left for me. Where did you find it?"

"The day before you arrived, I came to bring the flowers and it was on the terrace between the iron gates and the door. I do not know who brought it."

"Thank you." That could mean only one thing and she'd bet a million toucans that they tossed her house. Just like the last time. Nothing appeared to be out of place, but then how would she know? She hadn't been here in three years, and although everything was as she remembered leaving it, that doesn't mean they didn't have a go at it. "And how has the weather been lately?

"*Ay, dios mío*, it was very bad last week, *lloviendo sapos y culebras*!"

"Raining toads and snakes?" Maya laughed.

"*Sí*. It was very serious."

"I guess that's no stranger than raining cats and dogs."

"Oh, no, Doña Maya, *sapos y culebras* are much, much worse. They can kill you."

Maya's phone rang again. Another call from someone whose number was not in her directory. She answered and muttered hello.

"I am so happy to have finally reached you. I left several messages over the last few days. Did you get them?"

"To be honest, I haven't even checked my messages. Who is this?"

"Oh, darlin', I'm sorry. Of course, you don't know who this is. My bad. This is Louise Henry. We met briefly at your husband's magnificent show at the museum a few years ago. Tragic what happened to him. I am so sorry. I hope your time in France was good for your healing. I called because I read the article about you in the local paper and I wanted to tell you that you can always count on me if you need any uh, information. The article said you would be featuring various expats and what they are doing here since they arrived. And, well, I do know some interesting tidbits."

"I see. Well, Louise, the magazine isn't a gossip rag, but we will be featuring profiles of people. I'll certainly keep you in mind if I need an interesting individual to write about."

"Will you be at the luncheon this Friday?"

"Yes, Maybelle called me earlier. I'm planning on being there."

"Fabulous. We'll talk more then. Everyone is so excited that you are back. I think you'll be quite surprised at the changes that have occurred here in the last couple of years. And then we have all these new people moving in. Well! We'll get to all of that at lunch. See you Friday. Toodles."

There were eighteen messages, but rather than listen to any of them, she deleted the whole bunch, and turned off the phone.

"Magda, I'm going to town to get some things. Just lock up when you leave if I'm not back."

"*Claro*, Doña Maya."

Chapter 7

Louise was certainly right about the changes in San Pedro. Maya hardly recognized the little town. It had gone from a sleepy agricultural enclave to one of the hippest places in Central America, outside of Antigua, Guatemala. The new buildings, ultra-modern with dazzling glass fronts and fancy signage, were the first thing she noticed. Thankfully, they were still no taller than two stories, but they looked incongruous in this old colonial town. Then there was the area around the park, the north side of which had been transformed into a walking street with bricked pathways, elaborate garden beds overflowing with tropical flowers, and an espresso cart on either end of the one-block street. Her favorite restaurants were still there, but now there were a couple of new additions catering to vegetarians and vegans, in a country that prided itself on the high quality of its meat products. There were several day spas that looked as though they had been airlifted right off Rodeo Drive, offering every kind of hair and beauty treatment available. And what surprised her the most were the yoga and Pilates studios – way too many for a town this size. She had a hard time envisioning the local farmer's wife on a Pilates Reformer. There were security cameras on the corners of almost every building, and some were mounted on trees in the park. But what really shocked her was the recent addition of a stoplight at the intersection south of the main cathedral. There wasn't even a stop sign when she lived here three years ago. Now every intersection had one along with the ubiquitous security cameras mounted on poles high above the street.

Maya's first stop was Banco Nacional de Malpaís where two somber, armed guards monitored the line of people waiting to get in. Everyone had a grim expression and shook their head when she inquired why there was a line in the first place. When she finally got to the door, the guard asked to see some identification to prove she was a client of the bank. She retrieved her wallet, removed her debit card, and held it in front of the guard's face. "*Pase, pase,*" he grumbled, holding the door for her to enter. Everyone took a number and waited in the two rows of chairs for their turn to talk to a bank employee. It took ten minutes before Maya's number appeared on the television screen mounted on the wall.

"*Buenos días,*" she said to the dour faced gentlemen sitting behind the desk. "I would like to see Esteban Lopez, please. He handled my accounts."

Gerardo Campos, the name plaque on his desk read, leaned forward, and rested his arms on his desk. "I'm afraid that will not be possible. But I would be happy to assist you. Please give me your bank card and your passport or residency card to prove your identity."

Maya fished them both out of her handbag and slid them across the desk. Gerardo studied them for a few seconds, then typed something on his laptop. He didn't offer any explanation for what he was doing or why she couldn't see Esteban.

"Can you please tell me what is going on here? I really want to have a word with Señor Lopez. Why all this security, and armed guards no less? It wasn't this way when I left for France three years ago."

Gerardo removed his glasses, laid them on his desk, then pulled a handkerchief from his pocket and wiped his forehead. "Señora Warwick, if you were out of the country then perhaps you do not know what happened here. There is good news and bad news, as you say. The bad news is that Esteban Lopez is in prison for embezzling toucans and dollars in an amount equal to roughly five million dollars. The good news is that your accounts have not been affected in any way. Or, if he did steal from one of the accounts, the money has already been replaced. Your deposits appear to be intact and perfectly fine. You have nothing to worry about."

"How is that possible, Señor Campos? I knew Esteban and he was a very good banker."

"Yes," Gerardo exhaled heavily, "*too* good. So good that he diverted funds to an offshore account in the Caymans for over a year before anyone realized what he was doing. The last million he stole right under our noses, walked out with a suitcase full of money, and went straight to the airport. The customs officer noticed how nervous he was, so they brought sniffer dogs and when the money was revealed, he was arrested immediately. We are very sorry for any inconvenience this has caused, but as I said, your deposits are safe."

"I don't know what to say. My main purpose in coming here today is to make a withdrawal. Will you be able to do this, or do I need to go to a teller?"

"I'll be very happy to accommodate you. How much would you like to withdraw?"

"Five hundred dollars." Then she had a flash memory of when Esteban called her to set up a meeting during which he would reveal how her husband had tried to blackmail him. Her response was something along the lines of "I hope you are not calling me to tell me the bank was robbed, and I have no money in my account." Esteban made a little choking sound, meaningless then but made perfect sense now.

Gerardo opened the top drawer of his desk and pulled out a one-page form and handed it to her. "You must fill this out. Indicate the amount you wish to withdraw in the top line, and the purpose of the withdrawal below that."

"I only want five hundred dollars. What is this nonsense?"

"Hmm, I guess you didn't learn about the new banking rules either while you were abroad. Any amount over one hundred dollars must be accounted for. You must list what you intend to do with this withdrawal," he said, pointing to the first line on the form. "You can put something as simple as household expenses, salaries, food items. It doesn't have to be exact or even very detailed."

"Why these new rules?"

"It seems that the U.S. government has taken a huge interest in accounts held by its citizens. If you were a Malpaiseño, you could take out your entire balance and nobody would blink an eye. But as a U.S. citizen, you must comply with these requirements or our bank can be fined, and your accounts frozen, perhaps confiscated. They might even attempt to say you laundered this money, and if that is the case, you will never lay eyes on it again. I am sorry for this troubling news, but things have changed a lot in the three years while you were away."

Maya scribbled furiously on the form, signed her name with a flourish, and handed it back to Gerardo Campos. "Yes, I see they have. It's very disconcerting to have these kinds of restrictions. Not to mention the shocking news about Esteban Lopez."

Gerardo nodded affirmatively. "Wait right here. I will return with your money in a few minutes."

Maya took the cash, put it in her purse, shook hands with Gerardo Campos, and left the bank. She was still trying to process that Esteban Lopez was a thief, but there he was, locked in a prison cell in a third world country. All she wanted to do now was go around the corner to Café Café and mainline a shot of the best espresso.

Fifty meters to the corner and twenty meters to the right, Maya was relieved to see that Café Café hadn't changed. It was still a hole in the wall with six tables and a counter where cookies and pastries were displayed. She sat at a table against the wall and waited to be served. Normally, the place was empty this early in the morning. Today one table hosted three fit and stylish women in expensive work-out clothes, with one chair dedicated to holding their yoga mats and other paraphernalia. Even from across the room, Maya could see the rocks the women sported on their left ring finger. One wore a tee-shirt with "East Hampton" emblazoned across her chest and another wore a sweater with "Sag Harbor Clothing Co." They chattered well above a normal speaking volume as though they wanted the world to hear about the urgency of finding cashew cheese, something called Fakin' Bacon, and tofu crumble. Maya shook her head. There certainly were changes and she wasn't happy about the things she had seen so far. And she'd only been in town for an hour. She downed the espresso in one gulp, left a few toucans on the table, and darted past the babbling women on her way to the door.

Something was also different about the atmosphere of San Pedro. It used to be a quiet, unpretentious agricultural town, and a common sight was to see a farmer strolling the main street leading a cow, a horse, or even a thousand-pound pig, or carrying a basket of corn on his head. Sometimes there were oxen-drawn carts loaded with vegetables on their way to the market. People were casual and friendly, and greeted you as they passed you on the street. If you ran into someone you knew, it was hugs and kisses all around and the perfunctory questions about how they were doing, how their families were doing, and if everything was okay. Now, she sensed a subtle shift in attitude. People walked briskly with intended purpose instead of promenading and making small talk with their companion. Everyone seemed to be in a rush, and their ever-present smile was replaced by a look of worry, or maybe it was disappointment at what their town was becoming. Maya also noticed that prices had increased. A lot. Inflation would be natural in a three-year period, but the cost of her shot of espresso had doubled, if that was any indication of where things were headed.

She walked past Ramón's art gallery, but it was closed. Peering through the window she didn't see any of Lucien's work on display. If any of it sold, it would be found money, but nothing she counted on. The supermarket that had been a very basic store was now decked out with elaborate food displays with a list of new products they carried in response to their customers' requests. This was where those three women should come to buy that Frankenfood they were prattling about. Maya was shocked at the transformation. She could have been in Dean & DeLuca or Balducci's. She wondered if the locals still shopped here because with the high-end food items they offered, the average farmer would not be able to afford these things, nor would he eat these things. The basic diet was still very Mesoamerican and a lot healthier than any of the processed "health" foods she saw on display. It was overwhelming for Maya who was still reeling from the news that her banker was in the slammer for embezzlement. She selected the things she needed and went to the check-out line. She had been in town for just over an hour and all she wanted to do was go home where it was quiet and peaceful.

Chapter 8

Everything was one big blur as she drove the winding road over the mountain. Even that seemed to have changed or else she didn't remember the road being so narrow or so treacherous. By the time she reached Finca Azahar, she was trembling and relieved that Magdalena had left for the day. She put water on for a cup of soothing tea but abandoned that idea and opted for a slug of vodka on ice, even though it was only noon.

Out on the terrace she heard a faint whooshing in the distance as the sky unleased its fury on the far end of the valley. It would move slowly across the landscape until an *aguacero* brought intense and violent rain. Watching the afternoon storms approach was to behold the magic of nature. The rains here were so predictable you could set your watch by them. Afterwards, the air would be fresh and fragrant, the clouds would move to the west, and it would be sultry until the sun went down. For Maya, this was the perfect time of day.

She put her empty glass in the sink, fished in the brown envelope for the William Balthazar Hastings-dedicated iPhone, hit his number, and waited for him to answer. She hoped she wouldn't say anything she'd regret later. That shot of vodka had gone straight to her head. Will answered on the third ring.

"Will, it's Maya. Do you have time to talk?"

"For you, of course. I was wondering when I would hear from you. How are you settling in?"

"Uh, that's what I want to talk to you about. Where the hell am I? This is not the place I once lived. It only took me an hour in town to see the changes, none of which were to my liking."

"Anything in particular?"

"For starters, my banker is in prison for embezzlement. There are security cameras everywhere, stop signs, and a traffic light, too. My favorite café was taken over by Long Island yoga *devotées*, probably some of your neighbors in East Hampton, judging by the advertisements emblazoned on their tee-shirts. The local grocery, which heretofore only carried fresh fruits, vegetables, meat products, and essentials such as toilet paper and soap, now looks like an ersatz Dean & DeLuca, with shelf after shelf of processed fake food catering to vegans. What the hell is cashew cheese?"

Will laughed. "Is there such a thing? You found it a bit disconcerting, is that what you're trying to tell me?"

"That would be an understatement. Before I went to town, I had two phone calls from women I have never heard of in my life who welcomed me back and invited me to a ladies' luncheon on Friday. Per your instructions, I accepted, but both mentioned that they had read about my return in the local paper. Exactly what does everyone know?"

"I told you we did a few press releases in the local newspapers, both English and Spanish, along with strategic announcements on certain Facebook pages for expats in the area. We were trying to make your re-entry easier, but perhaps you don't see it that way."

"It's too soon to make that assessment but Maybelle – yes, that's her name – and Louise something or other were both gushing over the idea that I would be writing about expats."

"That's good. You need to have your supporters in place. They are the ones who will have their ear to the ground looking for information they think you can use. Relax. You'll do just fine. Anything else?"

"No, but Will, I have to say I feel as though I've time-traveled back to a former life that doesn't even exist anymore. It's like trying to reconstruct a dream but the details keep dissipating. I guess I'm still in the adjustment stage. I'll report back to you after the luncheon on Friday." A few seconds later, Maya shrieked, "OH, MY GOD!"

"What?"

"The whole house is shaking."

"It's only an earthquake. Get outside, away from anything that can fall."

How did he know that, she wondered, as she staggered across the room and bolted out the door. "I'm on the terrace and it's still moving. It's like being on a boat." Maya paused for four or five seconds, then said, "Wow! That was a long one. I wonder what it registered."

"Six-point-two on the Richter scale according to the USGS website. That's pretty big."

"It was, Will. Long and strong. Oops, that didn't

come out quite right," she laughed, blushing. "Prolonged would probably be a better description."

"As long as you enjoyed it. That's all that counts."

"I wouldn't go that far. But you're pretty funny."

"Has it totally stopped now? If so, go take a nap and chill out. It's going to rain in the next few minutes anyway."

Maya looked at the darkening skies and wondered how he knew that. "Is there anything you spooks don't know?"

"Not really. Talk to you soon."

Within fifteen minutes, it was raining toads and snakes. From her bed, Maya watched the torrents of water sluice off the overhang of the terrace. Between the pounding rain and cascading water, the noise was deafening and there was no way she could take a nap. It was nice to lie there, her face buried in a silk-covered pillow, listening to the mesmerizing rhythm. Suddenly, she chuckled out loud as the conversation with Will came to mind. Even now she felt embarrassed describing the quake as she had, but Will's response that she seemed to enjoy it was the remark that made her laugh. Up until now, there had been a palpable tension between them. His raillery about her gaffe made her think that underneath that East Coast prissiness, he had a sense of playfulness. After getting emotionally involved with Harry Langdon, her previous handler, she knew better than to even think about going "there" again. Besides, Will was younger than she and by his own admission was anything but relationship material. Just as well, Maya thought, because he would surely be trouble, but she was relieved that their relationship had accidentally skidded into a more relaxed tone.

Chapter 9

Friday arrived and Maya prepared to tackle her first expat luncheon at Café Roma. What to wear was her big dilemma: dress up, dress down, look professional, or be super casual? She knew from previous experience that some in the group would criticize her if she showed up in a potato sack. She opted for a pair of Jeans, a white linen shirt, red espadrilles, very little make-up, and her signature pink pearls and hoped the cackle of hyenas weren't hungry for fresh meat.

Parking was scarce in town this time of day, so she wound up several blocks away and took advantage of the opportunity to amble to the restaurant, looking for changes she hadn't noticed previously. When she arrived at Café Roma, she went directly to the patio. There was a long table with one empty chair. A woman with an over-permed head of hair in a metallic red not found in nature, sprang from her chair, and waved her arm frantically, beckoning Maya to have a seat. "It's me, Maybelle, in case you didn't remember," the woman trilled.

"We saved you that seat next to Louise and Sharon."

Maya approached tentatively, nodded politely to the others, and sat down.

Louise Henry reached over and patted Maya's hand. "It's so good to have you back and we're happy you could join us."

Maybelle picked up the table knife and her water glass and tapped the edge several times. "Ladies, let's welcome Maya Warwick. For those who don't know, Maya is one of the old-timers who's been living in France for a couple of years. She's returned as the senior editor of *Neotrópica*, that fabulous new magazine we all read about. Thank you so much for joining us today, Maya. Let's everyone introduce yourselves and then we can order lunch."

For the next ten minutes, the women commented about how happy they were to meet her and rattled off their names one by one. They seemed friendly enough, but Maya didn't remember ever having seen any of these women before. She figured she would get their stories soon enough though.

The menu was surprisingly diverse featuring typical lunch items as well as pastas, fresh fish, and even wood-fired pizza. Maya ordered an arugula salad and the sea bass filet. When the server brought her food, she felt mortified. Everyone else had ordered huge plates of everything, with extra bread, extra fries, and jugs of soda. It would explain why almost every woman at the table needed to lose at least thirty pounds.

The overlapping chatter made it difficult for Maya to concentrate, causing her to piddle at her food. With every bite she took she felt the disapproving glances from the other women. When everyone finished eating and the plates were cleared away, Maybelle whispered conspiratorially across the table, "Did ya'll hear what happened to Sandy and Raymond the other night?"

The table responded in unison. "NO! Do tell."

"Well," she gasped, clamping her hand over her breast, "they were in bed watching TV and six masked men came in through the skylight and tied them up with those plastic thingys. One guy stood over them with a gun to their head while the other five proceeded to loot their house – for three hours. Can you imagine? The horror! A truck was parked outside into which they loaded everything and then drove off."

Louise, a diminutive woman who was as wide as she was tall, with a face like a rabbit, including a nose that twitched constantly, exclaimed, "That's positively awful. What did the police say?"

"The police shrugged their shoulders as if to indicate that living in a home the size of most office buildings was justification for the robbery. It's positively awful what's been happening here," Maybelle lamented.

"What has been happening here in my absence?" Maya asked.

"Oh, darlin'," Maybelle sighed, it's been a wild ride."

By the time lunch was over Maya had a headache from the cacophony of voices. On top of that, she got two names wrong, and a couple of the women gave her the stink eye after that and chatted amongst themselves in such a way as to totally exclude her. This didn't surprise her even though she had been friendly and attentive, even feigning interest in the latest reality show or what the Kardashians were doing when in fact, she hadn't heard of most of the celebrities they seemed to be obsessed with. She tried her best to be gracious, but there was no denying the undercurrent of hostility. Maya got up from the table and got Maybelle aside, handing her one of the business cards Will supplied, and said, "I enjoyed having lunch with you and the other ladies. Unfortunately, I have another engagement, but perhaps we could get together, just you and me, and you could clue me in on things that have happened in the expat community during my absence."

Maybelle's eyes lit up. "Oh, yes! That would be lovely." She looked down at the card, studied it for a few seconds, then said, "How does next week sound? You could come to my house in Nuevo Paraíso."

"Where is that?"

"It's just outside San Pedro, across the river, on the road going to the coast. It's the newest development. We built Bert's dream house. I'd love for you to see it." she said, squeezing Maya's hand.

"Hmm, that sounds lovely. Give me a call in a few days and we'll pick a day and time."

"I'll do that, and thanks for coming, Maya. It's so lovely to see you." Maybelle leaned in and gave Maya a hug, before turning her attention back to the gaggle of gringas staring disapprovingly.

Maya left the restaurant, sighing with relief, and walked through the park to her car. She felt light-headed from the stimulation of so many simultaneous conversations, and the hostile glances she got from two of the women gave her anxiety. It reminded her why she hated these types of gatherings. Having lunch with Maybelle, who seemed to be a wellspring of gossip and insider information, would be easier to handle. Maya would wait patiently for her call and take it from there.

Chapter 10

Maya followed Google's instructions to get to Maybelle's house. As she meandered through town, she found the new construction shocking. This side of town used to be a quiet, unassuming residential neighborhood of mostly middle-class locals, with well-maintained wooden houses in the style typical for this part of the isthmus. Now, there were two new luxury apartment buildings, and dozens of vacant lots displaying For Sale signs where the charming old houses had been demolished. Small houses with lovely flower gardens facing the street were replaced by structures that occupied the entire footprint of the lot, leaving no green space at all. Rather than a Spanish colonial theme, most were ultra-modern with lots of glass and metal. By the time Maya reached the main road to the coast, she felt a bit sad for the way this little town had changed.

Once she reached the turn-off to Maybelle's house, the road hugged the mountainside and presented expansive views of the ocean in the distance. She drove a kilometer until Maybelle's house came into view. Maya gulped and slammed on the brakes. "WOW! She wasn't kidding when she said you couldn't miss it!" There it was in all its gaudiness: architecture straight out of medieval England or *Harry Potter*. It was a citadel painted neon teal with a dayglo magenta trim, probably ten thousand square feet, with turrets and parapets on each side, an imposing steel gate, and surrounded by iron fencing with concertina wire on top. Maya wondered if there was a moat with alligators or crocodiles, or maybe water moccasins. Once the shock wore off, she drove the last five hundred meters to the house laughing to herself. The gate rumbled opened as she approached. She drove in and parked behind the black Range Rover. Maya looked up to see Maybelle standing on the second-floor balcony, waving, sunlight forming a halo around her gleaming red hair. The wall surrounding the balcony was decorated with jagged up-ended bottles, obviously meant as a deterrent to anyone thinking of climbing up the side and over the wall. "Come through the side entrance. I'll meet you there."

A demure local woman dressed in a black uniform overlaid with a starched white apron opened the door and ushered Maya inside. Maybelle practically floated down the curved staircase, her long floral dress billowing behind her. It was an entrance worthy of a cameo on an episode of *Dallas*. She extended her arms to embrace her guest. "I am so happy you to see you again. Let's go out to the side patio." Turning to the docile servant whose hands were clasped behind her, Maybelle said in the worst Spanglish Maya had ever heard, "*Por favor*, we will have drinkos and luncho on the patio. And please bring el wino firsto."

"Wow, this is some house," Maya declared, staring at the suits of armor lining the far wall and the impressive display of swords, muskets, and other Medieval tools of torture, destruction, and mayhem.

"Yes," she sighed, "Bert is into all this stuff. I would've been happy with a two-two ranch, but having a castle was his dream."

More like a nightmare, Maya thought to herself. She dutifully followed Maybelle through the living room and out the French doors to the terrace where a round glass table was set for lunch.

"Would you look at that view," Maybelle said leaning on the wall, careful not to cut her wrists on the broken bottles. "We get the most magnificent sunsets almost every day. And if you look carefully, you can see fishing boats off the coast. Have a seat. Luci will serve us. But we must be patient. I'm still training her. It's been challenging because she doesn't speak one word of English."

"Aha, yes, that's an issue, but perhaps it would be easier if you learned Spanish," Maya gently suggested.

"I didn't need to speak Spanish with the hired help in Texas."

"But you're not *in* Texas."

"I know. Thanks to Jesus for that."

"Why all this security?" Maya pointed to the cameras and spotlights mounted everywhere she looked.

"Oh, darlin', after what happened to your poor, dear husband, may he rest in peace, we got a bit spooked. Bert said he would rather be over-protected than a victim, so he went full bore on security devices. Personally, I think he overdid it and now we have so many keys to so many locks that I feel like the jailor in a maximum-security prison," Maybelle bellyached.

"Yes, I can see where you would feel that way. So, tell me what brought you to San Pedro?"

That was the only question Maya needed to ask and Maybelle blabbed non-stop for the next thirty minutes. She didn't even let up when Luci approached in stealthy silence with the wine, then some appetizers. Her litany of complaints about the United States were the usual: immigrants stealing jobs, sucking off the welfare system, avoiding taxes, and refusing to learn English. Oh, and of course, they were responsible for all the crime, on top of every other ill. After each complaint, Maybelle sighed as though she had escaped a dystopian hell. She only stopped for a few seconds as Luci placed their lunch before them.

"This looks divine," Maya said, staring at the huge lobster tail on her plate, with a small dish of melted butter off to the side, a medley of lightly steamed vegetables, and a separate plate of salad. She hoped to change the subject from Maybelle's incessant complaints to something more interesting. "But your life here is quite nice, isn't it?"

"Oh, yes, I have no complaints, other than the increased crime we've experienced in the last three years. It seems it exploded right after your husband, uh, you know, disappeared. There were gang shootouts in San Pedro last year. Something about turf wars over drugs and prostitution. I didn't follow it too closely because it was *muy* depressing. I thought we had escaped all of that when we moved here. There's not supposed to be crime in Paradise. I must say, though, some of the changes have been for the better."

"Such as?"

"For starters, the local supermarket now carries that creamer I like. And they've started importing some packaged foods from the U.S. You know gringo junk food was forbidden before, right? Now, I don't have to eat those blasted sweet potatoes; I can get Kraft Macaroni & Cheese, Pop Tarts, Folger's coffee, and a few other things I really missed."

"You don't like the coffee here? It's some of the best in the world."

"I guess I'm just loyal to the Folger's brand. It makes me think of home."

"I get it." She didn't, but all she could think about was how to extricate herself from this woman's clutches as soon as she ate the last bite of lobster and pumped her for information about any of the characters on the infamous list.

"Enough about me and my petty complaints. Tell me about your experience in France. I've always wanted to go, but Bert won't go where they eat frogs and snails. And what brought you back to this God-forsaken place?"

"The magazine primarily. Plus, I missed my house and the life here." She was surprised at how convincing she sounded.

"I think the magazine is a fabulous idea. There is so much to learn about this country, so I'm looking forward to reading every issue. Will it have a particular focus?"

"Mostly it's going to be about life on this part of the isthmus. The culture, the people, some history, interesting things to do and see. I'm still exploring those ideas, so if you can think of something I might not otherwise know, I'd welcome suggestions."

"What about the new swinger's scene in San Pedro? Have you heard about that?"

"No. Tell me."

"Right after you left for France, we had an influx of those people from Generation Y and Z, or whatever they're called – the ones who work remotely and all they want to do is party and do drugs. One of them opened the nightclub in San Pedro and it was met with angry mobs who didn't want the noise and congestion in their neighborhood until five a.m. The city made them shut down at midnight, but they were just getting going so they started a swinger's club, and they would go to a specified location, swap partners, and party till the sun came up. I thought that nonsense went out with the seventies."

"I did, too." Maya made a face. "But what can you tell me about the ladies who were at the luncheon. Some of them seemed really interesting, but I find it hard to focus when I'm in those situations."

"Most of them came after you left, or maybe right before. They're okay, just your normal Americanos. We have get-togethers on the weekends or go on field trips to other villages or down to the beach. There's no shortage of social activities here. And that couple that got robbed and held at gunpoint? They used to have these huge parties, maybe two hundred people or more. They charged outrageous prices for drinks and said they were giving the money to charity. Personally, I think they were the charity because I heard they spent their last toucan building that mausoleum. If you think this house is gaudy, and I know you do," she smiled sweetly, "you should see that place. I told Bert it was only a matter of time before someone scoped it out figuring ways to get in, and then two weeks later it happened. That was when we were happy to have all this security."

"That's terrible, they must have been scared witless. I sure would be," she said, thinking of how her life could have ended if she hadn't outsmarted the thugs who were after her husband. "But are there serious things happening here?"

"That depends on what you consider serious. There were those two men who disappeared and were found murdered. You probably didn't hear about that either because I'm sure it never made the news outside this banana republic."

"What happened?"

"Single guys, retired, moved here looking for love. Found themselves young honeys who could have been their granddaughters and started acting all uppity, parading those scantily clad *chicas* in front of all of us at the expat gatherings. Now, don't get me wrong, I think it's possible for love to happen despite a forty-year age difference, but these girls, well, let's just say that it seemed obvious to me that they had another profession, if you get my drift. Rumor was that they plotted the murders with the help of their real boyfriends. But who knows?"

"Was anyone prosecuted?"

"Oh, heavens no. There was no investigation into either murder. A couple of dead gringos didn't really matter. One was found in a shallow grave on his property, and the other was found in, well, how should I say this, a few pieces in a plastic bag."

"That's shocking," Maya exclaimed.

"It is. But probably no more so than the god-awful things that happen back home. It's just that we are such a small number here and when an expat gets murdered it sends ripples of fear throughout the entire expat community. You just can't be too careful these days, no matter where you live."

"If I were to mention a few names to you, would you tell me if you know them or have heard anything about them?"

"Well, fire away, darlin', and I'll tell you what I can."

Maya reached for her bag under the table and took out the crooks, creeps, and crazies list and studied it for a few minutes. "How about this guy?" She rattled off the first name with no response from Maybelle. "Okay, how about this one?" Still no response. Finally, she got to Cary Caldwell, and Maybelle's face flashed with recognition.

"Oh, him," she sighed. "A real con artist if there ever was one."

"Can you explain?"

"He seemed nice enough, a real character. Talked a good line, constantly bragged about all the other bed and breakfasts he'd owned around the world. So, when he bought that B&B on the outskirts of town from that good looking Greek guy who was leaving for Asia, nobody raised an eyebrow. He gutted the place, made it real classy, but then ran out of money to finish it up. Started hitting up some expats for a loan – not much, five thousand, ten at the most, but in the end, he collected nearly a hundred grand, and suddenly the work on the B&B stopped, and he disappeared. Of course, nobody's getting a dime of their money back because nobody knows where he went. Some say he's in the Philippines, others say Thailand, or someplace round there, nobody's really sure."

"Why would people loan someone like that so much money?"

"Oh, darlin', he was so charming, with that South African accent, blond ponytail, buff bod, and the fact that he never wore shoes. Said he was a Bush Baby, and they don't wear shoes. Somehow those things endeared him to almost everyone. He was always the life of the party, and he had plenty of those, too, while the renovations at the B&B were going on. Had a real way with the ladies, always complimenting them, giving them hugs, whispering in their ears. A brilliant M.O. He was slick. When he needed money, he approached the women who then convinced their husbands to loan Cary the money. There's no bigger sucker on the planet for a few gratuitous compliments than an aging, overweight gringa whose husband is long past his expiration date. And if those husbands ever wanted to get any nookie again, they had better pony up the money."

"I see," Maya chuckled. "Did you loan him money?"

"Me? Oh, heavens no. I was on to him right from the beginning. Knew he was too good to be true and all my suspicions were confirmed when he asked another expat to do him a favor."

"What kind of favor?"

"The story goes like this: He called David and said he needed a favor. Maybe you remember him; he had the wife in a wheelchair. Anyway, David being David was all too eager to help, so Cary explained that he had a cashier's check that he wanted David to cash at the local bank."

"Why didn't Cary cash it?"

"Because that's the con. He wanted David to cash the check, wire-transfer eighty thousand to an account in

Ireland and give the other twenty thousand to Cary in cash."

"I must be missing something."

"The con goes like this: David cashes the check, which is counterfeit, sends the money, or gives the money to Cary, the bank gets stiffed, and they go after David's account for restitution. If he doesn't have the money, they begin prosecution. It's no small matter. By that time, Cary is who knows where."

"So, what happened?"

"David called me one afternoon and told me this saga and I said he was bonkers if he thought about doing that because it's a scam. David called Cary and told him he couldn't help him because I had told him not to."

"Oh, dear."

"Cary called me up in a total ballistic rage, told me to mind my own business; that this was a perfectly honest favor he was asking David to do. I laughed. You see, Bert was the president of a bank in Texas and these scams were prevalent a few years back, so I knew the con, and I told Cary that. He told me I was an officious old bag with an air of self-importance because I was the Grand Poohbah of the expat crowd. Right after that he started borrowing money then disappeared. It's been two years now and nobody's heard a peep. I warned them, told everyone he was a con artist, but they got all miffed at me, told me I was jealous or that I was too judgmental, and that I lacked basic trust in my fellow expats. Meanwhile, I'm not out any cash and they've all conveniently forgotten that I warned them. Cary's name is not allowed to be uttered in the expat community, so I feel vindicated."

"That's some crazy story. Nothing like this was happening here when I lived here."

"Because the floodgates hadn't opened yet with waves of gringos coming here to make a killing in real estate or to run their cons. A lot of them have left already for parts unknown, but there are still a few unsavory characters looking for unwitting victims."

"I see. I guess I have a lot of catching up to do. Maybelle, I really want to thank you for sharing this information with me, but I see storm clouds moving in, so I'd better get going. Thank you so much for lunch, and we'll stay in touch. Oh, and perhaps it would be a good idea to keep this conversation between you and me."

"Most definitely. Jealousy over the smallest things runs rampant in the expat crowd, but don't be surprised if you are overwhelmed with invitations to various functions because people will want to get close to you for a variety of reasons, and the main one will be to feed their ego."

Maya turned her car around in their circular driveway and headed toward the main road. Her head was spinning from the stories Maybelle shared with her, but were those events worth writing about? Within a few minutes the storm clouds arrived and unleashed their ferocity. The streets in town were already flooded from stopped-up storm drains. With lightning bolts flashing across the sky, people ran for cover. The rains were magical in one sense; they created the lush environment Maya loved so much, but their danger could not be overstated. By the time she got home to Finca Azahar she was drained and didn't feel like talking to Will or anyone else. There was always *manaña.*

Chapter 11

Rainy season mornings were usually filled with brilliant sunshine and cloudless, bright blue skies. The air was crisp and scented with fresh-cut grass, tropical flowers, and Maya's favorite smell of all -- wet earth. She poured her first cup of coffee and sat down to make some notes about her luncheon with Maybelle, she of the flaming metallic hair, bright red lipstick, and more eyeliner than a ring-tailed lemur. Maya was amused by her because she was the epitome of the Ugly American with money who moves to a third world country and pretends to be the Lord or Lady of the castle. In her case, *literally*. It was all very entertaining, and she was sure Will would think so, too. After breakfast and a shower, Maya would call him.

Maya entered her bathroom as something skittered across the floor of her shower. She cautiously peeked around the wall separating the shower stall from the bidet and screamed in horror. There, huddled in the corner, no doubt as terrified as she was, was the biggest spider she had ever seen.

"Oh no! What am I going to do?" She was terrified to turn her back on it but after a quick glance around the bathroom she spotted the rubber plunger. The hairy tarantula, the size of a salad plate, scooted along the bottom edge of the wall, eyeing its escape from the hysterical woman screaming and swearing at it. With its sights fixed on the bathroom door, it was about to make a dash for it when Maya plopped the plunger over its body. Then she ran from the room. There was no way she was using that shower. Not today. Maybe not ever again. "And this is why everyone should have two bathrooms," she said as she walked back to the kitchen to answer the ringing phone. It was Will.

"Good morning, Maya. How are you?"

"Oh, just fine with one small exception."

"What's that?" he asked innocently.

"There's a spider in my shower."

"Kill it."

"Are you kidding? It's the size of a baby rabbit and even has fur. It would make a huge mess, and besides, I don't like killing things."

"What did you do with it then?"

"I covered it up with the plunger. Now I'm going to wait."

"For what?"

"Until it dies, or I get someone to come here and remove it."

"If I were closer, I would do it. Spiders don't scare me. But snakes? Now we're talking real fear. Do you have those there?"

"I'm sure we do. It's the tropics, after all."

"Big snakes I don't mind; you know the ones that can

swallow a calf or small dog. You can see those coming, and besides, they move glacially slow. It's those other ones that terrify me. The ones that slither past you in a flash. If I lived down there, I'd have to have a mongoose."

Maya burst out laughing. "A mongoose?"

"Don't laugh. I'm serious. I gave this a lot of thought. I hate cats, and snakes can easily kill dogs. Ferrets are too weak, badgers too big. Mongoose? Just right. So, if I ever come to visit, you'll need to get one."

"Well, okay then, I'll see what I can do," she laughed. "I was going to call you this morning. I went to the expat luncheon in town, and yesterday I had lunch with one of the women who organizes a lot of functions."

"Did you find out anything interesting?"

"Depends on how you look at it. Most of it was basic gossip about who's doing what to whom, but I asked Maybelle about the names on that list and there was only one she recognized. Cary Caldwell. Seems he's disappeared after running a long con on the expat crowd and liberating them of a hundred thousand dollars."

"That's his forte. He's done it in at least a half dozen places now. Started out scamming white South Africans, moved to Zimbabwe, got run out of there, went to Canada where he screwed the wrong person and charges were filed against him, but somehow, he escaped and wound up in Malpaís. That's where we lost him. Does anyone know where he went?"

"Southeast Asia, China Sea, Philippines, nobody really knows, but he'd better not come back here."

"He never returns to a place where he ran his con. Always moves to the next target. So, this Maybelle, is she your trusted confidant now?"

"We'll see. She's one of those women who likes to stick her nose in everyone's business, but she does know a lot of people, so I'll use that to my advantage."

"That sounds reasonable. And please, do something about that spider. It'll die otherwise."

"I'll try. Maybe I'll save it for you."

"Get that mongoose and we're in business. Talk to you later.

Maya was still chuckling about Will's fascination with mongooses when her other cell phone rang. She saw that it was Maybelle calling and hit the answer button. Before she even had time to say hello Maybelle blurted, "Oh, thank God, I reached you. Quick. Turn on your television," she squealed.

"I don't have a television," Maya replied. "What's going on?"

"You won't believe what I just saw." Maybelle was breathless and her voice approached a hysterical pitch.

"Is it something I could see online?"

"I don't know. You can check."

Maya sat down, booted her laptop, and waited. "While I'm waiting, tell me."

"Do you remember Charlotte and Bradley Wilson? They came here just about the time your husband went missing."

"I recognize the names, but I don't think I ever met them. What's going on? You sound frantic."

"He's dead, gunshot wound to the back of the head, and she's in custody."

"What happened?"

"I saw her being led away in handcuffs, and well, my Spanish being what it is, I had to kind of figure out what they were saying, but it looks like she popped him. Then in the crawl it had the word suicide, so I guess that's what she's claiming. Suicide by gunshot to the back of the head? Right. And I'm Princess Di. They were an odd couple to begin with, so I'm not surprised."

"What do you mean?"

"They called him a Wall Street whiz kid, kinda like Gordon Gecko. Made a billion some said. Then he and his wife moved here, bought a thousand acres of land, and started a wildlife sanctuary down where those hippie, raw food people and wellness centers like the one in *Nine Perfect Strangers* are. They were on the news occasionally talking about how they were going to spend their money taking care of animals. Everyone thought that was a noble idea, but then there were rumors. Oh, my. A friend of mine met them at a party in Santa Lucia and said they were both 'off' if you get my drift."

"Actually, I don't."

Maybelle sighed. "Charlotte asked my friend if she could recommend a good doctor because she was having trouble with her medication. Said it wasn't working anymore. She confided that life had been very stressful, and she needed help to deal with the pressure of her marriage and the way Brad was spending money. Plus, the isolation of living in the jungle was starting to take its toll. According to my friend, Charlotte looked completely frazzled, hands shaking, a nervous twitch in one eye, and was skinny as a matchstick."

"But why would she kill her husband?"

"Isn't that the question we always ask? Who knows what went on behind the closed doors of that monstrosity they built? Oh, wait, hahaha, they didn't have doors. Did you ever see pictures of that thing? I don't know how anyone could live there. It looked like a parking garage. Nothing but concrete, pillars between the four floors, no walls, just these steel blindati that came down at night to keep the wildlife out. It was very strange. I thought you would want to get in on this news item right away. Might be good material for your magazine. Life in Paradise isn't always what it's cracked up to be."

"It certainly isn't," Maya said sympathetically, "and thank you for alerting me. I'll get online and see if I can access the local news stations. Please do keep me in the loop if you hear anything outside the official pipeline."

Maya immediately typed *Malpaís Noticias* in the search engine and there it was, video footage of willowy, blonde Charlotte Wilson being led away from the parking garage that doubled as their house and shoved into the back of a police van. Maya turned up the volume and was stunned by what she heard:

"We're here at the home of Charlotte and Bradley Wilson where Mrs. Wilson has just been arrested for the murder of her husband. At four fifteen this morning, the police received a frantic call from Mrs. Wilson stating that her husband shot himself. When the police arrived, they found Mr. Wilson, without life, lying in his bed, a gunshot wound to the back of his head. Mrs. Wilson claims that her husband had been depressed in recent weeks over business dealings and that he kept a gun in the nightstand. She claims she woke up in the middle of the night to see him pointing the gun at his forehead. A struggle ensued and he got the gun away from her and shot himself behind his right ear. Mrs. Wilson was hysterical when the police arrived, but after interviewing her, they concluded her story didn't add up, and immediately placed her under arrest. We will bring you continued coverage of this story. Stay tuned for updates."

Maya made a note of the reporter's name – Kendall Jacobs – and looked at the paper's website to find a phone number for Kendall to see what his take was on this situation. After all, she was the senior editor of *Neotrópica*. She dialed his cell number, but it went directly to voice mail. She left a brief but detailed message and asked that he please call her back. Then she went to the San Pedro Facebook page to see if there were other announcements. All she saw were a lot of gringos opining on what must have happened for her to kill her husband, and the leader of the pack was none other than Maybelle Stevens. It amazed her that people who didn't know the couple could have opinions about their marriage and what would lead to such a tragedy. Maya was all too familiar with the strange things that happen behind closed doors. Next, she looked at the local Spanish news outlets, but they were sharing Kendall's video with Spanish subtitles. Then her phone rang.

"This is Kendall Jacobs returning Maya Warwick's call."

"Thank you for getting back to me so soon. I just saw your broadcast and I was wondering if you could share your observations with me for a piece I will be writing for our new magazine."

"There's not much to tell at this point. I got there the same time as the cops. I could hear her wailing from the driveway. She was on the fourth floor of their house. The three cops and I entered and took the elevator to the top floor. It was not a pretty sight. She was frantic, hair all matted, make-up smeared down her face, dressed in a flimsy nightgown. She kept screaming, 'Why? Why? Why' as the police scoured the room for clues. Bradley was lying on his side, blood everywhere, and the weapon he supposedly used was lying on the floor on the opposite side of the bed. It looked as though he had been sleeping peacefully when he was shot. At least that was my first impression, and after the police had a little conference, they decided the same thing and slapped the cuffs on a screaming Charlotte Wilson. But what was more interesting was all the stuff they found in the bedroom."

"Like what?"

"On one side of the room were a half dozen wooden bins. When the police opened two of them, they found assault rifles and enough ammunition to start a small war, one bin was full of money – all kinds of money – euros, pounds, dollars, toucans, must have been a few hundred thousand dollars in there, maybe more. But the real jackpot came when they opened the last bin to find it full of gold bars, expensive jewelry, bags and bags of precious stones, gold and silver coins, and a couple dozen Rolex watches."

"Wow. Why would he have all those things stashed in his house?"

"The police want to know the same thing. I was listening to what they were saying amongst themselves and of course drug dealer, money launderer, and tax evader were labels being tossed around. The police ordered a forensics team to come and examine the crime scene and another team to remove all the loot."

"What's going to happen now?"

"She's going to be arraigned tomorrow, assuming she's coherent enough to appear in court. I'm sure a psychiatrist has been called in to sedate her. That's all I know. Obviously, this is a developing story, which I can assure you I will be following very closely."

"I don't blame you. I'm also very interested in what happens. Could you keep me in the loop? I'll follow you online, but if there's any big development, would you be so kind as to let me know?"

"Sure, Maya. Be happy to. I'm going to go down to the police station now and see if I can get an interview with her. I'll let you know how that goes."

"I'd appreciate it. And thanks for getting back to me so soon. We'll be in touch."

Maya intended to call Will after a quick Google search of the Wilsons. There were a dozen articles praising him as a financial genius who made a billion dollars then moved to Malpaís to start a wildlife preserve with his beautiful model wife Charlotte. It wasn't until Maya got to page five or six on Google that she found his troubles: The IRS was interested in what he did with all that money and why they didn't get their fair share. There were also a couple of stories about investors not being happy with their returns and suspected that he had been running a massive Ponzi scheme to the tune of six hundred million dollars. None of that mattered now because he was dead. From the photos of her taken at various events, Charlotte's focus was fashion and being seen at the most expensive restaurants in the most exotic places. Behind that fixed smile, a haunted, faraway look radiated from her eyes, a look that Maya knew all too well. That aside, she had to admit that the photos of Charlotte standing in the golden sunlight of the Serengeti plain, dressed in a luxurious white organza gown, the gentle breeze fluttering her long blonde hair, were stunningly beautiful. She was wraith-like and moved like a gazelle. A stark contrast to Bradley, who was built like a wrestler, thick neck, over developed upper body, and at least five inches shorter than her five-foot eleven frame. Despite those physical differences, they made a striking couple, radiating health and wealth. But why would she kill him? There was nothing online that indicated they were anything other than a perfect couple. But then everyone thought Maya and Lucien were the perfect couple and look how that ended. She picked up Will's phone and hit his number.

"Are you calling to tell me you got a mongoose?"

"Very funny, but the answer is no. I'm calling to tell you about the latest scandal. There's just been a high-profile murder, I mean, suicide, here in Paradise."

Chapter 12

At three a.m., Maya awoke to a sepulchral silence with neither a rustle of a banana leaf, nor a cricket chirping. The all-encompassing quietude was shattered when a band of coyotes in the valley began yipping and howling, celebrating their capture of some small animal and the meal it would provide. Their high-pitched screams rose and fell, then stopped as suddenly as they began. She desperately needed to go back to sleep because the previous two weeks left her totally enervated.

It was a whirlwind of lunches, dinners, charity events, and a few very large parties at the homes of various expats. Will kept reminding her that appearing sociable and congenial would encourage those who had inside information to confide in her. What she got out of the deal was an aching face from smiling, a sore back from standing in heels for hours, and a throbbing headache from listening to featherbrained twaddle and juvenile banter. Sometimes she wondered if any of them had ever had a serious thought. Maya took advantage of these social events to query other guests about the people lucky enough to have landed on a list she referred to as crooks, creeps, and crazies. Other than the con artist Cary Caldwell, nobody recognized any of the names. However, after spending so much time with the expat crowd, she encountered plenty of other candidates who would qualify for that list.

An hour went by, then two, and try as she might, sleep would not come. Finally, she decided to get up. It was *madrugada* -- the cusp of daybreak that would blossom into a brilliant sunrise. She shuffled to the kitchen to make coffee and while it was brewing, she saw messages on her phone from both Maybelle and Louise that had come in the wee hours of the morning. All three of the messages said, "Urgent. Call me as soon as you get up." She needed coffee first and then she would call Maybelle.

The phone completed one ring when Maybelle answered in a shriek. "Oh, my God, Maya, you won't believe what happened."

"Tell me."

"Bill Reynolds committed suicide."

"He did?" Maya racked her brain trying to put a face to that name.

"He was at the fundraiser last week. Tall guy, graying hair, looks kinda like an aging Don Johnson. He's married to Sue, the one with the platinum blonde beehive hairdo."

"Oh, yes, I remember. What happened?"

"Sue woke up at midnight and he wasn't in bed. She got up and saw the open door to the pool. Maybe he's outside, she thought, so she turned on the lights. And there he was. On the bottom of the pool with cement blocks tied to his ankles. She called 911, then me. She was downright hysterical. I got there as the police arrived. They removed the body and called an ambulance to haul her off to the ER. She definitely needed some heavy duty meds. I'm waiting to hear from her now." Maybelle's voice lowered to a conspiratorial whisper. "Between you and me, there were rumors that he was involved in some strange activities, although nobody could say what exactly. He certainly never seemed depressed, and Sue confirmed that. He was always a happy go lucky guy. Anyway, all I can say is my God!"

"That's just terrible. I'm so sorry. I see Louise left me a message, too."

"Yes, I called her after they took Sue away. It's very suspicious. Cement shoes to commit suicide. Well, maybe, but it sounds more sinister to me, like something the mafia would do. But what do I know?"

"Hmm, it does sound odd. I suppose there will be an investigation. Please let me know if you hear anything."

"Oh, I will, darlin', and I'm going to call Louise right now and tell her we spoke. We just wanted to keep you in the loop."

"Thanks, Maybelle. We'll speak soon then."

Maya stood riveted on the spot, her hands shaking so badly she could hardly hold the coffee cup. Did Bill Reynolds owe someone money? Was he engaged in illegal activities? Only an investigation would reveal those things if anyone cared enough to investigate. They sure hadn't when Lucien disappeared. And like Lucien, Bill was one less gringo they didn't have to deal with anymore.

Chapter 13

The rainy season was nearing an end, but tropical storms forming in the Atlantic brought unprecedented precipitation. Heavy black clouds moved rapidly towards San Pedro and Maya wanted to get home before the downpour. The rain began, gentle at first, but became intense very quickly. In another five minutes she would have arrived safely at Finca Azahar, but the universe had other plans.

The rain slammed down in blinding sheets rendering the windshield wipers nearly useless. As she approached the turn into the development, the run-off sluicing across the road made bad driving conditions even more treacherous. Her old car sputtered up the hill barely cresting the rise when it lurched a few times and died. By now, the *aguacero* was in full force. Sitting in her car with the windows steaming up, she realized she could be stranded here for hours. Her house was still a mile away. She could walk the distance, but she'd get drenched. Left with few options, she stuffed her cell phone deep into her pocket, grabbed the one bag of groceries, and ventured into the storm, locking the car doors behind her.

"Oh, God, why me?" she moaned as she trudged toward the house, dodging potholes sloshing with ankle deep water and slogging through mud. She wished she'd worn her new blue Hunter boots, but morning rain was a rarity. Her only consolation was that it wasn't freezing cold, and tropical rainstorms did have their own beauty if there was no lightning. She picked up her stride, barely able to see where she was going because of the rain pelting her face. Then she heard a horn honking. She turned around as a car pulled up next to her.

"Hi ho," the silver-haired woman said with a big smile on her face. "Get in. You can't walk in this. It's dangerous."

Maya walked around to the passenger side and opened the door. "I'm soaking wet."

"No matter. It's just water. Get in. I'll take you home. Where do you live? Oh, I'm Madeleine, by the way."

"Maya Warwick. Thanks for stopping. What a storm, eh? I live about a mile that way," she pointed.

"Oh, you're on the other side of the development. That's why I haven't seen you before. But look. There's a *derrumbe* just ahead and the road is impassable. You'll have to come home with me until we can get someone with a Bobcat to move that pile of mud."

Maya sighed. This was not how she wanted her day to go, but she had little choice at this point. "You could let me out near there and I could climb over that heap. My house isn't far from there."

"No, no, *no*. That's a bad idea. We'll go to my house.

I'll give you some dry clothes, you'll have a cup of tea, and we'll call Hernán to come move that dirt. It's all going to be fine," she said in a comforting tone.

"Thank you. Have you lived in this area long?"

"A year or two. Or maybe it's three or four. Who can keep track when every day is the same as every other day unless it's raining?"

"True. I'm surprised we haven't run into each other before this."

"Hubs and I stick close to home. Don't socialize much. We like life quiet and peaceful. Plus, we have plenty to keep us busy on our finca."

Madeleine stopped outside a large green gate, aimed the remote control, and waited for it to roll open. She pulled in slowly and turned toward the house which, thankfully, had a covered carport.

"Don't worry about anything. Come on in."

A bespeckled man with a shock of unruly gray hair, greeted them at the door. "I just saw the news. It's a mess out there. Did you have trouble getting home?"

"I didn't, but this poor woman's car pooped out just after the turn, so I picked her up on the road. There's a three-foot high pile of mud and debris at the entrance to her part of the development. Please call Hernán and tell him to come here quick. Now, Maya, you stand right there, and I'm going to get you something dry to put on."

"Howdy. I'm Richard," he said, taking the sack of groceries from her hand and setting it on the table in the entryway. "You're drenched. Poor thing. Well, my wife will fix you right up."

"Yes, she's been very kind."

"I'm going to put on the teakettle. You wait right

there. Then I'll make that phone call."

Maya smiled meekly while dripping water all over their Saltillo tile floors. As she waited for Madeleine to return, she glanced around the room filled with art, bibelots, antiques, and plants. Lots and lots of plants. And tiny fairy lights everywhere, along with incense burners pumping out plumes of frankincense. The skylight she was standing under was being hammered by the rain. That can't be safe, she thought to herself, moving to the side so that she was not directly under it in case it hurtled to the floor. Madeleine limped toward her muttering "damn sciatica" and handed her a large terrycloth towel and a Hawaiian print muu-muu. "This will do for now," she said. "Strip off your clothes, dry yourself off, and put this on. I'll run your things through the spin cycle and toss them in the dryer. Then we'll all have tea. Come into the kitchen when you're ready."

"You're so sweet," Maya said. "I really appreciate it."

"We'll see," Madeleine said over her shoulder as she walked toward the kitchen where the teakettle was whistling.

"Richard, why didn't you turn this thing off?" she bellowed.

"Can't," a faint voice called from some other part of the house.

"Why not?"

"Because Martha got in."

"Oh, dear me. Yes, that's a problem."

Martha? Who was Martha? Maya wondered as she padded barefoot towards the massive kitchen.

"Have a seat," Madeleine instructed, pointing to a chair next to the counter. "I'm making tea now. How about some biscuits? Richard is tending to Martha. He'll join us in a minute."

"Is Martha your. . ."

"Dog? Child? Grandchild?" Madeleine let out a boisterous laugh. "None of those. Oh, look, here he comes now."

Maya turned around to see Richard standing there with a peacock on his shoulder. "Wow," was the only thing she could think of to say. "That's a beautiful bird."

"Yes," Richard moaned. "But she's afraid of rain so she always flies to the terrace and then sneaks in the house. She was hiding under the bed. No easy task getting a peacock out from under a bed."

"I can imagine," Maya sympathized. "Do you have just one?"

"Ha! We don't have one of anything," Madeleine laughed. "The more the better is our motto."

"I see."

"Here's some nice chrysanthemum tea, lovey. And biscuits, too. Help yourself."

"Thank you so much. So, how many peacocks do you have?"

"We've lost count, to be honest. Maybe fifteen," Richard replied as he stroked Martha's head.

"Tell her about our other pets, Richard."

"Let me put Martha in the guest bathroom." A few minutes later Richard appeared with a large snaked wrapped around his shoulders. "This is Gertrude. Named after Gertrude Stein. She's harmless, unless you're a little mouse."

"Uhhh," Maya said, recoiling in horror. "Snakes are not my thing. She's lovely though."

Richard turned on his heels and retreated to the bathroom.

"He does love his pets," Madeleine said, slurping the hot tea. "How long have you lived here, Maya?"

"Off and on six years. I was gone for three years but I'm back for good."

"Oh, I know who you are. You do that magazine, right? I haven't had time to read it, but someone else mentioned it to me as a good resource for expats. We've just been too busy with our zoo to pay much attention to those kinds of things."

"Zoo?"

Madeleine laughed. "Might as well be. I've given up, truly I have. I just let him do whatever he wants. He's always rescuing things, but as long as I don't have to take care of them, it keeps him out of my hair."

"Uh-huh, I see," Maya commiserated, "you don't happen to have a mongoose you'd like to rehome, do you?"

"You'll have to ask the zookeeper."

Out of the corner of her eye Maya saw something scuttle in the front door, something small, furry, with a long tail. She let out a little yelp.

Madeleine swiveled her head. "Oh, dear, Bridget got in. Riiichaaard, your possum snuck in. What are you doing? Come out here and sit with us."

"I can't," said the faint voice. "I have poop to clean up here. Give me a minute."

Madeleine shrugged her shoulders.

"So how did you wind up in Malpaís?"

"Ah, that's a good question, isn't it? Mostly because Costa Rica wouldn't let us import our parrots."

"Oh, you have parrots, too?"

"A few."

"Riiichaaard, get in here," a voice screeched from

some part of the house.

"Who's that?"

"That's Hemingway. Our African gray. He and his sister are the primary reason we wound up here. Oh, and Abigail, Leslie, and Ginger – the cockatoos."

"So, you have mostly birds? Other than the possum and a big snake?"

"I wish," Madeleine sighed, stuffing a biscuit in her mouth. "There are a couple of mutts down in the barn. They herd our six sheep, then we have guinea hens, quail, chickens, turkeys, and the peacocks of course, plus a large pig who wandered onto our property about a year ago. I think he's going to be Christmas dinner . . . for the whole neighborhood. Figure he weighs about a thousand pounds."

"Good grief," Maya gasped. "You're sure you don't have a spare mongoose?"

"I don't think so, but you'll have to talk to Richard."

"Richard and his pig. Richard and his pig," Hemingway screeched from the other room. "I'm sick of this mess," he added.

Maya started laughing. "Why is he sick of the mess?"

"Oh, well," she said, raising the back of her hand to her forehead in a grand gesture. "I kind of lost it a week ago when Wilson, that's the pig, wandered into the house and pooped everywhere. I admit it. I started screaming at Richard. And now Hemingway won't shut up about it. Shut up, Hemingway," she yelled.

"You shut up, you shut up," came Hemingway's response.

"Oh, look," Maya said, pointing to the large picture window. "The rain stopped. I could trudge home now."

"Sit tight, your clothes will be dry in five minutes.

Hernán should have been here by now, too. I'll have Richard call to check."

"Thank you. I really do appreciate your hospitality and showing me all your wonderful pets."

"Richard is a real Dr. Doolittle, that's for sure.

"Actually, I was thinking it was more like an episode from *The Durrells*."

Madeleine gave her a blank stare as she walked to the laundry room to retrieve Maya's clothes.

"Thank you so much for your help. We must get together again. Next time, my house." *Not a chance*, Maya thought silently. Anxious to get out of the zoo, she pulled the muu-muu over her head and quickly donned her warm clothes. "No need to see me out. I'm just going to scamper home before the rain starts again," she called over her shoulder as she bolted out the front door. When she reached the top of the driveway, she sighed. "Just more expats in Wonderland."

Chapter 14

As Maya tramped towards her house, the idea for an article came to mind. She quickened her pace because she was eager to sit down and hammer out what was swirling in her head about ex-pats and the concept of Paradise, and because it was once again starting to rain.

Stripping off her clothes and shoes, she left them in a pile on the terrace. Once inside the house, she dropped the groceries on the counter, dashed to her bedroom, and found clean sweatpants and a cotton tee-shirt to wear. A quick look outside her bedroom window revealed the second wave of the storm approaching the valley. Thankfully, the laptop was fully charged because losing power was always a possibility in storms this violent. Then the iPhone rang.

"Did you make it home safely?" Will asked with parental concern.

"Yes, but barely. I have an idea for an article that started brewing in my head as I sloshed through mud and rain. I swear, Will, the cast of characters who wound up here is right out of a Durrell novel, or something Carson Beales wrote in the twenties. I'm going to make a cup of tea and have a go at it. I'll send it as soon as I'm done. Your staff can edit it however you like. The title is going to be Expats in Wonderland."

"That's fitting. Looking forward to reading it. And don't go outside. I'm monitoring the weather satellite and there's going to be lots of lightning, plus there's a cell over the Atlantic that may form into a hurricane. Gotta run. Stay dry and start writing."

Ninety minutes later, Maya sent the following article to Will, closed the laptop, and crawled into bed for a nap as the storm raged outside.

Chapter 15

"Expats in Wonderland"

Tales of expats living in foreign countries dubbed "Paradise" might very well be a modern version of Alice in Wonderland replete with beautiful gardens, strange smiling characters, unintelligible language, and societal customs that are rarely and barely understood. The uninitiated expat, after falling down the rabbit hole and then crawling through the tiny door to find himself – in this case, in Malpaís – will be greeted with nearly as many surprises as Alice, for it cannot be denied that Paradise is unlike any other place, right? Paradise is a cross-cultural concept, with references to this mythical place in every religion. It is generally accepted that Paradise is the opposite of the misery-filled existence of the real world. It is a place of contentment, peace, and happiness, and is often used interchangeably with Utopia or the Garden of Eden. In other words, Paradise represents that perfect state prior to the introduction of evil. The etymology of the word

Paradise goes back to the 5th and 6th Century Persia where the literal translation meant a beautiful garden enclosed by walls to protect you from the outside world – a mini-heaven on earth. Since 9/11, Paradise has become part of the collective consciousness because we've been exposed to the promise of Paradise as a weapon in the Jihadis' aggressive brainwashing and recruitment of young men to their suicide squads. Rivers of milk and honey, pastoral valleys, and of course, the beautiful virgins who await them upon martyrdom, are a far cry from the Paradise our expats are seeking.

Just google "Paradise in Malpaís" and more than a million references, all capitalizing on the "P" word are listed, including almost any service you could ever want: restaurants, hotels, real estate companies, weddings, travel packages, vacation rentals, maps, blogs, tours, boat trips, honeymoon spots, land developments, and photography. There's no denying that the word "Paradise" is an infinitely marketable commodity primarily because it conjures up images of white sand beaches with scantily clad, beautiful young women, swaying coconut palms, warm caressing trade winds, magnificent sunsets, lush tropical forests, exotic flowers, fruits, monkeys, and birds, and most importantly, a life free of stress and strain. And in Malpaís, there's that special enticement of eternal spring-like weather.

The expats come to Paradise, first and foremost, for financial considerations and the desire for a simpler and less stressful life than the one they had in the States. Websites and Facebook pages claim that it's possible to live in Paradise on a meager pension. When you consider that the average American only gets a little over a thousand dollars a month in Social Security, finding a place to live well on that amount of money is indeed a quest. But beyond the financial reasons for moving to another country, there are more human and emotional reasons that drive people to uproot themselves to travel to and live in an environment so unlike the place that they call home.

During my ethnological research among the Expat tribe, I discovered dozens of happy people nestled in all areas of Malpaís, from the cooler mountains where the best coffee is grown, to the tropical humid coasts. With more than thirty micro-climates there is a spot to suit almost everyone's needs.

Not everyone moves here because it is their first choice. Malpaís often becomes the destination by default because it reminds the future expat of someplace they would rather live but can't afford. As residency and financial requirements in other ideal retirement spots become more stringent, places they hadn't considered before now look enticing. "Looks like Hawaii, but cheaper," is the motto of one of the land development companies. And so, they come. Young ones, old ones, rich ones, poor ones, even potential expats with an entrepreneurial spirit who want to start a new life, or a new family, away from the former pressures of life in the United States. Sometimes the old ones come to take advantage of low-cost, high-quality medical services that are available for the final state of their life. The young couples often come with the specific intent of dropping an "anchor baby" to be born soon after their arrival to guarantee their access to legal residency. Regardless of their age or socio-economic circumstances, they arrive with suitcases full of hopes and dreams, but not everyone's experience of expatriation is positive.

When I first began thinking about this article, I met a woman (whom I will call "Jane") in a local expat hang-out. Jane was middle-age, attractive, well-educated, and had arrived a few weeks before. I first encountered her as she was busy searching the web for English-speaking schools in Malpaís that might employ her. She held a degree in English so she assumed that finding a use for her skills would be relatively easy. Her enthusiasm was boundless; she was sure that she had made the right choice to come to Malpaís. Several of us pointed out that even if she did find a teaching job, she probably wouldn't earn enough to support herself. By her own admission, she had come to Malpaís with only a small amount of money, had no pension or other resources on which she could rely, but nonetheless she was hopeful. A week later the shock of her suicide resounded through the expat community. And then the stories of other suicides arrived in my email. Stories of how an expat had taken up drinking after moving here, had isolated themselves, or never really integrated into any community, or simply became depressed because Malpaís wasn't what they hoped it to be. Most who sent me these stories echoed the familiar refrain: What clues did they miss? What should they have been looking for? Should they have been more watchful or curious when they didn't see that expat for a few days or weeks? Should they have been friendlier or more welcoming? The questions swirl for months, but nobody really has an answer. One email came with the subject line of "Don't move to Malpaís if...." The body of the email read: "Don't move to Malpaís if you are paranoid of home invasions and/or getting robbed, or if your relationship with your significant other has not already been tested. There are many divorces and separations at the hands of the pressure cooker of Malpaís. Don't move here if you are not comfortable living in a semi-socialist, left of center nation that has no military but does have national health insurance. Likewise, don't move here if you want to escape socialized medicine and government monopolies. If you aren't patient, stay home; and for God's sake, don't move to Malpaís if you are broke and poor. Don't move here if you think it is the easy way to solve all your problems, and lastly, don't move to Malpaís if you are from my old neighborhood. You are one of the reasons I moved here."

Given the expats' own interpretations of marketing and their ignorance about the land, the law, and the people who create the myth of Paradise, it takes time to learn to deal with the hypocrisy and the little lies told daily in Malpaís. Lies and hypocrisy are part of daily living in Paradise. People don't want to know the truth and with a few exceptions, Paradise is the same as any other place. The expat would rather maintain their unrealistic image of the country because this image serves them well when they are in the doldrums of daily life. In reconciling Paradise, it comes down to do you really want to know?

Paradise is not for everyone. For some, it is/was a form of Hell, but for many others it has lived up to their expectations, and they can't imagine living anywhere else. For those who ignore the warnings, their lives will surely become curiouser and curiouser. Knowing Paradise, with all its warts and limitations, also means you must know yourself, know the culture, and know the language to truly understand what Paradise is. . . and what it is not.

Chapter 16

After five months of socializing, sleuthing, and snooping Maya gave up trying to uncover information about the people on the crooks, creeps, and crazies list. She even entertained the idea that these people didn't exist, other than Cary Caldwell. The only intel she seemed to gather was a lot of idle gossip, rumors, and innuendo. It made Maya wonder what they were saying about her behind her back. And for that reason, she kept her personal life very vague. At any social gathering she usually wound up talking to the men because the women were only interested in sharpening their ornately decorated porcelain claws on some new arrival.

Bill Reynolds' suicide by cement shoes was still a topic on everyone's mind although there had been no new revelations as to what drove him to do that. The only other even vaguely interesting event was the murder of Bradley Wilson for which his wife Charlotte was officially charged. Rather than being confined to a jail cell, she was reportedly being held in a locked psychiatric ward at the hospital in Santa Lucia. Kendall Jacobs had no updates either because the authorities weren't releasing any information, and even Kendall's inside contacts had nothing to share. There was lots of speculation though. Had she had a complete nervous breakdown? Was she being heavily drugged? Would she wind up being a suicide? Everyone seemed to have an opinion, but none of it was based in fact. In Maya's last conversation with Will, she expressed her disappointment in not being able to uncover much of anything that was noteworthy about this patch of land on the isthmus. All of that changed on a hot and humid Friday afternoon as Maya left the farmer's market.

Heading towards Café Café for an espresso, she got as far as the park when the bags she carried became too burdensome. She sat down on the closest bench and proceeded to redistribute the items in the two shopping bags. At this time of day, the park was nearly empty because everyone had gone back to work after lunch. Without the usual crowds, it was a peaceful place to sit, surrounded by flower beds and tropical trees. A few white-faced monkeys lived in the park along with a couple of chickens who laid their eggs in the flower beds. After walking seven blocks from the feria in this heat, it was a relief to sit on the cool bench beneath the Flame of the Forest trees with their vibrant orange flowers. A few minutes later, a middle-aged man strolled towards her and sat on the bench across from her. He smiled bleakly and she reciprocated with a nod of her head and a quiet *"Buenas tardes."*

Ten minutes in the quiet shade and she was refreshed enough to walk the final distance to Café Café. She gathered her shopping bags and was about to stand up when she heard him say, “You’re Maya Warwick.”

“That depends.”

“Yes, of course,” he laughed.

Who’s this guy? Late forties, well groomed, expensive clothes, high cheekbones, and an aquiline nose indicating possible indigenous heritage. A handsome man by anyone’s standard, with a melodic accent-free voice.

“I have some information you might find interesting.”

“And what might that be?”

“Do you mind if I sit next to you?” Without waiting for her to respond, he approached and sat on the opposite end of the cement bench. After a few anxious, silent seconds, he reached into his jacket pocket and removed a brown envelope and placed it in the space between them. “You will want to look at this in private. If you’re as good a journalist as some have said, then you just hit the jackpot.” He stood up and turned toward the park entrance. “Have a pleasant afternoon.”

He quickly melded into the crowd gathered at the crosswalk and was soon out of sight. The envelope stayed on the bench. Hesitantly, she reached over and picked it up. It couldn’t contain more than a few sheets of paper. Maya wasn’t sure what to do. Her first impulse was to rip it open but his admonishment about looking at it in private stopped her. What could possibly be inside? As difficult as it was to curb her curiosity, she placed the envelope in her purse, grabbed her parcels, and strolled diagonally across the park and down the street to Café Café.

As she waited for her espresso, she decided to open the envelope. She undid the clasp and removed the contents. The first photograph was a satellite or drone shot of thick jungle with a road cut through the middle and a mound of indistinguishable material at one end. The second photograph, a long shot and slightly out of focus, was of a perfect crescent beach, white sand to the azure water's edge, ringed by dense undergrowth with coconut palms leaning towards the water. Two figures stood in the background near the trees, looking down at the beach. Their faces were obscured by distance and camera angle, but Maya's heart lurched as she zeroed in on shorter of the two men. The shape of his head was like that of a Damascus goat. With trembling hands, she placed the photos back in the envelope and shoved it in her handbag. Paralyzed by shock, she barely noticed the young woman setting a cup of espresso in front of her. So many questions blew through her mind. Who was the mysterious guy who gave her these photos and what was she supposed to do now? There was very little she could do without more information, but how was she going to obtain that? And more importantly, should she tell Will? She downed the espresso, grabbed her packages, and headed towards the cultural center where her car was parked. In the three-block stroll, she tried to calm her mind and approach this logically. If there was a story to be investigated, surely the person who gave her these photos had more information to share. The only thing she could do now was wait.

Once she arrived home, she took the envelope from her purse, and rummaged in the drawer for her jeweler's loop. Even with that, she could not see any details of the images, only that there were two men, one of whom had a very large head. She also had no idea what they were looking at. When she examined the other photo, she could see a mountain of metal parts, and what looked like an airplane wing. Maya sat quietly, deliberately what to do next. She didn't have long to wait long. Her phone pinged indicating an incoming text. She opened the app and saw this message: 11:00 a.m. Monday. Park bench. She didn't respond. He would know that she saw the message, so she left it at that. Monday was three days away. She would have to be patient.

Monday morning Maya went to town early, did some errands, and arrived at the park a few minutes before eleven o'clock. It was crowded but luckily that same bench was available. She sat down and waited, periodically checking her phone for messages. Then he appeared, as if out of nowhere, and sat down on the opposite end of the bench.

"It's a lovely day today, don't you think? Thankfully, the dreaded rains have ended," he said in that melodic voice. He shifted slightly toward her. "You looked at the photos."

"I did. Can you tell me more?"

"As a journalist, I assume you protect your sources?"

"Of course." Maya noticed that he fidgeted with the zipper on his jacket, a trickle of sweat near his hairline, which he wiped away with the back of his hand. "Do I get to know your name?"

"Miguel will do for now."

"Okay, Miguel. Where is that road, or is it a landing strip? And where is that beach? More importantly, do you know the identities of the men in the photo?"

"First things first. That airstrip is in a remote area near the Guatemalan-Mexico border. They've spent the last two years bulldozing the jungle to provide a way for the cargo planes to land."

"Cargo planes?"

"Yes, the ones bringing in tons of cocaine. From there, it's a short trip into Mexico and the route to the U.S."

"Who is 'they' and why hasn't anyone stopped this?"

"'They' are the cartel. And who would dare to stop this? The politicians and the local police are all in on it. And most of the population don't know anything that goes on in this country and couldn't care less if they did."

"About the picture of that beach. Where is that exactly, and who are the men in the background?"

"It's a beach south of the Rio Dulce and that is where the leg bone belonging to your husband washed ashore. The two men in the photo are part of the cartel called Lobos Locos – Crazy Wolves – and that is who your husband owed money to."

"Why are you giving me this information?"

"Miss Warwick," he exhaled before scowling disapprovingly, "don't be so naïve, and do not think I don't know what you're up to with your glitzy little magazine about life on the isthmus and the activities of a bunch of silly gringos. Your magazine is a front."

"I don't know where you would get that idea."

Miguel emitted a derisive laugh. "Do you not know the history of the CIA in this region? Do you think that those of us who know 'things' aren't aware of your timely appearance here in Malpaís as the country is about to explode? I doubt it's coincidence. My bet is that the CIA are behind your publication, but I see it as an advantage. That means you have an inside contact."

"You are totally wrong about that. More importantly,

why exactly should I be investigating anything you say?"

"Who better than *you*? After all, your husband was murdered by these criminals."

"So far, you haven't given me much to investigate. Two grainy photos and that's it. Oh, and the name of the cartel."

"Don't get overanxious. This is a process. I first had to establish contact and now we must build our relationship. I will be in to touch with you soon. *Que tengas una buena tarde.*"

As quickly as he appeared, he was gone, fading into the crowd, leaving Maya sitting there in the park wondering how this was going to unfold. Now that Miguel mentioned it, what exactly was the agenda of Will and his employer? It surely wasn't getting intel on low-level undesirables who may or may not have existed. It was time to approach Will and find out.

Maya arrived at Finca Azahar a few minutes before the *chaparrada* started. Because of the din she would have to wait until it subsided before she could call Will. Even though it was the end of the Green Season, it was not unusual to get an impetuous downpour, but it usually didn't last more than an hour. She made a cup of tea, made some notes, and tried to figure out how she was going to approach Will about what Miguel said about the magazine being a front.

Twenty minutes later, the rains let up and were now little more than a drizzle. She hit Will's name and the phone barely rang once before he answered.

"Good afternoon, Maya."

"Hi, Will. I need to talk to you about something."

"That's what I'm here for."

She told him about her first encounter in the park and about the envelope with two photos, which she described in detail. Will didn't respond, so she continued about meeting the mysterious Miguel in the park for the second time. She thought she heard a nervous cough, or choking sound, before he replied, "And who is Miguel?"

"I thought maybe you knew him. I doubt that's his real name, and besides giving me those photos, he made an interesting observation."

"About?"

"He said that my arrival here, and the launching of the magazine was suspicious, especially since the country was on the cusp of exploding."

"Anything else?"

"He said these things were a good indication that the CIA was fronting the magazine and that my role here was something other than monitoring the activities of a bunch of retirees."

"What did you tell him?"

"What do you think? I denied it all, although I don't think he believed me."

"Do report back to me if he contacts you again or gives you any other information. In the meantime, can you send me those photos?"

"Of course, but what about his claim that there are massive drug transactions taking place here?"

"Not your domain. Do what we asked you to do. Nothing more, nothing less."

"Considering what I've learned so far, you and your 'employer' must have another, larger agenda besides me reporting back to you about what the expats are up to. I've already established that the names on the list, other than one, don't ring a bell without anyone I've spoken to. There's some interesting stuff going on here, but it isn't exclusive to the expats."

"When you submit your reports, make notations of anything you think I should follow up on. We'll speak soon." Then the line went dead.

Chapter 17

Miguel's comment about Malpaís being on the verge of exploding rattled around Maya's head during the night. When she got up, she opened her laptop and went to the local Spanish newspapers to see if she could glean any insight into why he would say that. Admittedly, she had never been concerned with local politics, government corruption, or anything else that didn't directly affect her daily life. She was no different than other expats who moved here and proceeded to enjoy the last few years of their lives without worrying about what was happening around them. Most of them didn't speak Spanish well enough to follow the local news in print or on television; they were in their retirement bubble and were content to be oblivious to the perils of living in a backward Central American country. A country that was now on the verge of exploding. But how and why is what Maya wanted to know.

A quick glance at the online version of *La República*

told her that there was plenty going on here that she should be paying attention to. While she was flitting from lunch to the next dinner party looking for interesting tidbits about expats, the real action was taking place within the fabric of society. The first story was about three missing teenage girls. Beautiful young women, between the ages of thirteen and sixteen, who simply disappeared on their way to school, the store, to see friends. Their frantic families pleaded with the public to report any sightings or even the smallest detail about the girls' lives that the parents may not have known. Did they have a secret boyfriend? Were they involved in drugs? Did they get into a car with a stranger? The distraught face of one mother was featured in the story, begging for the return of her daughter, and holding up a photo that was taken just before her disappearance six months ago. Between tears and sobs, the poor woman managed to say, "My Ana would not run away. We had a happy family, she had everything a young girl could want. She must have been kidnapped." Towards the end of the article, the writer suggested that the disappearance of these girls was in some way related and perhaps they were kidnapped and sold into prostitution, possibly spirited away to another country where they would never be found. Another grim possibility was also proposed: that the girls were murdered, and their remains not yet discovered.

The next article was about two reputed mafia leaders ceremoniously assassinated in broad daylight in an exclusive area of the capital thirty-five miles away. The two Sicilian men left an upscale restaurant and stood near the street waiting for the valet to bring their cars. As they waited, a *sicario* wielding a 9 mm weapon with a silencer executed them with two precise shots – one to the chest and one between the eyes. The identities of the driver and the passenger of the motorcycle were impossible to detect because both were dressed completely in black, their faces hidden behind the shields of their helmets. It was suggested that the murdered men were involved in drug trafficking, although no other details besides their nationality were listed. There were no leads in the case.

The next page had stories that could have happened anywhere: fatal car accidents, domestic violence, armed robberies of local businesses, burglaries of homes owned by the wealthy, but one story really intrigued her, and had far-reaching consequences to the expat community. The current president of the republic had been in secret negotiations with the IMF for a massive loan to improve infrastructure. The details of the clandestine negotiations were leaked to the press by a member of parliament. To secure the loan of nearly one billion dollars, the IMF was demanding that a new VAT be added to all consumer goods, a three hundred percent hike in the toll for the new stretch of highway between San Pedro and Santa Lucia, which the IMF had financed in a previous loan, a property tax increase of two hundred percent, and an increase of one hundred percent on all yearly car registrations. Those things would surely have a financial impact for many retirees living on a fixed income. Maya planned to discuss it with Will. But the shocking story, buried on the third page when it should have made headlines, was how a container shipment of pineapples destined for Spain was intercepted at the port after an anonymous tip to local authorities indicated that the pineapples were filled with cocaine. The lax controls at the border allowed the container, originating in Costa Rica, to avoid detection. The tip proved to be a jackpot when more than ten tons of cocaine was discovered hidden inside hollowed out pineapples. A photo of a smiling customs official holding a brick of cocaine in one hand and a pineapple in the other accompanied the headline that read "Is Malpaís a Pineapple Republic"? Maya chuckled. That was certainly a new twist on the banana republic jokes. According to the story, no arrests had been made and there wasn't much of an investigation about who packed the pineapples, or how they were transported undetected to Malpaís in the first place. More importantly, where was all the money that was exchanged in this commercial venture?

Maya closed out the website and pondered why, with all these activities going on in the country, was she being asked to spy on a bunch of gringos? There were far more important issues to be investigated, but she also knew those issues came with risks, none of which she was willing to take. She had had enough danger in her life, but her investigative instincts were now sparked. What would she do with information she uncovered? And more importantly, when would Miguel contact her again? Did the rest of the world even care what went on here? Probably as much as they cared about the thirty-year civil war in Guatemala, the Iran-Contra affair in Nicaragua, or the Noriega caper in Panama. How many people could even find Malpaís now that it was officially on a map? And did she dare bring these issues up with Will? He seemed adamant about her staying the course and reporting on the activities in the expat crowd, but did Will need to know everything she was investigating? She had a sneaking suspicious that the CIA was using her as a pawn, and there was much more to this assignment than she was told. She knew very well she would never be privy to the machinations of the CIA; she had been recruited as an asset to do a task and whatever she was told was on a need-to-know basis. That much she had learned from Operation SHADOWHAWK.

A quick glance at her calendar revealed she had no expat functions for the next five days when there was a potluck at the Snyder's house in the same area where Maybelle Stevens lived. Maya was relieved to have these next few days to herself during which she would prepare her reports for Will.

Chapter 18

Although it was technically summer now with hot and dry weather, an afternoon shower was always a possibility in the highlands where she lived. The five-day respite from the social whirl gave Maya time to relax and putter in her garden. Thanks to her gardener Juan, she had an abundance of ginger lilies, shampoo ginger, *baston de rey*, stargazer lilies, and birds of Paradise for the dining room table and her bedroom. They would cost a fortune in gringolandia, but here they were hers for the time it took to cut and arrange them.

After a light lunch, she retreated to her bedroom for a nap, covered herself with a blanket, and buried her face in a silk-covered pillow, expecting to drift off as the gentle rain pattered on the roof. As she lay there, she detected a slight movement like a mild case of vertigo, followed by low creaking sound. Before she could focus on where it was coming from, the bed crashed to the floor. She lay there for a minute totally stunned, then crawled out of the bed frame and tried to figure out what just happened. The rails that once held the mattress in place had disintegrated into a fine dust. When her heart stopped racing, she laughed. However, there was nothing she could do about this now. She would wait for Magdalena to come in the morning to deal with it. With nerves totally frayed, she retreated to the guest room and once again tried to take a nap. The ringing of Will's phone woke her up just as she started to dream. She shuffled to the living room, retrieved the phone from her bag, and answered.

"So has the earth moved for you lately?"

"What?"

"I meant did you feel the earthquake?"

"Oh, right, for a second there, I thought. . ." She laughed nervously.

"No, no," he said, "there was a big earthquake in Guatemala about an hour ago and I figured you might have felt it."

"I might have. What time was it?"

"At twelve minutes past one."

"That's what I felt. It happened the same time my bed collapsed."

Will gasped. "Are you serious?"

"Yes, I am. One minute I was preparing to take a lovely afternoon nap and the next minute I was on the floor in a cloud of very fine sawdust."

"Why did that happen?"

"Good question. I have no idea, I'm sure my housekeeper will have an answer for me. Meanwhile, I'm camping out in the guest room. Did you call for a specific reason?"

"No, just inquiring after your safety. I saw the alert

about the earthquake in my news feed. Oh, I read your reports. Very well done. Keep up the good work."

"Will, we need to talk. I glanced at the local Spanish newspapers and there are some very troubling things happening here."

"Such as?"

"First, there was an article about a cocaine bust that uncovered several tons of blow stuffed inside pineapples destined for Spain."

"That's out of my purview, to be honest. Something on that scale is surely being monitored by those whose job it is. Why does that concern you?"

"Because you acknowledged that the Lobos Locos cartel is involved in drug trafficking here. I can't find anything that indicates there were any arrests, so I'm thinking that's because too many higher ups are involved. Something of this magnitude should be of interest to everyone who lives here."

"For most people, if it doesn't affect their lives, they don't care. Most likely, they will never come in direct contact with anyone involved in the drug trade. Your deceased husband, and you by default, were an exception."

There was an awkward silence until Maya said, "Considering both you and Miguel told me that it was the cartel to whom my husband owed money, my interest is personal especially since he was murdered by these thugs."

"My advice: Don't get involved. It's a dangerous route to take. Focus on the human-interest stories and leave it at that. Don't get out of your depth."

Maya seethed for a minute then responded, "You are right. However, there was one story I saw that surely would interest the expats living here and that was how the government was in secret negotiations with the IMF to borrow nearly a billion dollars for infrastructure improvements, the catch being that the IMF wants usurious taxes to be levied to help pay back the loan."

"That's worth noting, for sure. I'll get our staff right on that. Anything else?"

"Not really. Let's talk again soon. I'm going to try yet again to take a nap."

Chapter 19

"Before you do anything, come with me," Maya said when Magdalena breezed into the house. "I have to show you something." She beckoned Magda to follow her down the hallway to her bedroom. The two women stood in the doorway and stared at the mattress on the floor. It took a second for the scene to register and when it did, Magda doubled over laughing.

"*Ay, dios*," she exclaimed, clasping her hand over her heart.

"What happened to my bed?"

"Doña Maya, it is nothing serious. You were gone for three years, and during your absence little *bichos* made their home in the wood and started eating it. They make little tunnels back and forth," she said, waving her hands in the air, "until eventually, the wood is not strong enough to hold any weight. I hope you didn't get hurt when it collapsed."

"No, I didn't, but it was quite a shock."

Magdalena was contemplative for a few seconds before saying, "Let me tell you about my beloved uncle. He had a similar thing happen to him. He was a *borracho* for many, many years and eventually became very depressed at his condition, so he decided to commit suicide by hanging. He went into his *taller* where he repaired shoes and threw a rope over the beam near the *techo*. He stood on his workbench and jumped off, thinking he would get away, once and for all, from his demanding wife who he claimed was the cause of his drinking problem. *Entonces*, the same little bugs had eaten through that beam and when he jumped, the beam broke and he crashed to the floor in a heap and passed out because *por supuesto*, he was drunk at the time. *Mi tia* found him many hours later and kicked him a few times to see if he was still alive. When he opened his eyes and saw his wife standing over him, he started crying. He thought he was in hell, and bellowed, 'I can't even get away from you when I am dead.' She replied, 'No, José, you are very much alive,' which only made him cry harder."

"That's so tragic, Magda."

"*Sí*, but it was also very funny. After that he stopped drinking the white lightning we make here and spent his last few years sober as a priest, even though he was still stuck with his *esposa*. Do not worry about your bed. I will call my friend who can fix it in a few minutos. It's very easy to do," and with that she turned around and walked back to the kitchen, still laughing at Maya's misadventure, and called over her shoulder, "*bienvenido al Paraiso.*"

Maya was about to get online when her phone rang. It

was Louise shrieking.

" Calm down, Louise. I can't understand a word you are saying."

"I have to talk to you. Can you meet me in town?" she blubbed.

"Can you tell me what's wrong?"

"I will when I see you. Please," she begged, "meet me in an hour at Café Roma."

Café Roma was nearly empty. Maya spotted Louise hunched over a corner table, her little rabbit face looking ghostly pale, her hair disheveled, and her nose dripping onto her upper lip. A stack of paperwork was in front of her.

"Louise, what's going on? You're a mess. Here," she said, handing her a napkin, "wipe your nose."

"Honey, I know, but when I tell you what happened, you will understand."

"I'm here now and listening. Tell me what's got you so upset."

"Okay, well, about three weeks ago Bob and I were having breakfast and the police came to our front door. Of course, Bob being Bob, he was all friendly and everything, even invited the two officers in for coffee, and asked how he could help them. That's when they handed him this paperwork." She pointed to the file folder in front of her. "We had no idea what it was, because like everything else in this country, it's in Spanish so we couldn't even read it. Bob called our lawyer immediately, but the phone was disconnected. Our gardener was there during all of this, and he said his son spoke English and could tell us what the paperwork said. He called the son – he's a university student, nice kid – and he came right over since they live a hundred meters down the road. We gave him the papers and he sat at the kitchen table to read them. He said nothing except '*Ay, dios,*' over and over with a somber look on his face. Finally, after ten minutes he said, 'It's very bad news.' We begged him to tell us what it was, so he took this deep breath and said, 'You are being evicted from your home.'"

"How is that possible? I thought you owned your house like most expats here."

"We did, too. But in the closing documents, which we didn't read because we don't know two words of Spanish, there was a clause – just two little lines of text – well, that was our undoing. Those two lines signed over the house to our lawyer, free and clear, giving him the right to take possession at any time with thirty days' notice."

"That can't be legal, can it?"

"Apparently, it is because there was another clause that said we totally understood what we were signing, so what's our defense? That we didn't understand Spanish; that we trusted our lawyer? Then it becomes a he-said-she-said scenario. We talked to another lawyer who said this happens frequently here, and that's why when you do any transaction, you need two lawyers. One to do the job, and one to check on the first lawyer to make sure he did it right. We thought that was a joke – you know a gringo thing, so we laughed it off. Maybe we did fall off the proverbial turnip truck from Silesia. And you know how they read the documents out loud to you before you sign them? I'm sure he read that clause to us, in Spanish, but we didn't understand bupkis. Bottom line, we are screwed and must vacate our house. Oh my God, Maya, we are ruined. We sunk every penny we had into that monstrosity," she bleated before burying her face in her hands.

And it *was* a monstrosity. It was originally built by another gringo, who got it ninety percent finished before he ran out of money after being price-gouged during construction and charged double or triple for everything. By the time he was three hundred percent over budget, he threw in the towel and sold it as it, hoping to recuperate enough money to return to Alabama and buy a shack. Bob and Louise got it for a song, more like funeral dirge now, dumped another few million toucans into it, and finished it the way they wanted. It was spectacular when it was finished, but in all seriousness, why do two people need a seven thousand square foot house?

"Can't you have this investigated? If this happens as frequently as you claim, there must be other cases on record. Have you thought about filing a lawsuit and going before the judge?"

Louise pursed her little rabbit mouth and said in a perturbed tone, "Of *course*, we thought about *that*, so we hired a new lawyer. Then there were different problems."

"Such as?"

"He filed paperwork and asked for an emergency hearing to stay the eviction process until we went through legal channels. That did not work out as planned," she sighed, dabbing at her pink rabbit eyes with the soggy napkin.

"Why not?"

"The day before we were scheduled to have a hearing, the judge was arrested." Louise started sniffling again.

"For what?"

"Putting a video camera in the women's bathroom stalls and watching them on his laptop as they used the toilet while he was, well, you know, pleasuring himself."

"You're kidding." Maya shook her head in disbelief.

"Would I kid about something like that?"

"And then what happened? Couldn't the case be heard by a different judge?"

"If only things were that simple here," she whined. "Our case mysteriously disappeared. There is no record of it ever having been filed. Because guess what? The wanking judge was our scumbag lawyer's uncle. I swear, Maya, everyone in this country is related to everyone else. There is no justice here. Especially for gringos."

"I'm so sorry. What are you going to do now?"

"We're packing it in and heading home. We've been dealing with this for the last month with no results, and now we must vacate the house in a week. I wanted you to know about this because you need to expose this corruption and warn other people who come here. It's open season on gringos. And to be honest, we're so embarrassed this happened to us that we are quietly packing our stuff and leaving a week from tomorrow. Basically, we're slinking out of here with our tails between our legs. I can honestly say that living here has been the worst, and most expensive, lesson we've ever had. And nobody warns anyone about these things, especially about the lawyers who have the moral compass of a puff adder. But now, I'm begging you to do that. *Please*, don't let this happen to anyone else." Louise's bottom lip quivered for a few seconds before she burst into heaving sobs. Maya got up and sat next to her, putting her arm around Louise's shoulders.

"I will certainly do my best to expose this."

Maya left Louise sitting in Café Roma waiting for her husband, and sauntered back to her car, too shocked to do anything but sit there and gather her wits. She would put all these details in her daily report to Will. The marketing of Paradise was fraught with serious omissions about what life entailed here on the isthmus. Portrayed as the last Paradise, it seemed to be anything but that when she factored in all the nightmare stories she had heard lately. What worried her were all the things she still didn't know about this country. She found it appalling the number of incidents that befell the expats when all they did was come here to retire in tropical bliss.

When she pulled into the driveway of Finca Azahar, she didn't want to get out of the car. Once inside, she would have to write her daily report to Will, check her email and voicemail, and brace herself for whatever tale of woe someone wanted to dump in her lap. There were so many victims in the expat community and that made her wonder why they were targeted. Were they too trusting? Too ill-prepared for life in a third world country? Too lackadaisical about their own safety or business affairs? She would pose these questions to Will so his staff could address them in the next issue of *Neotrópica*. From her driveway, she looked across the valley, focused on the two volcanic cones, and watched as black clouds portended a tumultuous afternoon. Although it was summer and this area was not usually prone to hurricanes, climate change had brought an unusual number of violent storms and some of the worst weather on record. And judging by the blackened skies and the uptick in wind, this was going to be a doozie.

Chapter 20

The subject of the email read "EXCLUSIVE INVITATION" and originated from someone named Ginger Phillips, Executive Director of the Santa Lucia Writer's Consortium. Maya wasn't aware that there was such a group but was ecstatic to receive the invitation. Lately, she missed the monthly dinners with her writer pals in Aix, so this email arrived at a propitious time. Ginger extended a cordial invitation to Maya to be a part of the group, if Maya met the qualifications. "*If*?" Maya snorted. "That's a no-brainer." The next meeting was in five days and Ginger requested that Maya send a writing sample of five hundred words by return email for other members to peruse. "Sure, I can do that." Maya inserted the thumb drive that held the final manuscript of *In the Shadows* and selected a passage about the ways in which Nazi propaganda art influenced the worldview of German citizens during the Third Reich. She attached it to her reply, and graciously accepted the offer to attend the meeting on the

25th. The convoluted directions to this event were also included: Five hundred meters north and two hundred meters east of the church in Los Angeles de Santa Lucia, then right at the fourth palm tree and follow the dirt road to the iron gate. Sounded simple enough. And thankfully, the meeting was at one p.m. so she wouldn't get lost in the dark. For the first time in months, she was excited about an event that wasn't a potluck.

The day arrived and Maya was jubilant about this meeting. Surely, this would be a pleasant and stimulating way to spend the afternoon. The drive through the mountains outside Santa Lucia was challenging, given the narrow roads and the huge drop-offs into the sugar cane or coffee fields. She gripped the steering wheel for dear life as she went around some of the tight curves and was relieved when she arrived at her destination. There were other cars on the road, so she parked behind them near the gate. A doorway boasted an arrow pointing to the first house on the left where she was greeted at the door by an elderly and rather cadaverous-looking gentleman who introduced himself as Bill.

"We are so happy you could make it. Please, come in, and let me introduce you to our other members." Bill escorted her to the living room where a half dozen people stood around a table displaying drinks and platters of snacks.

After introductions and a few minutes of perfunctory comments about who lived where and for how long, Bill suggested that they take a seat at the dining room table, with Maya at the head. Was this the hot seat? In front of each place at the table was a sheet of paper that had been red lined with an overabundance of proofreader marks. Maya glanced down at the paper in front of her, took a deep breath, and tried to remain calm. Everyone sat down and turned toward Maya with penetrating gazes. Then Bill suggested that they go around the table so everyone could make comments about the passage Maya sent to be reviewed. Maya smiled but her gut told her this was not going to end well.

"I'll go first," Janet volunteered, waving her hand. "Maya, we are so happy you could join us today. We all take writing very seriously, and we assume you do, as well."

"Yes," Maya replied, "I have been writing since. . ."

"Please don't interrupt," Janet scolded, shaking her head back and forth. "That won't do. I read your submission, and it's quite interesting, however. . . I don't agree with your use of commas or semi-colons. You also seem to like gerunds. And there are too many run-on sentences for my liking. I'm also thinking it could have been more concise."

"I see," Maya replied meekly. *Funny, neither my agent nor my editor ever mentioned that.*

Before Maya could say anything else, Bill, with his sunken, pale blue eyes and straggly wisps of hair, weighed in. "It's a bit pedantic and I doubt anyone would really care about such a topic. I'm sure it bogged down the rest of the manuscript."

"But, Bill," Maya said cautiously, "that is one page out of a five-hundred-page book."

"Ginger asked that you send five hundred words. You didn't. This was only four hundred forty-seven words," Larry barked, waving the paper in the air like a flag.

"Uh, well, I-I apologize," Maya stammered. Maya's left leg began to twitch. What other ridiculous criticisms were coming, she wondered. She wasn't disappointed because Ginger's comment took the prize.

"Why do you think you are qualified to join our group?"

"Because I am a published author and I live here? And besides, you approached me, so I assumed you knew my writing history."

"We have a strict admission policy; I hope you understand that" Ginger said obstinately.

Around the table they went with each person throwing out more gratuitous reproaches: It was too wordy, too haughty, too condescending, too pretentious. Maya stifled the urge to interrupt these people, and the only way she could maintain her aplomb was by keeping her tightly clasped hands on the table. Finally, Maya had enough. "Before we continue, may I ask a couple of questions?"

"By all means," Bill replied.

"Okay, let's start with you. How many books have you written?" He didn't reply. "You have written some books, right?"

"Uh, yes. One book," he replied sheepishly.

"Oh, good. That's fabulous. And where might I find that book?"

He paused for a few seconds, then said, "You can't. It hasn't been published. Yet."

"And Ginger, what about you? What have you written that I might be interested in reading?"

"I write a lot of poetry," she replied, pursing her lips in a condescending fashion. "And I wrote an article for a local newspaper on the importance of *camotes* – you know, sweet potatoes – in the local diet."

"My, *my*, I'll bet that was a piece of journalism worthy

of a Pulitzer," Maya snuffled. "And what about you, Frau Satzzeichen Nazi?"

Janet glowered and wrinkled her face so fervently she resembled a Shar Pei. "I was a junior high school English teacher for thirty-five years. I know my punctuation."

"I'll bet you do," Maya laughed. "But have you actually written anything that's been published? *Anywhere*?"

"I have a book that's a work in progress. It should be done in the next year."

"Well, isn't that just fabulous," Maya said, clapping her hands together. To the gray-haired man sitting at the far end of the table, Maya asked, "Surely you must have something to add to this review. What say you?"

"Honestly, it was a bit over my head. German history is not my strong point," Steve replied and went back to examining his fingernails in exacting detail.

"Well, okay, then. Here's the deal, kids. That excerpt you so eagerly ripped apart came from the second book I wrote that was on the *New York Times* bestseller list. My first book also made that list. I want to thank you for inviting me to this meeting, but I doubt seriously any of you have so much as a scintilla of advice to offer me about writing." Maya rose from the table. "Please, don't get up. You all enjoy your afternoon." She grabbed her handbag from the table and dashed for the exit. When she got to her car, she sat there for a few minutes trying to decide if she should laugh or cry. Were these people serious? The sad truth was yes, indeed, they were. Maya turned the car around and headed down the narrow mountain road to the highway, relieved to be going home and getting away from these sanctimonious, *soi-disant*, aspiring scribblers.

Chapter 21

It was five days of nonstop rain. Not just any rain – not a *chubasco*, a *chaparrón*, not even a *chaparrada*, but the torrential rain they show you on the weather channel when Florida gets hit with a hurricane and the weatherman is blown sideways. Powerlines crackled and Maya's internet was out this entire time, so she had no way of checking news reports. All she could do was hunker down, keep the doors and windows closed, and put towels on the floor where the roof leaked. Luckily, she had enough food in the fridge and the cupboards to survive because it certainly wouldn't be safe driving in these conditions. Late in the afternoon on the fifth day, her internet came back, and she was shocked to learn that the entire Central American isthmus had been battered by Hurricane Elsie. Honduras, Guatemala, and Malpaís were hit particularly hard with widespread flooding, wind damage, and landslides that buried entire villages, killing hundreds of people. Rivers overflowed their banks sweeping away herds of cattle in the process. Dogs, cats, chickens, and goats all searched desperately for shelter. There were rescue groups devoted just to helping the poor animals. The Red Cross and local police assisted human survivors and rescued as many as they could from the mud and the swirling waters. It was a disaster of biblical proportions. By the time Maya spent an hour reading the reports, she was an emotional wreck. Portions of Malpaís were in terrible condition, mostly in the lowlands, but there had been plenty of *derrumbes* – landslides – in the mountain areas where she lived. It would take days before the roads were safe enough to drive, and the forecast said there would be at least one more day of dangerous weather before the storm lost its strength. With the internet back in service, she logged on to her email account to see a half dozen messages, all from people she didn't know.

Two of the messages were about armed home invasions that had occurred during the worst of the storm. Apparently, a gang of thieves used that opportunity to barge their way into houses where the occupants were hunkered down, forcing them to turn over their valuables, credit and debit cards with the pin numbers, and anything else of value they could cart away. With phone lines down in many areas, nobody in their right mind was going to leave their house to go to the police station to report these incidents, giving the thieves a head start on emptying bank accounts and fencing valuables. There wasn't much Maya could do about these incidents, but she would file them away for future reference.

One email stood out. As she read it, she imagined the demeanor of the author, upper class British by the way he constructed his sentences. It read, in part:

"My esteemed Maya Warwick: I would so like to take this opportunity to advise you of a most unfortunate set of circumstances that have befallen me and a group of friends who formed a partnership for the purpose of procuring land near the coast on which we desired to build our retirement homes. During our absence, and before we could commence construction, a band of squatters moved onto the property and built ramshackle abodes. Any attempts to have these squatters removed have been squelched by the courts in favor of the squatters. Much to our dismay, it appears that once squatters are ensconced on a vacant piece of property, their rights go into effect, and they cannot be removed. In essence, they have appropriated our land. After serious investigation, we have discovered that one of the most powerful families in Malpaís paid a rather large sum of money to these squatters to invade our property. This family owns the largest newspaper, a chain of supermarkets, a local real estate franchise, and a bank from which the money paid to the squatters originated. We have been engaged in legal machinations for more than five years with no end in sight and no possible resolution to our problem of how to gain control of our property. This fight has turned into quite a journey, and I have to say I have learned a lot about Malpaís, the most important being the way pressures (financial and social) work here...quite brutal in a 21st Century version of 'feudalism'!"

The email continued for three more paragraphs detailing the frustrations of all parties and beseeching Maya to expose this band of land thieves in the hopes that adverse publicity would shame them into doing the right thing. "The real elephants are the *deputados* and the prevailing culture of 'forelock tugging,' bribe-taking, and the one-term non-consecutive law which is useful for getting rid of disobedient bureaucrats. Until some of these 'Untouchables' are sent to jail nothing will change and that's never going to happen as long as the worst offenders remain free. Amnesty International says the culture of corruption here in Malpaís is the worst in Latin America."

Also enclosed in the email were several aerial photos of the property in dispute, as well as a map of the planned development. It was a forty-five-hectare parcel of land bordering a perfect half-moon cove on the Pacific side. Maya certainly understood why the land was so coveted. It had everything one could want in a tropical Paradise: An abundance of native trees, including tropical fruits, a mountain-fed stream stocked with trout and freshwater shrimp, and a magnificent white sand beach ringed by towering palm trees. The frustration expressed in Bentley Beresford's email was palpable, as if reaching out to Maya was his last desperate attempt to expose this corruption once and for all, having gotten no satisfaction from the courts and no exposure in the largest newspaper because the perpetrators of the theft controlled the flow of information. She hastily typed responses to these messages, apologizing for the delay and citing the lack of internet because of the hurricane as the excuse. In truth, she had no idea how she could help any of these people, but if Will and his editorial staff were looking for fodder to write about, here it was.

What Maya found particularly troubling were the number of incidents that seemed to portray two completely different Malpaíses: the one marketed to gullible gringos and the one that existed that no one talked about or even seemed to be aware of. Was it that nobody was paying attention or was there an underbelly of corruption and sordid activities that never made it past the victims' inner circle? Maya logged onto Facebook news groups in San Pedro and Santa Lucia and saw what was really going on in this tiny country. And none of it was pretty.

There were more desperate parents searching for their teenage daughters who seemed to have simply vanished without a trace. Maya immediately focused on the similarities of all seven girls: long, flowing hair, full lips, large eyes framed by perfectly microbladed eyebrows. There were also two or three missing teenage boys – also with similar features: finely chiseled bone structure, expressive eyes, and mouths with perfect white teeth. What had happened to these young people? Had they been kidnapped, did they run away, were they rebelling against their strict Catholic upbringing? Nobody had a clue. As troubling as this was, it didn't hold a candle to the stories she read about young prostitutes being murdered and dumped in a ravine where people disposed of their used appliances and furniture. Malpaís had the dubious distinction of condoning legal prostitution, but the articles indicated that the trade was controlled by a mafia who set the prices for the services the girls offered, and who housed and provided for these girls. However, how could these girls escape this life when they tired of being a sexual commodity if they were indentured? From what Maya could glean, there was no happy ending, and it made her wonder how many of these girls wound up in that garbage dump, tossed away like yesterday's trash when their usefulness waned.

What Maya found ironic was how the residency application of George and Betty was denied on the grounds that George had been convicted of soliciting a prostitute. . . thirty-five years ago. How self-righteous it was coming from a country where prostitution was perfectly legal. Some things made absolutely no sense.

The next morning Maya left for town early, intending to do a bit of food shopping and getting home before any threat of rain. As she stood in the check-out line at the grocery store, she heard a distinctive voice call her name and turned around to see Maybelle standing seven or eight people behind her in line, waving frantically. After paying for her groceries, Maya sat at one of the little tables near the entrance and waited for Maybelle to get through the line. She dropped into the chair opposite Maya and groaned loudly.

"I'm so glad I ran into you. Did you hear what happened to Charlotte Fellows?"

"No, because I've been *incommunicado*. My internet was out for five days. What's up?"

"The poor thing. They found her dead in her recliner chair, holding a full wine glass in her hand."

"That doesn't sound good."

"Did you ever hear her story? It's a humdinger. Two years ago, she came from the States to housesit for my neighbors. Before they left for Europe, they asked me if I would assist Charlotte if she needed anything. Of course, I said I would."

"How did that go?"

"About a week after she arrived, she asked if I would take her to the grocery store. She went into the store, and I went to the pharmacy across the street. I came out two minutes later, and Charlotte was standing there with two large sacks of groceries. I couldn't figure out how someone could shop that fast. Three days later, she again asked if I would take her to the store. Who am I to judge? I needed a few things at the market as well, so we both went in. When I got in line to check-out Charlotte was three people ahead of me. Do you know what she bought? Six boxes of that awful, cheap wine."

"Was she having a party?"

"No; I assumed she was stocking up. . . for three or four months. But three days later, it was the same routine. I asked her why she needed to go to the supermarket so often when most of us here usually only went once or twice a week. All I had to do was look at her eyes. They looked like road maps. She obviously saw the shocked look on my face, and blurted something about having allergies and that was why her eyes were so red. It wasn't convenient for me to go to town, but she pleaded and said if I took her this time, she wouldn't need to go for five or six days."

"Did you do it?"

"Yes, but all she bought was wine. Lots of wine. Later that night, I heard doors slamming and lots of yelling. It woke both me and Bert and so we went out to the terrace to figure out where it was coming from. We looked up the hill to the house where she was ensconced and saw all the lights on."

"What did you do?"

"Nothing. Went back to bed, but the next day I sent my neighbors an email telling them what had been going on and they begged me to keep an eye on her until they could cut their vacation short and come home.

The next morning, I walked up the hill to check on her and she was passed out in the hammock at ten in the morning. I peeked inside the house. Dishes everywhere, with the poor cat mewing its heart out, so I fed it, then left her a note to call me when she woke up. . . or came to. Long story short, my neighbors came back and booted her out, so she rented a little guest house on the property just below me. I had already distanced myself, but I saw a taxi come to pick her up three or four times a week."

"What a sad story."

"Seriously, Maya, you should write about this – it's a cautionary tale."

These stories upset Maya but what could she do? She made apologies to Maybelle about needing to get home before the rains.

"Oh, darling, I do understand. It's been miserable, hasn't it? What I find amusing is that hurricanes were never mentioned in the promotional ads for this place. You would think that would be an important item to warn people about. The longer I live here, the more I realize that we were all bamboozled by Mad Ave salesmen. Now here we are. Stuck in this place because who is going to come and buy these great big houses we built? I'll tell you who. No one. Let's have lunch when the weather clears up. It's been way too long."

"Definitely, Maybelle. I'll give you a call next week and if you hear of anything else happening in this Paradise, please let me know."

The rain started as Maya began her climb over the mountain road towards Finca Azahar. It was gentle at first but within two minutes it had become an *aguacero*

– sudden fierce, strong, driving rain that washed mud across the road and caused several *derrumbes* to dump large rocks onto the roadway. Maya was relieved to get home without incident. Running from the car to the terrace, she was drenched by the time she stuck her key in the door. Her first mission was to grab the stack of towels and put them under the newly formed leaks. Dealing with the turbulent weather was exhausting and a full-time job.

Chapter 22

With this ongoing atrocious weather, the social scene in San Pedro came to a screeching halt. No morning get-togethers, no luncheons, and no potluck dinners. Maya wondered what all the expats were doing without these activities to keep themselves occupied. For her, it was a welcome break. She used the extra time to delve into the local happenings in both San Pedro and Santa Lucia. After making a cup of *juanilama* tea, she logged onto her email to find a message from Bentley Beresford that included an attachment.

"My esteemed Maya Warwick: I do hope you have survived this monstrous storm that has disrupted all our lives here in Paradise. It would be my great pleasure to meet you and take you for lunch if you are so inclined to come to Santa Lucia when this storm passes. I received your email regarding our land fraud case, and I have much more to tell you in person rather than in this format. In the meantime, I thought the enclosed transcript of Charlotte Wilson's preliminary hearing would be of interest to you. Her trial is set to begin in a fortnight. Perhaps this case is interesting enough to be included in your magazine. I eagerly await your response about a future lunch. With kindest regards, Bentley."

Maya downloaded the lengthy document and opened it. As would be expected, it was in Spanish and there was the usual legalese at the beginning identifying the lawyers defending her and the prosecutor who brought the charge of murder. Maya skimmed through this section and looked for the juicy parts in Charlotte's testimony. She gasped as she read Charlotte's account of what happened that night.

"Bradley went to bed before me, after he took all his medication for his depression and bi-polar disorder. They usually knock him out cold. I went to bed about an hour later and he was sound asleep. But then I felt him stir and toss and turn a few times and even in the pitch blackness, I could see him holding a gun to his head. Of course, I panicked and yelled at him to put the gun down and he mumbled something about how he couldn't live like this anymore and that he would be better off dead. I told him that was not the answer and to give me the gun, but he wouldn't, so I reached for it and tried to take it away from him and that's when it went off. I don't remember anything else after that except screaming and trying to call the police. That is all I remember."

Maya continued reading the transcripts of the detective who arrived on the scene and found Charlotte in a most distressed state with her husband lying in the marital bed with a gunshot wound behind his right ear.

By all accounts, Bradley Wilson was predominantly left-handed. Maya read these sections several times and no matter how she analyzed it, she couldn't but wonder how someone who is left-handed could shoot themselves behind their right ear. Maya sat quietly for a few minutes and imagined the scene in her head. She pictured Bradley sound asleep, in a drug-induced dreamland, and his beautiful willowy wife lying beside him. How did she see a gun if the room was pitch black? What if Charlotte had gone to bed, saw him sleeping peacefully, and simply shot him in the head as he lay unaware of what was about to happen. It would make sense that she would throw the gun to the opposite side of the bed. It would also make sense that she was totally distraught afterwards. The more Maya read, the less sense it made to her investigative mind. She was eager for the outcome and if the rumors about their turbulent marriage would be exposed in the trial.

Two weeks later, the trial of Charlotte Anne Pearce Wilson began in a packed courtroom in Santa Lucia, presided over by one judge. It lasted two days. The judge handed down a verdict of not guilty and ruled Bradley Wilson's death a suicide. A jubilant Charlotte and her movie star handsome lawyer held a press conference on the steps of the courthouse announcing how happy they were that the judge weighed all the evidence and came to the right conclusion: Charlotte was not guilty. Haggard and frail, this ordeal, along with bad hospital and prison food, had nearly done her in. Her smile radiated relief more than anything. She waved to the crowd of reporters as her lawyer led her down the stairs and into a waiting sedan. Maya now thought that almost anything was possible on the isthmus, even a rich woman getting away with murdering her husband.

Three days later, the prosecutor once again filed charges of first-degree murder and issued an arrest warrant. To add insult to injury, Charlotte was dragged at midnight out of the luxury apartment in which she was now residing and taken to Buen Pastor, the local women's prison, where she was booked, fingerprinted, and tossed into a rat-infested cell. Maya could hear her screams of disgust and entitlement all the way to San Pedro. The following morning, she was once again arraigned but threw such a colossal temper tantrum in the courtroom that the judge ordered a mental evaluation. Rather than being returned to the prison, she was taken to the local psychiatric hospital which resembled something out of a nineteenth-century horror story. Denied access to the media, she was held in solitary confinement until her mental status was assessed. This is when Maya discovered that double jeopardy was a concept that did not exist in local jurisprudence. In less than two weeks, Charlotte would be on trial again, and if the prosecutors had their way, a verdict of guilty would be handed down.

They weren't disappointed. The prosecutors hired some hotshot crime investigators from the UK to review the evidence gathered at the crime scene, review autopsy reports as well as Charlotte's statements. They concluded that there was no way Bradley shot himself behind his right ear, and Charlotte Wilson was deemed guilty of first-degree murder and sentenced to twenty years in a maximum-security prison. She was literally dragged from the courtroom after feigning unconsciousness and tossed into the back of a dilapidated police van that sped away with the faint sounds of Charlotte's screams filling the airwaves. Maya shook her head in disbelief. This was not the end of the story, however, and Charlotte's lawyer petitioned the court for the return of all the personal items that were confiscated from the parking garage following Bradley's death. According to her lawyer, the value of those things exceeded fifty million dollars. Citing his client's dire financial situation, and the need for funds to launch yet another investigation and appeal, the judge summarily denied the request stating that taxes needed to be paid on those items and until then they were property of the state.

Maya could barely process this information. Two trials already and a third one about to be staged. How many times could this go on? What kind of justice system was this anyway? It was something out of Alice in Wonderland. She would watch for updates on this situation, and in the meantime, she accepted Bentley Beresford's luncheon invitation.

Chapter 23

Maya met Bentley at a restaurant called La Princesa on the outskirts of Santa Lucia. It was a seafood restaurant situated in an old mansion facing a park. A uniformed doorman ushered her in, and a *maître d'* escorted her to Bentley's table. He was staring at his phone when she approached, but immediately sprang up to greet her.

"I am so delighted that you could meet me. I assume you had no trouble finding this place."

"No, I didn't, thanks to Google Maps."

The *maître d'* pulled out a chair across from Bentley and Maya sat down. A menu lay in front of her.

"Do have a look at their offerings, but might I suggest the grilled lobster? I can attest to the quality of their food. Always impeccably fresh and well prepared and do give the gentlemen lurking behind you your drink order. They make a fabulous martini, which is what I am having."

"I think I will stick to a glass of white wine, and the

lobster sounds delicious."

Bentley gave the lunch order to the maître d' and then turned to the gentlemen sitting at the next table and told him to order whatever he wanted on the menu. The thick-necked Hispanic with a muscular build and coal black hair slicked back from his rugged face stared intently at the entrance. It was then that Maya noticed the two Malinois shepherds sitting on the floor near his table. Obviously, this guy was Bentley's bodyguard, which made Maya wonder if she was in any danger by having lunch with him.

"What did you think of the document I sent you?" he asked in his lilting British accent.

"It left me speechless, as I am sure anyone would be who wasn't familiar with the way things worked here. I've been following the case now through local news outlets, but the question that comes to mind is how many times can they try her for the same thing?"

Bentley laughed, amused by Maya's question. "As many times as it takes to get the results that make them happy. As for being shocked by such machinations, yes, well, it is business as usual here, I have found. Oh, by the way, the gentleman at the next table is Enrique and his two companions are Hannah and Lina. They're my insurance policy."

"Are they necessary? And should I be sitting with my back to the door?" she asked, looking over her shoulder towards the entrance.

"Don't worry, Enrique has eyes like a hawk, and nothing moves without his dogs taking note. This is probably the safest you will ever be in this country. By the way, I'm aware of what happened to your husband. It must have been a very traumatic experience for you."

"Yes, it was, but after five years, it doesn't dominate my daily life."

"I hope you had a good resolution though, at least to give you some peace."

"The authorities had almost zero interest in the case. And I am just now learning about the kinds of nefarious activities he may have been involved in that led to his unfortunate demise."

"Hmm," Bentley mused, "nefarious seems to be the operative word in this part of the world. I've had quite a bit of nefarious activities to deal with in the last five years."

"Can you tell me a little more about your legal issues here?"

"More like illegal issues. My lawyers, and I've had several since this nightmare began, haven't been able to do much of anything to speed my case along so it has become a loathsome boondoggle into which every spare *sou* I have is being thrown. Which is why I contacted you. I've seen your magazine and if your goal is to realistically write about life, customs, and the culture of the isthmus, then incorporating the culture of crime might also be of value."

"I couldn't agree more." Maya placed her phone on the table and looked up at Bentley, whose placid face showed no emotion, except for the devious glint in his pale blue eyes. Maya guessed he was nearing seventy, but still had a full head of silver hair, and with his trim physique, he cut a dashing figure, and probably was – or maybe was still – a lady's man. She was willing to bet he was a product of one of those ritzy Swiss boarding schools that groomed the sons of the uber wealthy for the life of privilege and prominence to which they were accustomed. "Could you start at the beginning, and because I'm a terrible notetaker, I'd like to record our conversation. Is that okay?"

"But of course," he replied, eagerly leaning forward. "Shall I begin?"

"Please."

An hour later, Maya hit stop on her phone and looked directly at Bentley. "That is quite a tale. Basically, what you've told me is that the most powerful families in this country are engaged in a pattern of systematic theft of land owned by foreigners."

"Oh, not just foreigners. But the locals, too. That new luxury hotel going up at the beach? Have you seen the photos of that? It's on par with a Four Seasons and the land on which it is being built was appropriated under a specious eminent domain law. The family that owned and lived on the property for the last two hundred years were summarily evicted, and the main house and other outbuildings were bulldozed. Construction started the following week."

"But surely the family was compensated for this, weren't they?"

"Ha! Fair compensation by any standards would have been in the millions because those four hundred acres were a prize piece of land bordering the ocean with several small coves and pristine beaches. As it stands now, the family got not a quid, and although they have filed several lawsuits, nothing ever gets resolved. Meanwhile, the eighty-five-year-old widow is living with one of her sons in Santa Lucia. The son contends that the judges are all in on it and simply bury the pleadings under the mountain of paperwork that the judicial system is famous for here. If I had to guess, it appears that they simply do not want anyone owning prime real estate other than those who belong to their cabal. And with a plethora of crooked lawyers falsifying land transfer documents, there is almost no way to end this practice."

"What do you hope to gain by making this public?"

"My thought is that exposing these families and their far-reaching tentacles of corruption would deter anyone from coming here and investing in this country. As I said previously, when we first bought our parcel of land, nobody had ever heard of this place. Within a year or two, the marketing campaign began and well, you know the rest. After all, you fell for it, too."

"Yes, I did. And I'm grateful nothing has come up that would be a red flag considering who I acquired my property from. I've had my lawyer check the registry and the chain of ownership, and so far, it all looks okay."

"You are one of the lucky ones, then."

"I am starting to realize that."

Chapter 24

Maya checked her email and saw nothing from Will or anyone in the expat crowd. She was about to log off when this appeared:

"Dear Maya Warwick: I have been reading your new magazine *Neotrópica* with great interest. I am one of the people who got lured into moving to this third world dung heap by slick and deceptive advertising. You see, after getting a hard sales pitch from a well-heeled con man, I decided at the age of sixty to fulfill my lifelong dream of becoming a Euell Gibbons character, buying a piece of land where it doesn't snow, and trying my hand at growing coffee. It didn't quite work out as I envisioned. I hope at some point your content strays away from local customs, anecdotes about history, and those endless recipes for *camotes* (my God, I don't know how anyone can eat those things) to something more substantial. Let me give you some fodder for future articles.

"After only five years of living in this teeming backwater my life is totally ruined, my entire savings evaporated, and my dreams dashed. Robert Vesco was right. When asked how to come to Costa Rica and leave a millionaire, his reply was "come with two." The same applies to Malpaís. I didn't come here as a millionaire, but my nice nest egg is *adios*, having gone to a herd of crooked lawyers to clean up one mess after another caused by the unscrupulous way business is done here. Then there was that totally manipulative Latina beauty who set her sights on my pension and my property. If I sound angry, I am. My shrink is on vacation, the pharmacy ran out of my anxiety medication, and I'm about to blow a gasket.

"They say this is a developing country. Are they kidding? About the only thing they've developed is a way to ship massive amounts of cocaine to Europe stuffed inside pineapples. This pineapple republic is run by a bunch of inbred, white-collar carpet baggers and thieves. There are only a dozen families who control everything, and they're all related. How do I know that? Well, there are only fifty surnames in this country. When people have two last names that are the same i.e., Carlos Lopez Lopez, you can be sure that somewhere in the family tree someone married a cousin, brother, sister, or uncle.

"And these customs. Talk about exhausting. The first immutable custom is that you never, ever walk into a business without saying hello, good morning, good afternoon, how are you, I hope you are doing well, how's your family. Forget that quick stop in the local *pulperia* (their version of 7-11). By the time you've gotten through all the perfunctory greetings, you have wasted fifteen minutes on a task would've taken only sixty seconds back in the US. Those who refuse to engage in these little rituals run the risk of price gouging. Don't believe me? Try it and see how they jack up the price of something because you didn't ask about their sick mother-in-law.

"Being ten degrees north of the equator, our days and nights are the same length every day of the year. It gets so monotonous that you don't know what day it is unless you look at a calendar. Your circadian rhythm resets here. Until I came to this wretched place, I was a night owl. Now I'm going to bed when I used to eat dinner and am getting up when I went to bed. Dinner is at three p.m., and I'm flat on the sofa by six fighting to stay awake until I can go to bed at eight. Who does that? Chickens, that's who. God*damn* chickens.

"Let's talk about the weather. We have two seasons. Rain or no rain. Also referred to as summer or winter but often it's simply referred to as the land of eternal spring. That's about right because spring weather is unpredictable just about anywhere, but especially here. Summer is supposed to begin in November but for the last five years we've had three or four hurricanes during that month. Nobody warned me about that. The slick ads deliberately omit any mention of a third season called wind! This is different than the hurricanes and is known as the Vientos de Navidad – the winds of Christmas. Even Gabriel Marquez writes about them in his homeland of Colombia. Nice name but holy crap, they are often gale force and start in early December and last through February. Last year, the wind blew eighty mph for nine days, ripped the roof off my neighbor's house in big sections, and sent them flying. There's nothing like being awakened in the middle of the night to a resounding crash and discover you can see the stars through the yawning gap in your new roof. That was fun.

"September and October are the rainiest months. You go to town early and get home by one p.m. to hunker down. You don't want to drive in one of those tropical downpours – you know the ones I'm talking about? Where the pelting rain obscures your vision and walls of water containing tree trunks, branches, animal carcasses, and other garbage often washes cars right off the road? Yeah, that rain.

"Dare I even mention how they drive here? Let me be frank: they drive like they're either drunk or on crack. Many have never taken a driving lesson, most have no license, and rules of the road are mere suggestions, same with stop signs, traffic lights, and road signs. I guess it wasn't too long ago that riding a mule or using an oxcart were the only modes of transportation. But does anyone warn us that driving here is a life-or-death situation? Nope. Not a word from the glitzy ad men. Don't even get me started on motorcycles but the stat that more people are killed on motos than in cars speaks volumes. Anyone with half a brain doesn't drive at night here. The roads are poorly lit, unmarked, and because the pedestrians have no sense of personal safety, they often walk on the side of the road (we have no sidewalks) dressed in black. God forbid you hit them because you will be hauled off to the hoosegow on the spot. Welcome to the land of Napoleonic Law. Guilty until proven innocent. The last thing on anyone's bucket list should be going to jail in this third world hell hole.

"I wanted to warn of the dangers of old men getting involved with beautiful young women, but my experience is so embarrassing, I still can't talk about it, except with the shrink. Let's just leave it at this: That twenty-two-year-old babe was not in love with a sixty-three-year-old man, but rather what few assets he had. It was so perfectly orchestrated that he will have to support her, the kid she had with her drug dealer boyfriend, and her extended family. Forever. Of course, I feel foolish having been so naïve to think I was getting a second chance at romance at my age. She, on the other hand, did quite well for herself. She managed to take possession of my house based on some arcane law that left me barely enough to live on until I die. However bad it is, it's better than winding up in a shallow grave as that other guy did who was just as dumb as me.

"The country motto, or rather advertising slogan, is Pura Paz. It means pure peace. It's also a way of life and is responsible for Malpaís being named one of the happiest countries in the world (by whom I want to know!) The locals use this term as a greeting, to say goodbye, everything's wonderful, life is good. Don't stress about little things, live in the moment, and don't worry about the past or the future. Therefore, stopping their car in the middle of the road to chat with a neighbor, even if they are holding up traffic, is more important than someone getting to work on time or a doctor's appointment. You have two choices: risk your life going around the car stopped on a blind curve or sit and wait.

"Stealing is a national sport rivaling soccer. In fact, if what you steal is valued at less than a thousand dollars, it's not even a crime. Every family has a thief. For this reason, who you let into your house is very important. Maids are notorious for tipping off thieves (often their cousin or brother). Maids also steal your jewelry, toilet paper, a packet of meat, that expensive scarf. They come to your house empty-handed, but that doesn't stop them from stashing the goodies in their underpants or their bra. It's open season on gringos who come and show off. After all, they've got tons of money to replace what gets stolen. These things are only ever spoken about in hushed tones amongst friends because people who want to sell their houses don't want to scare off prospective buyers. Thefts in broad daylight have become more frequent. Don't pull out an iPhone on the street, don't wear that Rolex watch, and don't sport those gigantic rocks that your philandering husband bought you. Better to look like a bag lady or a homeless man than be a target. You can lose a finger or even earlobes as that one woman did. You didn't read about that in the paper because it was hushed up.

"Our electricity, with the highest rates in Central America, is provided by the government monopoly. It too is run by a bunch of high salaried thugs. People love working for the government because one can never be fired, and their pension plan rivals any Fortune 500 company. My bill here is higher than it was in a Maine winter even though we have frequent power outages and Internet is unreliable during bad storms, which is six months a year. It also helps if you are a prepper and know how to dehydrate food, grow the basics, stash water and candles, and chop wood. Nobody told me that at retirement age, I would need these skills to survive. Instead of being Euell Gibbons, I reinvented myself as Bear Grylls because life here is one continuous episode of *The Survivor*.

"The only truthful thing in the brochures was the information on the Farmer's Market. It has hundreds of vendors selling every kind of fresh fruit and vegetable you could imagine. You can also buy meat, fish, chicken, milk and cheese, flowers, soap, plants, pots and pans, hay, cow manure, potting soil, and underwear. Some fruits have hair, fuzz, and spines. One fruit looks like cotton candy on the inside, and there're other abominations called custard apples and water apples. I just want a Granny Smith instead of something I must kill with a machete before I eat it.

"What's with all these holidays? Every month the country shuts down for three or four days. For Christmas, all government offices and most businesses are closed from December 15 to the second week in January, and don't even get me started on Easter week, which should be renamed Easter Month. No liquor is sold during these holidays so if you didn't stock up beforehand, you're out of luck. I didn't realize I had a drinking problem until I forgot about a holiday weekend.

"Don't come here if you don't like bugs. Right now, there's a monster-sized cockroach under a plastic glass in the bathroom. I'm waiting for it to die so I can scoop it up and dispose of it. Leafcutter ants are my nemesis. My entire coffee crop, consisting of three hundred plants, was wiped out in two days by those buggers. Then there are the Army ants, who attack in a squadron approximately ten inches across and forty or fifty feet in length. Big black ants the size of my thumb that you can see coming from a hundred yards away and raid your house in about fifteen minutes. They are the cheapest cleaning service around and clean up the carcasses of other bugs and crumbs that the maid missed. I'm sure I've left out some other annoying items, but those are the highlights of my life and I feel a bit better now for letting it all out.

"Quite frankly, I am counting the days until I go back to civilization, even though I am broke and broken. The conundrum is how a tiny country, with such majestic beauty and an abundance of natural resources can be a repository for every ill afflicting mankind. Malpaís isn't Paradise but rather one of those circles of Hell Dante wrote about. You can have it; I'm going back to the woods. But do your faithful readers an enormous favor by telling them the truth about this place. Sincerely yours, Orville Richardson."

Maya set her laptop aside and leaned back in the chair, stunned by what she had read. She didn't know whether to laugh or cry at poor Mr. Richardson and his sarcastic litany of bad experiences and complaints. She had to agree that many important details were being omitted from the unbridled and salacious ad campaigns. The Malpaís depicted in the captivating TV and print ads was quite different than the one of daily life. No, this is not a permanent vacation, as the ads claim. In fact, living here is a full-time job. Even the smallest tasks take monumental effort to accomplish. Dealing with the labyrinthine bureaucracy is daunting for even the most patient and organized person, so it certainly wasn't a mystery why very few people lasted longer than two or three years, creating a revolving door of expats coming and going on a regular basis. Maya sent Orville's email to Will to see what he had to say about some of those topics. Everything he listed could easily fill an entire issue of *Neotrópica*.

Chapter 25

"You weave words as a spider weaves a web," Will said when she answered the phone.

"Well, I haven't heard from you in a while. I guess you've been doing spook things, huh?"

"You could say that. Mostly, I've been focused on your regular reports about what you are seeing and hearing, especially this last report about Bentley Beresford. I must say that his story raises some interesting issues that have not been addressed previously, mainly land theft by legal means. It warrants more investigation, and it certainly warrants an article in *Neotrópica* which our editorial staff is working on now."

"That's good to know. I'm glad you found it of interest. He's a totally engaging character so I am going to keep in touch with him because he seems to know who the real players are on this little plot of dirt."

"It certainly seems that way. We'll be in touch, Maya, and keep up the stellar work."

Maya was still trying to figure out why what Orville Richardson wrote troubled her so. Maybe because underlying his disgust and indignation about his experiences, there was a profound sadness, even desperation. Maybe it was his line about going home broke and broken that gripped her. She knew very well what being broken felt like and if her friend Liz had not been there, who knows how it would have ended when Maya finally realized that her husband was a deceitful, predatory sociopath. Her instinct was to reach out to him, but she didn't want to appear solicitous or patronizing. She sent him a very short email thanking him for his observations and asked if he would be amenable to having a café in town at his convenience. Less than sixty seconds after hitting the send button, he replied that he would indeed like to meet with her and for her to name a time and place sometime in the next three days because he would be leaving thereafter. They agreed to meet tomorrow at Café Roma.

Maya's routine of spending an hour reading the local news sites and various Facebook pages populated by a variety of people with an equally wide variety of complaints had become a source of entertainment. She couldn't believe how much moaning and griping they did about almost everything, from inadequate water supply to electrical outages, to the rising cost of living. One of the pages she was fond of was the local police page where every routine crime was reported to alert the citizenry of potential danger. As Maya scrolled the page, she stopped when she saw a notice in Spanish, "We need help identifying this person whose remains were found last week. Anyone with any information is invited to call this number. Your report can be anonymous." Maya stared at the sketch, analyzing every detail. It took a minute but then the full impact of what she was looking at sank in.

"That's Miguel." No wonder he hadn't contacted her after their last meeting in the park. According to the article, his partially decomposed body was found in a field, but a forensic artist created a likeness as he might have looked when he was alive. The local papers always revealed gory details about murder victims, and it was no exception with Miguel, whose tongue had been cut out, giving rise to suspicions that he was a snitch of some kind. Because his hands had been cut off, they had no fingerprints to run through any database. The article added that the cause of death was a single gunshot wound to the base of his skull, execution style. Maya felt queasy reading the article. How could she not wonder if the same people who murdered her husband were responsible for this? It seemed like a logical conclusion. She slammed her laptop closed. Now she was concerned for her own safety and intended to discuss this with Will. She made it very clear at that luncheon on her terrace in Aix that she wanted no part of anything that would put her in jeopardy, no matter how much she was being paid. Considering what happened to Lucien, it was obvious she had been in danger the entire time they were married.

Chapter 26

Maya was nervous about meeting Orville. She arrived at Café Roma fifteen minutes early hoping to gather her thoughts and formulate a few questions she could ask him that wouldn't be too intrusive. She jotted some notes on her iPad then set it aside when she sensed the presence of someone standing near her. Looking up she saw a tall, lanky gentlemen with unruly white hair, wearing tortoise-shell rimmed glasses and dressed in Levi's and a denim shirt. The slump of his shoulders was the first clue that he was shrouded in sadness. "Are you Maya?"

"Yes. You must be Orville," she smiled, extending her right hand. "I'm glad you agreed to meet me. Please, have a seat."

The waitress, who had been hovering nearby, came to take their orders of two espressos.

"It's I who should be grateful. Maybe I can leave this wretched place with at least one good memory."

"Your email touched me in so many ways. Would you

be willing to expound on any of those events you wrote about? I'm sure your experience will serve to benefit others."

He removed his glasses and set them next to the water glass. Maya noticed that his eyes were a shade of blue she had never seen before – something between glacier and teal and even with their sorrow they radiated warmth and kindness.

"I haven't really discussed any of these events outside of my doctor's office and when I wrote that email to you, I was scooting toward the edge of a precipice. I had had enough, and once I started writing, it all came bubbling out. I never expected you to respond. In fact, I'm a little embarrassed that I went on about my troubles. And for the record, I had never seen a psychiatrist in my sixty-five years until I came here."

"Tell me whatever you would like to share. If it's too personal, it will remain confidential between us, but I would like to write about many of those things you brought to my attention."

Orville sighed. "You seem like a very astute and worldly woman. Can I talk about my relationship with the person who ruined my life?"

"Of course. Maybe I can give you some advice or at least some consolation."

Orville dumped a sugar packet into his steaming espresso, stirred it for ten seconds, then looked directly at Maya. "You see, right before I got caught up in that guy's sales pitch, I was coming out of the nosedive of losing my wife of thirty-five years to cancer. Despondency doesn't even begin to describe my mental status, having spent the previous four years taking care of her. After she died, I was desperate to do something with the rest of my life, but mostly I wanted an escape from the profound grief I was experiencing. Moving to Paradise seemed like a good way to do that."

"I'm so sorry to hear about your wife. That must have been difficult."

"It was. We had a solid marriage. She was my anchor and best friend. Our life together was good and rewarding even though we never had children. It was just us and an old dog, and he died three days after she did. I was five years older than she was, and I always assumed I would predecease her so when she got sick, it threw me for a loop. When it was all over, I was left totally adrift. At least when I was taking care of her, I felt useful and needed. Then suddenly, I was alone – I mean alone. In retrospect, I didn't think this move through very well. I was obsessed with a new beginning and simply thought I had nothing to lose. I couldn't have been more wrong.

"The first couple of years here I focused on the house I built and my coffee farm. I never really made any close friends. I didn't know how to do that, or even where to meet them. My farm was a bit out of town, and I only ever came to San Pedro for supplies. One day I was standing in line at the supermarket and this beautiful young woman started talking to me in broken English. She was charming as hell, very coquettish, flirtatious. I was flattered, old man that I was. Having been married most of my adult life I didn't have much experience with women. On an impulse I asked her name and if she had time for a café. Her name was Liliana. She was twenty-two years old. If it sounds trite to say there were fireworks, well, so be it. But I'm not kidding, rockets went off for me. She was attentive, humble, caring, and very gentle and didn't seem to mind that I was old enough to be her grandfather. It was lovely the first six months, but then it all started to fall apart. She would disappear for a day or two, come back smelling of alcohol with a pallor the color of slate which made me suspect drug use although I had no idea what kind of drugs they might be. We started arguing – mostly me scolding her for being reckless, but she would get violent, hurling plates and glasses at me, scream, and swear in Spanish, which I didn't understand, and then storm out of the house and disappear again. After a year of this, I had enough and packed up her belongings and set them outside for her to retrieve when and if she ever came back. Of course, she did, only to inform me that there was no way I could kick her out of *her* house now that she was pregnant with *my* child. The next thing I knew I was served papers by the local police and ordered to vacate. I felt like the dumbest man on the planet as I gathered one bag of belongings before the police escorted me off my property. Two days later her real boyfriend moved in. I checked in to a local hotel in San Pedro, brooded for a day or two, contacted a lawyer and a shrink because I knew without some counsel, I could very well wind up in a prison here."

"That's understandable. I'm glad you had the good sense not to act on your anger. That would not have ended well for you."

"No, it certainly wouldn't. One night, after six weeks in that depressing hotel room, it hit me like a tsunami. Here I was a widower, who abandoned a nice quiet life as a retired professor, with a perfectly lovely little house in the Maine woods, and completely lost my wits over some vixen. I didn't just feel foolish. I felt totally broken. Everything I had worked my entire life for was now gone and for what? Because I bought into the dream of living in an exotic Paradise, with year-round sun, beautiful beaches, lush rainforests, and fields of sugar cane, but where did I wind up? Sitting in a run-of-the-mill hotel room, in a town where I knew no one, trying to figure out how I was going to reconstruct my old life back in Maine. On the bedside table was a copy of your magazine. I leafed through it, and the urge to write to you overcame me. I confess that I felt much better afterwards," he said with a slight grin, "but I figured you would think I was off my trolley, and I probably was, but at that point I had nothing else to lose, not even my dignity. Something inside of me crumbled into a million pieces. I was humiliated and embarrassed, and all I wanted to do was get the hell out of here. Thank God, I still have the house in Maine, so that's where I'm going."

A tear trickled out of the corner of Maya's eye which she brushed away before he saw it. His story was heartbreaking, and she could only imagine the inner turmoil and self-castigation he had subjected himself to. She forced a weak smile and said, "You are a very brave soul, Orville Richardson. I think everyone has a disastrous love affair in their history. I know I have, so I can totally sympathize with what you went through. If there is a bright spot in this scenario it's that you still have your house in Maine, and you are going back to a life you knew, albeit a different life than the one you had previously."

"I am totally ambivalent about doing that, to be honest. What am I really going back to? An empty life. My working career is over; I have no other family. It will be a supreme effort for me to integrate back into that community; many of the folks I used to know have passed on. I've been gone five years and didn't do a stellar job of keeping up with what few relationships I did have. The soul-searching I have had to do has been painful and yet in a way I learned some things about myself I hadn't ever thought about. If I'm lucky, I still have a few good years left. It occurred to me that most people who come here are either running away from something or running to something. For me, I was running from the painful memories of losing my wife and running to what I thought would be a whole new existence surrounded by magic. In the beginning it was. I was in awe of the beauty of this place, and I had so much hope, but how totally naïve I was. I saw what I wanted to see and little by little, the underbelly of this place became all too apparent, and I wasn't prepared to deal with it."

Maya was about to reach across the table and touch his hand when she saw Maybelle Stevens march into the restaurant followed by a stream of expat women, somber as a group of funeral goers. Orville turned his head to see what she was focusing on.

"Do you know those women?"

"A few. And it looks like something serious has happened by the dour looks on their faces."

"I need to get going now. Still have things to do before my departure. It was a pleasure to spend time with you, Maya. If you write about any of the things I mentioned, I'd love to see a copy of the article."

"You can subscribe to the magazine online."

"I'll do that. Take care and thank you for your kindness."

"Safe travels, Orville. We'll be in touch." Impulsively, she got out of her chair and threw her arms around him and gave him a hug. He reciprocated, then gently slid from her embrace, turned, and walked out of the café. Maya felt like crying, but instead took a deep breath and walked to the outdoor patio in the back where the eight women were gathered.

"Maya, come and sit with us," Maybelle implored. "Grab a chair from one of the other tables and join us."

"What's going on? Why do you all look so glum? Has someone died?" *Again.*

Maybelle sighed, "No, dear, but Anna here," reaching over to grab the elderly woman's hand as she continued to explain, "had a very traumatic incident and we are trying to console her. Aren't we, dear?" she asked the gray-haired woman who looked down at her lap.

"What the hell happened?"

"I got robbed," Anna said in a soft voice

"Did you call the police?"

"The police robbed me."

"What?" Maya gasped.

"I know, right? Early this morning I was outside, and a police car came to my gate. There were two officers. They spoke a little English and said that they were here to check my premises and make sure I was safe because there had been a few robberies in the neighborhood. Of course, I let them in. They walked around the outside of my house, looked at my security cameras and motion detectors, then wanted to see the inside of my house and whatever security I had in there. But a few seconds after they entered, they closed my front door, and one of them grabbed me from behind and put his hand over my mouth, while the other one tied my hands and feet together with those plastic handcuffs. Then one of them put duct tape over my mouth and tossed me onto the sofa while they ransacked my house. I didn't have much of value, a few hundred dollars, an equal amount in toucans, and a few pieces of jewelry. I thought I was going to have a heart attack, but it was all over in a few minutes and after they left, I was able to scoot to the junk drawer where I got the scissors to cut the plastic restraints."

"What did you do then?"

"I called Maybelle and she told me to call the police, but I told her it was the police who robbed me. Now who do I call?"

Maya looked at the faces of the other women, some of whom she had seen around town, but whose names she didn't know. By their expressions, they were all very upset over this. Maybelle, as usual, had made it her mission to get poor Anna some recourse. If expats couldn't trust the police to protect them, who could they trust? Maya knew the answer to that: Absolutely nobody. Expats were on their own here and were little more than moving targets for a large segment of the population whose goal it was to take advantage of them. Maya looked at poor Anna with all the sympathy she could muster. The woman must have been scared out of her wits and now several hours later still looked to be in shock.

"Do you live alone?" Maya asked.

Anna looked up from her clenched fists resting in her lap. "Yes. My husband died shortly after we came here. I have two cats, but well, they're cats." Anna shrugged.

"Maybe it would be a good idea to have someone come and stay with you for a while," Maya suggested. "Do you have a family member who could come down for a bit?"

"I called my daughter, but she's busy with her own life

and her kids, so she can't come, but she suggested that I come to live with her."

Maybelle chimed in, "I've offered Anna my guest-house until she calms down, and then I can help her with whatever she decides to do."

"I don't want to be here anymore," Anna whined, bawling into a paper napkin. "That was the most terrifying thing that ever happened to me, and with Max gone, I feel so vulnerable now. The only sensible thing for me to do is go back to the US."

The other women nodded in unison. Some dabbed at their eyes, and a couple were visibly upset with scrunched up faces and tears rolling down their cheeks.

"There, there, dear," Maybelle soothed, "you're going to be just fine. I'll watch over you until you decide what to do."

Maybelle had found her calling as the Patron Saint of Expats in Crisis. If Maybelle couldn't fix it, nobody could, and Maya felt relieved that Anna had someone she could lean on until she could escape this Paradise. Anna seemed a bit older than the other women; if Maya had to guess she would say she was in her late seventies, and that made Maya feel all the sorrier for her. She and her husband Max had obviously come her to live their remaining years in a Paradise only for Anna to find herself a widow and a victim of a brutal crime. If it were Maya, she would probably pack up and leave, too. There wasn't much else Maya could say or do so she extended her apologies to Anna, wished the other women a pleasant afternoon, signaled for Maybelle to call her when she had a minute, and headed for the exit. She walked to her car in a daze. Between Orville's story and what happened to Anna, Maya was wondering how long it would be before she, too, became a victim. The longer Maya was here, the more she realized that this was no longer the place she moved to six years ago. It had transformed into a pit of predators who viewed expats as easy and vulnerable targets. Will had assured her that she would not need to be here more than six months to a year, and Maya figured she had only a few months left on that sentence. This whole ordeal was starting to wear her down and she needed some clarification on just how long she was going to be indentured to "them" and reporting on the expats' trials and tribulations.

Chapter 27

Three days passed and there was no contact with Will. She used this time to decompress by turning off her phone and not going to town. The weather was calmer because the rainy season was nearing an end. The mornings were a bit foggy but as the sun encroached on the horizon, the skies cleared, and the dew made everything sparkle like a field of diamonds. Maya walked down to the orchard and picked a basket of oranges and tangerines, lemons, mandarinas, a few limes, and a couple of *maracuyá* – passion fruit --- that grew on vines covering the chain link fence. When all else seemed overwhelming, she found solace wandering among the trees and marveling at all the fruit that was hers to pick as she needed. In a far corner of her lot, she found a spot that faced the vast valley and sat down in the shade, peeled a grapefruit she just picked, and thought about Orville Richardson. She hoped he made a safe and uneventful trip back to Maine and decided to send him a quick email just to say hello.

Being totally alone in the world was a familiar state for Maya but she knew it was harder on others than it was for her and letting him know she was thinking about him seemed like the human thing to do. She was sorry that she didn't get the opportunity to know him better, but she totally understood his urgency to escape this Paradise while he still could. She gathered her fruit basket and trudged up the hill to the house.

Scouring the local news pages on Facebook, one item in particular caught Maya's attention. It was the arrest of five high-ranking police officers in a theft ring that authorities believed were responsible for thirty-three separate robberies netting more than one million dollars in goods. The article said that these robberies had been taking place in several areas around the country and while most of the time they targeted businesses such as jewelry and liquor stores, the gang was also responsible for a half dozen home invasions. Were these the same police who robbed Anna? She cut and pasted the article into an email to Maybelle and asked her to make sure Anna was aware of this and perhaps there was a way for her to get back her stolen items. Maybelle would certainly use this opportunity to her advantage in raising holy hell with the police who had preyed on an elderly woman living alone. What did this say about a society that these police officers would target the most vulnerable among them? It was certainly not a selling point to other elderly people wanting to move here, but Maya knew this information would never make it into any slick brochure for property sales or vacation tours. It would continue to be billed as the last true Paradise and people would continue to flock here looking for something that didn't exist. Maya wondered how many more victims there were besides the ones she encountered just in the expat community of San Pedro. It was a grim reality because she knew that many people would never admit to being a victim of crime for fear of being judged for their naïveté, inexperience, or downright stupidity. It made Orville Richardson's story even more important because he had the temerity to tell his tale so that others could avoid his fate.

Chapter 28

"Okay, ladies, there's going to be a new session of Spanish classes starting next week," Maybelle announced at the next Monday get together. "It will be a six-week course, twice a week for an hour, to be held in the little museum courtyard. I, for sure, am signing up. Who else is interested? I don't mean to lecture, but we *are* living in a country where the primary language is Spanish, and if we don't want to be viewed as outsiders and interlopers, it would behoove all of us to learn some basics."

"I wholeheartedly agree with that," Margo moaned. "I'm signing up because I am tired of making a complete fool of myself."

"What do you mean?" Maybelle inquired.

"I've got the basic '*hola*' and '*muchisimas gracias*' down, but after that I'm a complete dullard."

"Can you give us an example?" Helen asked.

"It's embarrassing, to be honest," Margo said quietly.

"Come on, you can tell us," Maya pried.

"Okay, but if any of you laugh at me, I'm going to be very upset."

"We wouldn't think of doing such a thing, would we, girls?" Maybelle crowed.

"So, you know how the country motto is Pura Paz, which means pure peace? And they say it for everything? How are you? Pura Paz. How's your day going? Pura Paz. How's your family? Pura Paz. Only I could screw up something as simple as that," Margo groaned.

"How? Do tell us," Maybelle pleaded.

"Okay, it's the little things in Spanish that count, right? How that accent over papa changes it from daddy to potato?"

"I know that example," Maya volunteered. "The phrase is 'my daddy is forty-seven,' or in Spanish, *mi papá tiene quarenta-siete años*, but if you leave off the accents you change it to my potato has forty-seven rectums."

The whole group burst out laughing.

"I kid you not," Maya said, shaking her head. "Come on, Margo, tell us what your big goof was. We're dying to know. How did you screw up Pura Paz?"

"I got it in my head that paz was spelled with an 'e'," she said, waving her hand in front of her face. "Spelling was never my strong point, just ask my fifth-grade teacher. Paz or pez, surely, they were the same thing, right? Anyway, I decided I would try using that phrase as the locals do. Whenever I ran into someone on the street and they asked me how I was, I proudly said, 'Pura Pez' and then watched their face go completely blank. I thought that was odd, but hey, maybe I was mispronouncing it. So, I practiced. Pura Pez, Pura Pez. I was determined to incorporate that phrase into my exchanges with any locals because surely, that would endear me to them, right?"

"And?" Maybelle prompted.

"My gardener came to work the other day and he said '*Buenos días*, Doña Margo, *cómo estás*?' And I bravely replied 'Pura Pez, Manuel. Pura Pez.' He stared at me, the same stare I got from others when I said that. By now, I am starting to wonder what the hell? Then he started laughing. And laughing. Finally, I ask him in my cryptic Spanish what was so funny? And you know what he says?"

"No, what?" everyone chimed.

"He says, in the most serious way possible, 'Doña Margo, why you wish me pure fish?' And I'm like HUH? What do you mean? And he says, '*Pez* is fish, so when you say Pura Pez, you are saying pure fish. What you should say is Pura Paz. *pura* peace. Besides, I don't like fish.' And then he lumbered off laughing to himself. So, yeah, I'm signing up for those Spanish classes. I'm afraid to even open my mouth now after that incident."

Chapter 29

It was a blustery morning, cold and misty, and Maya didn't feel like getting out of bed to do anything other than make a cup of coffee. She then gathered her phone and her laptop and settled back into bed to check her messages. Her spirits picked up when she saw a reply to her email to Orville. She opened it expecting to have him tell her that he had settled back into his old routine and that he was fine. Instead, what she read broke her heart.

"Dear Maya: You were probably expecting a reply from Orville, but I have taken the liberty of responding to your email. My name is Barbara Mercer, and my husband and I are his closest neighbors. I saw your email when I accessed his computer, which thankfully was not locked with a password. It is with a heavy heart that I share this sad news, but Orville passed away five days ago. The coroner said it was a heart attack. Frankly, I think he just withered away. He didn't talk much about his experience in that other country, but his demeanor was very different when he returned. We figured he was suffering from culture shock. My husband Archie and I tried to help him settle in again here, but he stayed to himself, so we let him be and kept an eye on him to make sure he was okay. We saw him leave the house to stroll through his copse of birch and maple trees as he did every morning, but when he didn't return, we went looking for him and found him sitting under the tree where his dog Spike was buried. He looked peaceful for the first time since he got back. Orville was such a dear soul, and we were happy to have him back in our community. He will be missed. From what I can tell, he read your email, so I wanted to thank you for reaching out to him. With nobody to organize a funeral service, he was buried next to Helen. Please say a prayer for him. Sincerely, Barbara"

Maya's heart sank. Thinking back to their short meeting right before he went home, Maya thought Barbara's comment that he had withered away was an astute observation. Malpaís had drained the life out of him, and he admitted he was going home broke and broken. Orville Richardson was collateral damage in this place called Paradise, a victim of the undercurrent that nobody sees, talks about, or warns others about. By the time Orville escaped the lure of Paradise, he had been stripped of his assets, his dignity, and his hope. Maya could only imagine how difficult it had been for him to admit defeat. The image of him sitting under one of his trees was imprinted in her mind now and made his passing all the sadder. What could she possibly do to warn others? Most people wouldn't believe the negative things anyway when the marketing campaign was so full of beautiful images and the promise of a peaceful life in this barely discovered Paradise. They usually had preconceived ideas about a place and what their life would be like. It would be almost impossible to dispel those fantasies and replace them with a vivid picture of reality. Whatever ills plagued Malpaís, those things surely wouldn't touch them or shatter their dreams of living in the tropics without the harsh winters or the unbearable heat of summer, where the land of eternal spring conjured up powerful images before they had even set foot in the country.

Since Maya's return, she had heard one grim tale after another – suicide, murder, property theft, disillusionment, all things that were dire enough to drive people back to where they came from, leaving a trail of wreckage nobody would ever talk about because of the shame and embarrassment those people wore for having failed to thrive in Paradise. Everyday Maya received emails from people with a litany of complaints about everyday life here. The smallest inconvenience was enough to launch a tirade about the inefficiency, the stupidity, and the cultural void they had found themselves in. As if Maya could do anything about these problems. Her only response was to thank them for their email and leave it at that. But there was one woman whose daily ritual was to get Maya to acknowledge her great inconvenience by having moved here.

Brenda's annoyances were always the same: the internet was slow, the water was a dribble, the electricity went out, the power surges blew her TV and refrigerator, she couldn't find her favorite foods or supplements, the language barrier was beginning to wear on her, the traffic was terrible, the humidity caused mold to which she was allergic until Maya finally did what she swore she wouldn't do – she blocked Brenda. It was a relief to stop the assault of complaints. A week later, Maya was in a small vegetable market on the outskirts of San Pedro and Brenda was standing at the counter paying for her items. Maya said hello and went about her shopping. Brenda came up behind her and said in a snarling tone, "You know you did me a favor by blocking me."

"How so? Don't take it personally. I only did it because I simply don't have the time to devote to helping you solve the issues about which you complained relentlessly."

"No, actually, you did me a favor because I was getting sick of your narcissism. The sad part is that you don't even know you're a narcissist, so yes, it is a relief to not have to deal with you anymore."

"I'm sorry you feel that way, Brenda. But your incessant complaining about a place you chose to move to was getting to be too much."

"You could've helped me, but you're so into yourself and your stupid little magazine to do anything for anyone. Oh, and I might as well tell you now, *nobody* likes you. Not one single expat." And with that Brenda turned on her heels and stomped out of the store.

For a few seconds, Maya was completely stunned. Then relief set in that she would never have to deal with this person again.

Chapter 30

Magdalena sashayed into the house promptly at nine a.m., humming a tune as always, a radiant smile on her face. Maya had never known anyone so consistently content with their life and who always found something about which to be grateful.

In her arms, she cradled something long and cylindrical, shiny, and brown, and gently laid it down as one would an infant, then stood back and lovingly admired it.

"What is *that*?" Maya asked, making a face as she inspected this thing that resembled a gigantic sausage about ten inches in diameter and over a foot long that was resting on her kitchen counter. Maya lightly touched its surface to discover that it was hard like an eggshell.

"This is a *cohombro*. And it is very special to us here," Magda said, a glint in her obsidian eyes. She stroked it tenderly as one would a sleeping pet. "I don't know botany, but it is something between a cucumber and a squash. This one is still very fresh," she said, thumping its hard exterior with her index finger, "but in three or four weeks it will start to rot, then it will release the most beautiful perfume you have ever smelled." She closed her eyes and took a deep breath, swelling her ample chest. "Believe it or not, in the middle of the last century it was common for every household to have one of these in the doorway of the house. It's a smell from another time, a smell of Christmas, and thanks to our *abuelos*, they invented the first air freshener. I am going to tie it up outside near the entrance to the terrace and you will see, in just a little while, how beautiful it really is. Every time you come home you will be embraced by the scent that will make you think of heaven."

"Hmm," Maya mused, "if you say so, although it's contradictory that something in a state of decomposition would actually smell good, but then what do I know?"

"But Doña Maya, you are in a different world now where you will experience many *cosas* you didn't know were possible. Magical things happen every day here if only we open our *ojitos*. Our fascination with *cohombro* is just one of them."

Maya couldn't disagree with her because sometimes a sense of derealization engulfed her when she tried to make sense of unexplainable things she had experienced since she first landed in Malpaís. Leaving Magda to her chores, Maya picked up her laptop, grabbed her cup of coffee, and walked to the terrace where she settled into the settee to read the latest local news.

For years, she had resisted the temptation of joining any social media platforms, and as Will pointed out on their first meeting, she was elusive – no Facebook, no Twitter, just an email account, the same one she'd had since AOL's inception. She wasn't even sure what the point of all those social media sites was except to portray one's life as being something of fantasy when it was probably very mundane. Joining Facebook groups that were based in Malpaís opened her eyes to the social structure that existed here. The local news groups told her more than she wanted to know about the culture, the types of crimes, the complaints, and the characters who fueled these sites. Until now she had no idea what Malpaís was all about. It was not just what was depicted in slick ads. There was a whole other side to Paradise, but most of it went unnoticed by the expat crowd unless they were an actual victim of this dark side. Although her original assignment was to spy on these expats and report any unusual activities to William Balthazar Hastings, what she discovered was a whole world of interesting history, legends, characters, customs, and attitudes, thanks to her housekeeper Magdalena Sanchez. Magdalena was determined to expose her to the real-life tribulations of Malpaiseños, and to make her understand that this little country was unique in ways most foreigners never experienced since these things were not discernible at first glance, and so vastly different than the culture from which they came. It would take a particular type of person to be able to grasp the elegance, the rhythm, the wisdom of a place that was only known to the world as the last Paradise on earth. "Malpaís is not just a place. It is a state of mind, a way of being. A way of seeing the world and all its mysteries," Magda insisted. Even with all this mystery and magic, all Maya had to do was open Facebook to be slapped in the face with a different reality. She took a big swig of coffee, opened one of the pages she subscribed to and saw some very disturbing articles.

Noticias de Malpaís featured the story of the *hijo de pápi* – spoiled rich boy – who chucked his girlfriend's cat off an eighth-floor balcony and filmed it flailing desperately before splatting on the cement below. The graphic video was posted to the page. Maya couldn't bear to look at that. Public outcry demanded that this son of an elected official be arrested and charged with animal cruelty, but the consensus was that nothing would happen to him because his family had enough money to make it go away. The occupants of the luxury apartment complex had other ideas and insisted that he be booted from the building otherwise who knows what could happen to that little brat? They weren't saying, but the warning was clear. The cat killer was now in hiding after an angry mob gathered outside the building and threatened to toss him headfirst from the roof.

The *Expats in Malpaís* page had some interesting entries. Mostly it was new arrivals wanting to know where they could locate certain items or services, and of course each inquiry was prefaced by the need for the person to speak English and for the thing they needed to be cheap. When Maya first arrived in San Pedro, the only people who spoke English were the gringos, but now almost every business establishment had at least one English speaking employee to cater to the lazy newcomers who wouldn't learn Spanish. Maya scrolled through a few more pages but closed her laptop when she heard Magdalena let out an audible gasp and mutter in Spanish. A few seconds later, Magda came out to the terrace, tears running from the corner of her eyes, and stood in front of Maya.

"What's wrong, Magda?"

"Oh, Doña Maya, I have some very bad news for you. Juan has gone to the angels and is now in his heavenly home, wrapped in the arms of our blessed Lord."

"Juan? The gardener?"

"*Sí*, he has been welcomed into the kingdom of glory and love for all eternity. It is so very sad," she said, wiping her tears on the sleeve of her *blusa*.

"What happened?" Maya choked back her own tears waiting for an explanation.

"Yesterday, that old *caballo* of his kicked him in the head. Death was instant and he did not suffer, and heaven is happy to have such a humble servant. The angels welcomed him with open arms, and now he is in the real Paradise." Magda shuffled back to the house and resumed her tasks.

Maya sat frozen for a few seconds trying to process what Magda told her. Juan had been working for her from the first day she bought the property. The beautiful gardens planted with so many exotic flowers were Juan's creation. He tended the fruit trees, trimming them regularly so they would produce abundant harvests, and every year he painted their trunks white to repel ants and fungus. The reason her property looked like a well-manicured park was because of all the work Juan had done. Maya felt shaken and sad and without saying another word walked into the house and straight to her bedroom where she sat in the corner chair and cried a river of tears.

Juan shared his story one day when she asked about his family and how he knew so much about plants. He was a humble man, a true *campesino*, from a remote village founded and occupied by his family. Eventually, with the passing of his last living relative, he became the sole resident of the village where he had spent the first fifty of his seventy-eight years. They were a large extended family of farmers who lived with the scarcest of amenities, their tiny houses barely a notch above a sty for animals. Other than a central well for drinking water and a church, there was nothing else in the village. The only education he or anyone received was how to work the land and lovingly coax it into providing an abundance of food, some of which was sold to the few passersby who found themselves on this deserted road to nowhere. He never married because his choices were relegated to either a cousin or a niece, something he found unpalatable even though it was a common occurrence in the remote villages. With literally nothing left for him in a speck of a town and destined for a solitary life that would end in loneliness, he made the decision to walk the entire distance between the only home he had ever known and San Pedro. He hoped that being amongst others would help him find meaning in life and relieve him of his crippling solitude. He arrived with not one toucan in his pocket and slept on the steps of the cathedral until the bishop took pity on him and gave him work in the gardens. He knew more about plants than anyone. He was one with them, fused in an ethereal understanding of the cycle of life. One of Maya's early memories of him was watching him talk to the plants as he prepared to put them into the ground. It was a conversation filled with meaning and respect, and made her heart convulse with joy as he spoke so softly and gently to the hibiscus or heliconia, and their response to his tenderness was to grow to immense size and flower constantly. She would miss him, his gentle ways, and his smile that radiated kindness and love for all living things. Her spirit sagged under the weight of the loss.

Magda was busy with her chores in the kitchen, and despite the sad news of Juan's death, was still humming. Maya walked stealthily through the house to the terrace and down the stairs that Juan built on the hillside to the flat park-like area below. At least she would always have the beauty he created for her. She lay on the carpet of thick grass, between a mango tree and a cluster of banana stalks, some bearing the traditional yellow fruit while others had pink or blue bananas. In the delicate silence of that space, she listened to the lullaby of the breeze and the song of the plants that Juan loved so much. After reflecting on how much he had taught her about life on the isthmus, she sat up and out of the corner of her eye saw him pass by for just a second, his dirty khaki pants tucked into his white rubber boots, with his machete, sharp enough to cut off a man's head, dangling from the rope that served as a belt. She blinked and shook her head. Of course, he wasn't there, except in the ether, in another dimension, on the way to his heavenly home.

In a daze, Maya trudged to the terrace and saw Magda getting ready to leave. "But you just got here," Maya said, puzzled about her sudden departure.

"No, Doña, I have been here three hours. It is almost noon."

"But I was in the gardens for only a few minutes."

"Oh, no, *mi amor*, you were on a journey of more than two hours."

"How is that possible?" Maya looked at her watch.

"Have you not yet learned that anything is possible here? You were in a state of reverie, somewhere between here and there, where time has no relevance and where the souls of the departed wander freely. Do not worry. It is something beautiful, and we cherish those little forays into another dimension. I must hurry to catch my bus now. Do not feel sad about Juan. He celebrated many springs and his journey to that special place is a fate we will all embrace one day and then we will all be together in the glory of heaven."

Chapter 31

As far as Maya was concerned the day was now lost. She was not motivated to do anything. Will expected a report from her today or tomorrow but she had nothing worth reporting on. Opening her laptop, she made a concerted effort to divert her sorrow over Juan's death into something productive, but all she found was even more distressing news.

The headline on one of the online news groups announced the brutal murder of a prominent female doctor, found wrapped in a sheet on the bed in the luxury resort on the coast where she went for a three-day vacation from her rigorous schedule at the main hospital in Santa Lucia. The article detailed the wounds that had been inflicted – bite marks on various parts of her body and limbs, a broken neck, a crushed skull, and signs of a sexual encounter. It was the work of someone filled with rage. Comments under the article vacillated from horror and outrage to curiosity – who would do such a thing to such a promising young woman who, according to colleagues or friends, had never uttered a harsh word or done anything to incite the ire of another. Her life was spent caring for those who couldn't care for themselves. Speculation about how this occurred seemed to be the common theme – who had she hooked up with? Was it rough sex gone south? Was it a random perpetrator or a sexual deviant? It was too early in the investigation for anything other than wild conjecture but according to the report, the police had a few leads and video of her and another person, a male stripper, sitting at a table on the terrace several hours before the estimated time of death. A picture of the vibrant doctor was posted next to a photo of a buffed-out male, his body gleaming with sweat, wearing a jock strap and a Lone Ranger mask.

The next story on that same news site was an account of the assassination in broad daylight of an alleged drug kingpin. It was a typical hit – two men on a motorcycle approached the target as he was dropping off his daughter at her private school. Even though he was surrounded by bodyguards, they were still able to get a kill shot to his head. There were no suspects and Maya doubted they were looking too hard, since a dead drug lord was a good thing and saved the police the trouble of bringing him to justice. The story alluded to a rival gang as the perpetrators, but who really knew? She had just finished reading the story when her phone rang. It was Will.

"I was starting to worry about you. It's been crickets for the last five or six days. Everything all right?"

"Depends on how you look at it." Maya choked back tears, "I found out my gardener died in a tragic accident, and then I read about a young female doctor who was murdered. Honestly, Will, I had no idea how twisted society was here. For some reason I thought this was a place immune from the usual societal ills. How could I have been so naïve? Women getting murdered is not a rare occurrence here. There were three other femicides in the last month. Why would a prominent doctor, from a good family, hook up with a bi-sexual male stripper? I'm sending you a photo of him."

"Hang on while I check my email."

After fifteen seconds of silence Maya heard what sounded like a snicker. Will replied cheerily, "I kind of look like that, minus the Lone Ranger mask. Maybe I could be your stripper concubine. Ah, but you have snakes. I would need mongooses, or ferrets, or something. I'm too hard-wired for danger. I'd never chill out there. What else have you heard about this murder?"

"The stripper and another friend have already been arrested but now it seems that the teeth marks on her face and her arm match the teeth of the owner, a known homosexual with a penchant for young boys. Another news article said that the older guy was invited to come to this country to open a hotel by one of the former presidents."

"Interesting. Any updates about the murder of the Swiss tourist?"

"The police published pictures of her body found on the beach. It was minus her head, which was found in another location. But this makes no sense because why would her head have been severed if she drowned? The other interesting news item is that the police raided a house on the edge of the jungle owned by a judge. They recovered two hundred kilos of cocaine and arrested two Colombians who were living in a guest house. Maybe the judge didn't know they were drug dealers but I'm betting he did and got a kick back for turning a blind eye."

"There is certainly no end to the crazy stories. Don't you have any good news?"

"Only if you consider my citrus harvest good news – I picked a big basket of oranges, grapefruits, and tangerines. That's the highlight of my day."

"Very good," Will said, "maybe I could pitch a tent on your lower property and live off your citrus orchard and be your stripper boy toy."

"What?" Maya laughed.

"Just joking. I'm trying to cheer you up because you sound totally depressed."

This wasn't the first time Will had made suggestive comments, but Maya always dismissed them as things guys – even spooks – say when they think they are engaging in playful banter. Maya never took it seriously. But there was something about the tone of these comments that made her wonder if there was some undercurrent to their professional relationship that she had overlooked. She chalked it up to what he said: that he was just making a joke to cheer her up.

"Anything else you want to share with me?"

"I'm sure my struggle with five extra pounds from going to all these luncheons and dinners really isn't your main concern."

"You're worried about five pounds? That's nothing. If it weren't for the snakes, I would come down and train you and the five pounds would disappear quickly." Will snickered. "Gotta run. Stay safe. I'll be in touch.

The next day Will sent her a video of a praying mantis killing small rodents and a snake with a one-line note: “If you could get some of these things, I’d consider coming for a visit.”

Their light-hearted banter was amusing. Will was handsome and engaging, but Maya knew better than to entertain any romantic notions even though it had been five years since her husband’s demise. Any male attention seemed foreign to her. After the disastrous relationship with Harry Langdon, her previous handler, she was not interested in repeating that scenario.

Chapter 32

If Maya had to pick one word to describe the last few Monday get-togethers, tame would be a good choice. Life was once again normal in the expat crowd, although Maya had little to add to their lamentations about the things they missed from home or how difficult it was to adapt to a Spanish-speaking culture. She was about to excuse herself when a tall, handsome guy, stylishly dressed in khakis, pale blue shirt, and Mephisto shoes with wire-rimmed glasses and a head of graying hair approached the table and stood nervously until Maybelle finally piped up.

"Well, *hello* there. Would you like to join us old hens? We're always happy to see a new face. Have a seat."

"Thank you," he said, sitting down in the chair at the end of the table.

"Normally, we have a bigger crowd, but today it's just me – I'm Maybelle – and this is Susan, Margo, Diane, Maya, and Helen. Introduce yourself and tell us why you decided to join our group."

"Pleased to meet you all. My name is Mark Connor and I've been living in Malpaís for almost a year. Someone turned me on to that magazine *Neotrópica* and I saw the article about this weekly get together. I thought it might be worth my time to come and see what you all are up to."

"Maya, who's sitting next to you, is the senior editor of that magazine. She's our expert on how to adjust to this culture. Tell us about yourself, Mark. How did you wind up here and where in San Pedro do you live?"

"I live on the other side of town. How did I wind up here? I'm still trying to figure that one out. Basically," he said, fidgeting in his chair, "I took early retirement from my position at a local newspaper in Sacramento. After a bad divorce I needed a change of scenery. With my share from the sale of the marital home I came here, thinking I would build myself a little house, have a nice, easygoing lifestyle, and devote my time to writing a book."

"How's that working out for you?" Diane asked.

"Not exactly what I had in mind," he said, his face drooping. "And that's why I'm here. I'm wondering if any of you could recommend a good builder. I need to fire the one I used before I do something that lands me in jail."

"Oh, dear!" Maybelle gasped. "What happened?"

"Long story short, I bought a lot on the other side of San Pedro. A small development with maybe eight other houses, some expats, some locals. At a party given by one of the other residents I met a building contractor. He seemed nice enough, was very forthcoming about building codes, how long the process would take, and the costs. He and I drove around one day as he showed me other houses he had built. I was impressed. They were nicely designed, well-constructed with local materials, and were in the price range I could afford."

"But something happened?" Maya asked.

"You could say that. One of the houses he showed me had this nubby texture on the outside. It looked as though they had plastered river rock all over the outside walls. I didn't think too much about it until the contractor, Diego, asked me if I liked that house. What was I going to say? I said yes, it's quite nice."

"So why is there a problem?" Maybelle asked, leaning her elbows on the table.

"About four months later when I was back in Sacramento wrapping up the last details of my life, I got an email from a neighbor I became friendly with. The subject of the email was "A Million Little Pills" – referencing that book that came out some years ago. Included in the email was a picture of my house that indeed had one million cement balls slapped on the exterior walls."

"But you said you liked that finish," Susan interjected.

"Yes, but I didn't say I wanted it."

"You don't like it?" Diane asked.

"That's not the half of it. You know how we all have names for our houses here? Well, I had a great name all picked out. Casa Pasando or Happening House. My goal was to get in tight with the local community, have parties, and enjoy expat life in Paradise. I thought the name was appropriate since I envisioned it as a gathering place for like-minded folks. Unfortunately, the neighborhood gave it other names."

"Like what?" Susan wanted to know.

"I'm getting to that. I gave Diego a color swatch for a particular shade of blue but instead it got painted the exact color of Viagra, and with those oval-shaped balls of cement slapped on the outside, it got named The Viagra House. Someone even drove by the other day as I was outside and asked me why I had Viagra all over my house? Now it's the butt of jokes in the neighborhood. What I want to do is hire somebody to sand blast those balls and give me a normal house. In some other color. Any color. We have a hard enough time assimilating into this culture without being the butt of a bunch of sex jokes."

"House castration," Margo mused. "That's a new one."

"The house of blue balls," Diane said innocently, then clamped her hand over her mouth and giggled.

After a few seconds of silence everyone, except Mark, started twittering like junior high girls who'd just seen a penis for the first time.

Margo snickered and quietly said, "The Boner House."

Mark groaned.

"How about Hard Rock House?" Helen asked.

"Dear, you got it backwards," Susan scolded. "It's Rock-Hard House.

"Okay, I get it. It's amusing. But please stop making fun of my pre-*dic*-ament. Now do you understand why I need a new contractor?"

Maya retrieved a business card from her wallet and handed it to him. "Send me an email and I will give you the contact information for the contractor I used. He's very good and can probably help you out."

"That's so kind of you," Mark said with a sigh of relief. "I'll get in touch with you as soon as I get back to my Hard On House – yes, that's another one they joke about." And then, he, too, started laughing.

"You need a very good sense of humor to survive this

place," Maybelle opined. "Without it, you would lose your ever-lovin' mind."

"That's about where I'm at," Mark mumbled.

"Okay, ladies, and Mark, I've got to run," Maya apologized. "I'm up against a deadline."

She waited until she walked out the main door of Café Roma before she shook her head in disbelief. "You just can't make this stuff up," she said out loud. Hopefully, Will would be as amused as she was by this comical situation poor Mark had found himself in.

Chapter 33

"I'm sorry to call so early; I hope I didn't wake you, dear," Maybelle warbled into the phone. There was a huge sigh before she continued. "Several of the expat women want to get together on Friday for lunch. It seems some of them are in dire need of emotional support because they are not transitioning very well to this new culture. It could provide some interesting material for your magazine." There was a muffled giggle.

"You seem to find this amusing."

"Have you met Marianne? She was at the last potluck. Mid-sixties, long blonde hair, a little on the plump side, and dresses like a thirty-year-old."

"Oh, yes. What's her problem?

"Yesterday she called me from Santa Lucia sobbing, hopelessly lost trying to follow directions her architect gave her for some store with interesting lighting fixtures. She said his directions were, you know, the usual convoluted malarkey. After hours of driving around aimlessly she found someone who spoke English who explained that the park had been demolished fifteen years ago, and the fig tree hadn't been there for fifty years. Before she hung up, she said she was going to kill herself from the frustration of living here if she didn't get some support."

"Oh, my," Maya said, trying to contain her amusement. Who didn't know about the crazy directions in this country? It was one of the first things Ryan McAfee explained to her. "So, lunch Friday. Where and when?"

"We decided Baci was in order, something lavish and elegant to soothe her and the other two who are also on the verge of having breakdowns. I made a reservation at noon for ten of us. See you there."

Maya was still chuckling when Magda walked in.

"Why are you laughing, Doña Maya?"

"I heard something amusing about someone who got lost in Santa Lucia trying to follow directions using landmarks that hadn't been there in years."

"*Ay dios*, that is very funny. It is one of the things I love so much about my country. We don't follow convention, even when it comes to addresses like the rest of the world."

"Can you help me understand why those directions even exist."

Magda put her handbag on the counter and sat in the chair opposite Maya with a big grin on her face.

"Malpaís has addresses, or at least I am told they exist, but I have no personal knowledge of them. Neither does anyone I know. *Mi mamita* told me once that they tried to make addresses, but nobody seemed interested. We were set in our ways. Santa Lucia is characterized by total disorder. The more the city expanded, the less addresses made any sense. So, we stopped using them. Besides, what would we use as an excuse for being late for something? *Es verdad* that no one really knows where they are going. If they arrive at all, it is the will of God."

"But why use landmarks that don't exist? How is anyone supposed to know what was there before they were even born?"

Magda shrugged. "Changes are very hard for us. We don't like them, and we cling to silly ways because even though they are inefficient or troublesome, for us, it's a secret language, a code for insiders. To be honest, Doña Maya, we are not too happy that Malpaís changed so quickly. We don't like modern things. We like our old ways and there is something about our *loco* addresses that connects us to the past, a connection of what is now with what was then. Can you understand what I'm saying? It's yesterday and today all rolled into our address. And that is what makes us happy; that we do not forget what was before. Let me put it in another way. *Mi primo's* address is fifty meters north of the mango tree and one hundred meters west of the *pulperia*. The mango tree is long gone, as is the *pulpe*, but when we use that address it conjures up our past and those of us who remember these things have pleasant memories. *Por ejemplo*, when I was a *niña*, the *pulpe* was where we got penny candy, and then on the way home, if we were lucky, we found ripe mangoes that had fallen on the ground. We would eat them and go home covered in mango juice, but we were happy. Sometimes we even have memories that our *abuelos* experienced. Memories are generational here and those things which no longer exist still linger in our minds and hearts, and we like to relive those pleasant memories, so we do not forget our history. *Entiendes*?"

"That's a lovely explanation. I understand perfectly what you are saying."

"*Bueno*. Yesterday and today, the past and the present, are contained in our silly addresses. Our past is very much a part of us, and we do not want to let it go or it will be forgotten in the *basurero* of time."

Chapter 34

With an egotistical smirk plastered across his face, Will leaned back in his chair, clasped his hands behind his head, and reveled in the recent successes of Operation LUCIÉRNAGA. It had only taken a few months of Maya poking her nose around the expat group and flaunting the success of her new magazine *Neotrópica* to flush out Miguel Espinoza, whose aliases were El Verdugo, (the executioner), or El Mano Derecho (The Right Hand) because that was the hand used to wield the guillotine-sharp machete that severed a rival's head. Will hadn't expected it would happen so quickly, but this fortuitous twist of events meant they were one step closer to outing "Gordo" and "Chucho," the top-level goons operating the largest cocaine cartel on the isthmus. It hadn't been difficult to track Miguel and put him out of his misery, but even Will hadn't expected the wet work team would do such a thorough job of making it look like a routine cartel hit. Cutting off his hands was an unexpected bonus that hadn't been included in the job description. Neither was cutting out his tongue, but those things turned the investigation towards an inside job, thus deflecting any suspicion away from anyone else. The only unanswered question was why had Miguel contacted Maya in the first place? Was he getting ready to blow the whistle on the cartel? Or was he gloating about killing her husband? Nobody would never know. Now, it was only a matter of time before "Chucho" and "Gordo" surfaced from their rat hole somewhere in Malpaís or Guatemala. All Will had to do was sit tight and keep a close eye on his inquisitive and rebellious asset.

He had to admit that he felt a twinge of transient guilt knowing the danger Maya was exposed to. According to the agency shrink who did a thorough review of her file, she would have never agreed to such a mission had she known the real role she was to play, which was altogether different than the agenda Will laid out for her. During Operation SHADOWHAWK her mission was to flush out the neo-Nazi leader who was the president of the pharmaceutical company that made the drug her best friend was taking when she killed herself. Maya wanted revenge for Thea's death. But why would she help find her husband's killers especially when she facilitated his murder? Wasn't she relieved that he was dead? After all, his demise saved her from an expensive divorce and insured her future security. Had he not been murdered she might never have been totally free of him, nor would she ever feel safe.

Assuring her that she was in no danger from the cartel to whom her husband owed a tidy sum was no easy task. Suspicious by nature, she had been hesitant about going back to Malpaís, the scene of so much misery and trauma, and Will considered it a major triumph when she finally agreed to their terms. Blackmailing her guaranteed her compliance. The threat of prison was a great motivator. Maya would not do well in such a setting. Nope. Not at all. She was too independent, too accustomed to luxuries most people dreamed about, and too obstinate and headstrong to be a model prisoner, and Will preyed on those weaknesses. His end goal was to bring down those responsible for flooding the market with cocaine, trafficking young women, and operating prostitution rings. Thankfully, the black bag operation installed surveillance equipment in every room of her house except the bathrooms and the laundry room. Should she be in danger, an exfiltration team would descend in less than five minutes, removing her to safety and eliminating any threat. This was cold comfort considering the cartel's reputation for violence.

On a less serious note, Will reluctantly admitted that he was amused by her routine reports of expat activities. Thorough in describing the players, their physical characteristics as well as their temperament, she was a keen observer of human nature and always managed to create reports with a dramatic and comedic flair. Will laughed at some of the incidents she described and more than once he mused how their antics would make good television, maybe a series called *Expats in Paradise*, although it seemed to be anything *but* Paradise if her detailed reports were even remotely accurate. His self-satisfying reflection of his current operation was short-lived when a ping on his phone displayed the message "Wheels up Istanbul 1400."

Chapter 35

After a ten-hour flight, during which he could not sleep, Will checked in to the Hilton Hotel and ordered a room service dinner before taking a shower and falling into bed. Just as he was drifting off, he noticed several calls from Maya. With the nine-hour time difference, it was too late to call her now. He would do it after some much-needed rest.

Six hours later, he awoke refreshed and ready to tackle the assignment he had been sent to do. As he waited for his breakfast to arrive, he phoned Maya.

"I see you called several times. I hope it's nothing earth shattering."

"Not exactly, but since we hadn't spoken in a couple of days – more like a week, actually – I was just checking in."

"Hold on. Room service is here."

"Where are you?"

"Istanbul."

"Why Istanbul?

"A little task I have to do. Nothing major."

"Istanbul is on the other side of the world. How long will you be there?"

"Depends."

"On what?"

"On whether I get someone straightened out or not."

"Sounds ominous."

"Not really. Pretty routine."

"I suppose you can't tell me what it's about, can you?"

"It's better you don't know."

"I hope you have time to go to the bazaar and see some of the sights. Some places there have always intrigued me. Hot air ballooning in Cappadocia, the Flintstone town, but especially the markets and all those beautiful rugs."

"It depends on how much I get done. I don't mean to cut you off, but I've got to find someone today, so I'd best call you later. Or when I get back to the US. But if there's anything urgent, you can leave a message, and I'll get back to you. With the time difference, it might be the middle of the night."

"Well, okay, then. Good Will hunting."

Later that morning, Maya received a message from Will. No text, only a photograph of him lying on his side on a hospital gurney surrounded by medical equipment, a surgical cap on his head, an IV in his arm, and a sober expression on his face.

"WHAT THE HELL? You went all the way to Istanbul for a colonoscopy?"

Five minutes later, he responded. "No, never, it was something else. Pain. Lots of pain."

"From what?"

"A bad choice."

"Come on, tell me. Nobody winds up in a hospital in Istanbul for no good reason. Did something happen to you?"

"You could say that. I underestimated the guy I was looking for and found. Let's just leave it at that."

"If you say so."

A few seconds later another photo arrived. This time it was Will with his hair cut to his scalp, sporting a three-day beard, and wearing a striped abaya, the traditional kaftan worn by Muslim men in the Middle East.

"It didn't take you long to go native."

"I had to blend in. Not happy about no hair, but what's a guy to do?"

"I need to talk to you about something serious. You know that journalist I told you about? The one who was covering the Charlotte Wilson trial? Somebody tried to kill him the other day."

"How?"

"He was driving on the main highway, and someone pulled up alongside his car and fired three shots into the driver's window. A real stroke of luck he wasn't hit, but he did have cuts from flying glass."

"Any suspects? What about motive?"

"My guess is it's because he has been dogging the authorities about all the items they confiscated from the murder scene – you know, those bins full of jewels, gold, weapons, etc. Will, I've got to go. I'm having lunch with the gaggle of gringas and I'm going to be late. I'll report back later. Stay safe, it's a wicked world out there."

Chapter 36

For a weekday, Baci was packed. Maya walked in and looked around. Squinting until her eyes adjusted to the dim light, she spotted Maybelle and her gleaming metallic hair seated at a round table in the far corner.

"Good afternoon, ladies. I'm sorry I'm late. International phone call that I had to take," Maya shrugged as she sat in the empty seat and nodded to each of the women. Sitting next to Maybelle was Marianne, the one on the verge of a nervous breakdown. She dabbed at her eyes with a napkin. Maybelle patted her quaking hand in a show of support.

"After we order, we'll let Marianne tell us about her harrowing adventure in Santa Lucia." Maybelle touched the woman's shoulder with a patronizing squeeze. In the meantime, the women were chattering about nonsense and basically talking around Maya as if she wasn't even there.

After the waiter took their orders, Marianne cleared

her throat before crying, "I don't know how much more of this I can take. What is the matter with these people? How do they find their way anywhere in this country?" She blew her nose into the napkin and lowered her hands to her lap. After a deep breath, she continued, "My architect said it was easy to find. I believed him, but after three hours of driving around aimlessly, I learned from a helpful local that the landmarks I'd been given hadn't been there in decades. What's up with that? How was I supposed to know the park had turned into a parking lot or that the tree was cut down by the power company? Seriously, this is the dumbest place I have ever lived. I just want to go back to Florida where we have good roads, and I can drive seventy miles per hour without fear of crashing my car in a monstrous pothole. I won't even mention the way people drive here. My God! I want to be able to go out any time of the day or night, to eat Mexican food, Thai food, shop on Amazon and Trader Joe's instead of going to ten places here to look for something only to discover they don't have it and if I buy it online and have it shipped in it costs three times as much. I just miss home, I guess," she whimpered.

As if this was a prayer meeting, all the women chanted "Amen" in unison. Maya stifled a giggle. After a sip of her iced tea, Marianne picked up where she left off.

"And the mail service here. How can it take two months to get a letter from the States? Is it coming by mule train? The only reason I know it arrived is because I asked the clerk at the post office if there was anything they hadn't put in my box. Why am I paying thirty-five dollars a year to have a post office box? Beats the hell out of me," she grumbled before rearranging the massive French twist at the back of her head. "And the rain. Did you all know your lives would revolve around the weather? It's six months a year that I can't go out past one p.m. or risk getting caught in some gully washer that might sweep my car away."

Maya said quietly, "It is the tropics, after all."

All heads turned towards her, and glaring eyes let her know that her comment was not appreciated. She'd forgotten that injecting facts into these laments was frowned upon.

"There's rain, and then there's this rain. My life revolves around it, and I don't like it. And then there's the fog. So thick you sometimes can't see the end of your car. But I don't know how I am going to get out of here now that I've sunk all my money into buying that stupid house."

Maya wanted to add, "Don't worry, there are plenty of suckers out there," but she kept quiet and let the other women soothe Marianne's frayed nerves.

"It's approaching winter in the U.S.," Maybelle said, gulping her martini and signaling the waiter to bring her another. "Now would be a good time to list the house in places where it's colder than a witch's tit. Don't despair, sweetie, you're just upset right now, but if you're really serious about leaving, I don't think you'll have a hard time selling to someone else who wants a taste of Paradise."

"Oh, God, I hope so. I have never been so miserable in my life and the three-hour tour of Santa Lucia was the cherry on the sundae for me. I just want *out*. I feel like I'm trapped. What am I saying? I *am* trapped," she sobbed.

Lunch arrived and for those few minutes as the waiters served everyone, there was a lull in the litany of complaints from this malcontent. Maya doubted that Marianne was happy wherever it was she was living before she came here. Where on the planet is there no weather? If it's not hot, it's cold, then there's rain, hurricanes, tornadoes, snowstorms, ice storms, heat waves, polar freezes, and floods. And where is it she wants to go? Oh, yeah, Florida. Good choice. It never rains there, and didn't Florida win some poll for the worst drivers in the world outside of Afghanistan? It wasn't Maya's job to tell her how ridiculous she sounded, and with any luck at all, she would indeed pack up and go back to wherever she thought she would be happy, because it surely wasn't here.

As the self-appointed group therapy leader, Maybelle asked a general question. "Does anyone have something they would like to get off their chest. I know living here can be challenging, so if you have an issue, maybe someone here can help you with that."

A woman Maya met once before at one of those gringo potlucks slowly raised her hand and smiled, revealing teeth befitting a thoroughbred. Maybelle encouraged her to speak up.

"I want to know why they *have* to speak Spanish," she said in a Southern drawl, smoothing the side of her platinum pixie-style haircut that was almost as white as her chompers.

"It is a Spanish-speaking country, dear," Maybelle added.

"I know that but why can't they speak English, too? How do they expect to communicate with us? I had one year of high school Spanish, but they speak a different dialect here, I guess."

"Give us an example," Linda with the shimmering chestnut hair, over-plumped lips, and unevenly tattooed eyebrows asked.

"Well, for starters, nobody says Merry Christmas here. It's Feliz Navidad, but the real problem is that Happy New Year phrase. You know the one I mean?"

"Feliz Año Nuevo?" Maya asked.

"Yes, that one. I am almost ashamed to bring it up, but with Christmas coming soon, I feel a need to warn ya'll. So, that word *año*. That's the problem, and I learned the hard way. Last year at Christmas – I mean Navidad – I gave my maid a bonus and put it in an envelope with a note written in my best high school Spanish. Two weeks later, Maria came to me and said she had to tell me something. She was talking a mile a minute and I didn't understand some of it but then she said that I had wished her a happy poopy hole."

Everyone at the table gasped.

"Ya'll, if you leave off the little squiggly thing over the 'n' you change the word from year to anus. Can you imagine a language so dumb that this one little mistake makes you look like an idiot?"

Because you are an idiot, Maya thought to herself. Everyone else snorted and giggled.

Maybelle couldn't stop laughing and had to be slapped on the back after choking on her third martini. At this point, Maya had reached the saturation point of all this bellyaching and quickly finished her lunch while trying to come up with an exit plan. Work was always a good excuse. She finished the last of her crab ravioli, placed her napkin on the table, and announced, "Ladies, it's been a wonderful lunch, but I have a magazine deadline and need to get back to work. And Marianne, I hope you have good luck selling your house and I'm truly sorry Paradise has been such a disappointment for you. I'm sure you'll be fine in Florida." Maybelle wished everyone a good afternoon, but the women totally ignored her as she got up from the table. Maya got the feeling that they were glad she was leaving because now they could complain without anyone pointing out how absurd they sounded.

Maya walked out of the restaurant into the glaring sunlight, snickering to herself. The entire lunch with those women was surreal, right down to the Happy New Year anecdote. As for Marianne, Maya wondered how much she was asking for her house because it crossed her mind that she should buy it just to hasten this woman's departure.

Chapter 37

With her laptop, a fresh shot of espresso, parrots squawking in the orange and lemon trees, Maya thought that she was as close to Paradise as she would ever get. It was a typical workday for Maya as she hammered out the requisite report to Will. Magdalena was busy in the kitchen, humming and singing to herself. At the end of Magda's three-hour shift, she almost always had an interesting anecdote to share about life and the culture of Malpaís. Maya looked forward to their chats because she learned about the old traditions which broadened her understanding of how and why the locals did things the way they did. It was fascinating to Maya and gave her insight into this culture that most expats never experienced.

Their conversation today was about why the blue church on the opposite side of town from the main cathedral was referred to as the "green church." It was like their squirrelly directions – didn't make a lick of sense to those who didn't know, but to the locals it was an insider's code and they understood it completely.

"When that church was built fifty years ago, the priest chose the color of the church. Green was his favorite color. Not any green, but a tender, soft green, like the color of a tender leaf about to emerge. Father Rodelio was well loved in our community. He took care of his flock as the Lord would have wanted him to. He baptized our babies, he prayed for the sick, he blessed the dead, and even conducted the St. Francis tradition of blessing all the animals."

"That's sweet," Maya said, totally enraptured by where this story was going.

"Oh, it was a wonderful ceremony, and people came from all the outlying villages and brought their donkeys, horses, pigs, cows, sheep, chickens, cats, dogs, birds, whatever animals they had and loved that needed a blessing. It was one of the best celebrations in this area. Stalls were set up for water and food for the animals, and of course, for their owners as well. It was a day of *amor* and kindness to all living things. One little boy brought a pet snake. but Father Romelio refused to bless it because snakes made him very afraid."

"Just like Will," Maya said.

"*Qué*?"

"Never mind, I was thinking out loud. Go on."

"*Ay, dios*, after many *años*, Father Romelio got very sick. He was *muy viejo* by now, maybe eighty or ninety, and everyone was afraid he would die so they came to the church and brought all types of green things for him, and they made a huge pile in front of the church to help him recover. But the Lord had other plans. *Ay, que tristeza*. He was welcomed into the heavenly kingdom on a beautiful sunny day. The entire town grieved and closed all the *tiendas* to attend his funeral and to walk the procession to the little cemetery. More than one thousand people walked for three miles behind his coffin." Magda wiped a tear that trickled down her cheek. "It took several weeks before we got another priest. He was young and ambitious, and he wanted a fresh start in this community, but the shadow of Father Romelio was very long. The first thing he did was paint the church. No, people cried, it must stay green to honor Father Romelio, but Father Francisco had it painted blue anyway. He said it was the color of heaven where we would all go one day. *Bah*! We weren't in heaven yet, and while we were still here on this earthly Paradise, we wanted the church to stay green. Even if it was painted the color of a papaya, or a passionflower, we did not care. It was green. And it was going to stay green. Nobody ever refers to it as the blue church. That would be a sacrilege. We do not expect it to make sense to people from *el norte* because they do not know our traditions and how we do not like change. I know you understand because you are not like most of them. You honor and respect our customs and that is why you are very loved in this community."

"Oh, Magda, that is a beautiful story. Thank you for sharing it with me and telling me about my role in this community. That means more to me than you will ever know. Every time you tell me one of your stories, I fall more in love with this country and its people. I have you to thank for that."

"*Con mucho gusto*. Oh! I must hurry to catch my bus. *Buenas tardes*, Doña Maya. *Hasta viernes*."

Maya sat quietly mulling over the story Magda told her. For the first time in many months, a wave of peace enveloped her. She wasn't sure why, especially since this house, this country, held so many bad memories but at this moment in time, they receded so far into the background that Maya only had this moment. A moment of pure bliss. All the painful moments that had come before no longer dictated her state of mind. At times, she missed the stone house in Provence with its Mediterranean blue shutters and the lavender field below, but right here, right now, she was happy. Out of the corner of her eye she detected movement in the driveway. A second later, a woman was standing at the gate to her terrace.

"Excuse me," she said, waving a manicured hand back and forth. She pushed the oversized sunglasses up on her perfectly highlighted blonde blunt cut and held her hands in supplication as she continued. "I hope I am not disturbing you and I apologize for just showing up like this. My name is Laura Huxley and I live in that house on top of the hill behind you."

"Hello. Come onto the terrace. The gate is unlocked." Maya closed her laptop and stood up to greet the woman. "Maya Warwick. Pleased to meet you. What can I do for you? Have a seat."

"Thank you so much. We moved here three months ago, and I'm so flustered I don't know what to do. I don't speak Spanish – not one word – but someone suggested that you might be able to help me.

"I'll try. What is the problem?"

Laura reached into the pocket of her Lululemon yoga pants and retrieved a tightly folded piece of paper. "This is my electric bill. For one month. It's eight hundred toucans. That's roughly four hundred dollars. How is that even possible? When my husband and I bought this property two years ago, Ryan McAfee said that electricity rates were very cheap here. This is not what I would call cheap, even by Beverly Hills standards."

"Let me see it, please."

Maya perused the bill, focused on the consumption chart, did a quick calculation, and handed the bill back to Laura.

"It seems to be calculated properly. Have you been using any machinery that uses 220?"

"No, not at all," she said, shaking her blonde head. "We've been done with construction for months, so it's just what we use on a normal basis. I really don't understand. I want to go to the electric company to complain but," she shrugged helplessly, "without Spanish, I'm useless. Whatever you want to charge me for your time is perfectly fine with me, but I would appreciate it so much if you could go with me and explain to them how this is all wrong."

"No need to pay me. I'd be happy to help you. When would you like to do this?"

"Tomorrow morning? Say, ten a.m.?"

Maya thought for a second, "Yes, that would work. I'll meet you there because I will have other errands to do in town afterwards. Do you know where the office is?"

"No, but I'm sure I could find it."

"It's one block south of the green church."

"What green church?"

"The one on the West side of town."

"There's only one church there and it's blue."

"Yes, that's it. The green church." Maya laughed to herself as she watched the expression on Laura's expression morph into total confusion.

"Why is it called the green church if it's blue?" Laura

was clearly befuddled.

"Don't ask. I'll meet you there a few minutes before ten."

"Thank you so much. Maybe after we can go for a coffee or lunch, my treat."

"Sounds good," Maya said, standing up to indicate their visit was over, and walked toward the gate. "I need to get back to work now. See you tomorrow."

Laura walked up the driveway and Maya heard her mumbling "What were we thinking when we moved here?"

Maya parked the car two blocks away and strolled leisurely to the main entrance of Malpaís Electricidad y Agua. Laura was already there, looking nervous and agitated. "I just got here, and look, there's a damn line here just like everywhere."

"Don't worry. I know the receptionist. She will move us quickly to the front."

They only had to wait five minutes before they were summoned to approach a cubicle where a beautiful young woman welcomed them with a big smile. "*Siéntate, por favor.*" Her name was Alejandra Muñoz and after Maya introduced herself and Laura, began to explain in Spanish why they were here.

Alejandra asked to see the bill, which Laura handed to her. Maya studied Alejandra's flawless face and watched the muscles around her eyes twitch uncontrollably as she saw the amount due. With great restraint, she placed the bill on her desk, smoothed out the creases, and made a concerted effort to contain her laughter. She shot Maya a furtive glance and rolled her eyes.

Finally, Alejandra spoke directly to Laura, while Maya

translated.

"Señora Hookslee, I do not understand your problem. This bill is very clear and easy to understand. Do you see this chart here that shows your electricity consumption?"

Laura nodded.

"The chart shows how many kilowatt hours of power you used in a certain period. Normally, the chart starts at zero. Your chart starts at five hundred."

Laura looked confused. She turned to Maya, "Tell her this is a mistake. Someone must be stealing our power, or maybe the meter is broken."

"No," Alejandra replied in halted English, obviously understanding what Laura said. "The amount you were charged is correct for that high consumption rate. Can you tell me please how many appliances you have, how many hours a day you use the lights, and how many people live in your home?"

Laura pouted at the audacity of the question before replying, "Stove, refrigerator, washer, dryer."

"That is *all*? Alejandra asked.

Laura heaved a sigh. "Okay, two televisions, two computers, dishwasher, water heater, air conditioner, big freezer, coffee maker, coffee grinder, espresso maker, wine cooler, Cuisinart food processor, blender, toaster, toaster oven, ten lamps, ceiling lights, outside lights, and lights along the driveway."

"Anything *else*?" Alejandra asked, her eyes twitching uncontrollably.

"No, I don't think so," Laura sighed. "What do you think is the problem? Can you send an electrician?"

"How many people live in your house? And what hours do you keep?"

"Just two people. We get up around nine a.m. and go to bed at midnight."

Alejandra looked down at her elegantly manicured hands, examined one of the brightly painted nails studded with rhinestones, before looking directly at Laura with all the patience she could muster.

"Señora Hookslee, you and your husband consume ten times the amount of electricity that a typical family of four in Malpaís uses. Most people do not have so many *chunches*. We do not have dishwashers, that is what your hands are for. We do not use dryers, that is why God made the sun. We do not need air-conditioning because God provided us with a breeze. We do not have coffee makers because we use the traditional white sock that fits over a wooden frame for our coffee. I do not know what a toaster is. We do not have freezers because we shop for fresh food every week. We typically go to bed two hours after the sun goes down and we rise when it comes up. We do not have water heaters. We wash our dishes in a special soap that is made for cold water. Most families here do not have hot water anywhere in their house. In fact, we think the obsession you from *el norte* have with taking a hot shower is, how do you say it, *frívolo*. It is much healthier to have a cool shower in the morning to invigorate you. We do not have lights in our driveway, because most of us do not own a car. We do not have coffee grinders because we use a hand crank grinder that may have been in our family for generations. It grinds corn, meat, coffee, whatever you need. I am very sorry that I cannot help you, but you are using very much electricity for all your expensive toys. I hope you have a nice day." Alejandra got up, walked away, and clasped her hand over her mouth.

Maya and Laura walked out of the office and two seconds later Laura started sobbing like a child. "What's wrong?" Maya asked.

"I couldn't feel more stupid if I tried. She made me seem like a totally spoiled gringa. I'm so embarrassed, Maya. And Robert is going to have a cow when I tell him that if we want all these gadgets, we're going to have to pay for them. I need a drink."

"It's ten-thirty in the morning, Laura."

"I don't care. I need a Cosmopolitan."

"Good luck on that. I doubt anyone in this country even knows what that is. How about a shot of the best espresso you will ever have in your life? I know a great little place called Café Café and it's only a short walk from here. Maybe ten minutes."

"*Walk*? We can't drive?"

"It's easier if we don't. Parking around the plaza is hard to find. Walking will do you good."

Laura blew her nose and took a deep breath. "Okay, if you say so."

Café Café was six blocks away, but they were not in a hurry. They strolled leisurely towards the main part of town, crossed the diagonal path through the park, then down the side street towards Banco Nacional. Along the way, Maya said hello to whoever they passed. "*Buenos*" was the typical greeting, whether it was morning, noon, or night. Whoever she greeted smiled and returned a hello, or sometimes said "*Dios te bendiga*." God bless you.

Laura was puzzled. "Do you know all those people?"

"No, I don't know any of them. By name, anyway. I see some of them here and there."

"But why do you say hello to them?"

"Because that's the custom here. It would be rude to pass someone on the street and not acknowledge them. I think it's a lovely gesture, don't you?"

"I don't know. I never thought to do that to strangers."

"They aren't strangers. They are people whose names you don't know yet. They might be your neighbor, or a family member of someone you do know. They will say to other family members that they saw you on the street, that you were looking well, and that you were gracious enough to greet them. It's a very small act of kindness and recognition in a world where so many people are invisible."

"It never occurred to me to view it like that. Nobody would ever do such a thing in Los Angeles. Who even walks there in the first place? We drive everywhere. I'm going to be perfectly honest with you, Maya. I've learned more from you in one hour than I learned the entire three months I've been here."

"That's a good thing. It changes your point of view about this place, and the role each of us plays in the lives of others. A simple hello and a smile to someone who might be having a bad day could change everything."

"Speaking of bad days. This started out being one of my worst, but it's now one of my best, thanks to you."

Chapter 38

Café Café was surprisingly busy. Maya's usual table at the back against the wall was available so she headed straight for it with Laura following behind. This gave Maya the vantage of being able to see who came and went. After they ordered, Maya focused on the three East Hampton ladies sitting at a table near the window. Their yoga mats were propped up against the wall and like last time, they were perfectly coiffed, decked out in their diamond rings, tennis bracelets, and designer workout clothes. The three of them huddled close together and whispered, obviously discussing something or someone and didn't want to be overheard, unlike the last time. Every few seconds one of them would glance in Maya's direction and then resume the huddle.

"Do you know those women?" Laura asked in a quiet voice.

"No, not at all. They were here once before."

"They're the first women I've seen here under sixty-five, well, other than you. Everyone else seems to be a year younger than dirt."

"I'm curious, Laura, why did you move here? It seems to be a stressful experience for you."

"It was my husband's idea. He's a developer, so he got this notion in his head that we could build something, flip it, and make a pile of money. So far, it doesn't seem to be going in that direction."

"What do you mean?"

"We bought the biggest lot and built the biggest house thinking that people who moved to Paradise would want that. But many of the expats are downsizing from large homes they had in the U.S. and aren't interested in the upkeep of a ten-thousand-square-foot house. None of our friends are interested either. We also thought it would be a much hipper crowd. There's no nightlife to speak of, so we wind up sitting home watching TV from the States. Robert hasn't made any friends because everyone is too old to play tennis four hours a day, so he's bored and getting on my nerves. I don't know how much longer we can last."

"That must be disappointing."

"You can say that again. Plus, it's a drag flying back and forth to L.A. every three weeks to get my hair cut and colored."

"I can imagine," Maya smirked.

The huddle was still going on at the other table until the woman with long auburn hair and a three-carat rock on her ring finger pushed her chair back, glanced over at Maya, and smiled.

The woman leaned in, whispered something to her friends whose mouths formed a big "O," placed both hands flat on the table, and announced, "I'm going for it!"

In three long strides, the woman with a BMI of twenty was standing next to their table. "I'm sorry to intrude. But aren't you the woman who does that magazine?"

"Yes. That would be me," Maya replied with a smile.

"Well! My girlfriends and I were just discussing how we are going to expose what happened to us and we thought maybe you'd be interested in our story."

"A lot depends on your story. Have a seat. What is your name?"

"Belinda. But everyone calls me Bel. I'm so happy to meet you. And you, too," she said to Laura, extending her hand.

Maya gave her the once-over. Very East Coast; definitely *nouveau riche*. "What happened to you and your friends that would be of interest to others?"

"We came here for an extended vacation. We're all into health and fitness, so we signed up for a three-week stay at that new organic, raw, low carb vegan, yoga health spa down on the coast. Have you heard about it?"

"I haven't. Tell me."

"It was created by this drop-dead gorgeous hunk of a guy who goes by Sat Siva Joyous. He claims to be a shaman and the absolute best when it comes to teaching a certain style of yoga. He promised to get us in perfect shape in those three weeks. There were two other women there besides us and everyone had their own little glamping set-up. It was very charming. And quite luxurious, too, with wonderful beds, expensive sheets, and a view of the ocean when you were lying down. Damn well should be luxurious for five thousand dollars a week. Plus, there was a saltwater pool, and a fabulous yoga platform. Lots of lush vegetation, parrots, monkeys, lizards, the whole tropical nine yards. We were totally enchanted and couldn't wait to settle into the routine."

"It sounds really lovely," Maya said. "Seems like you were getting your money's worth."

"We thought that, too. At first. We did yoga in the morning, then had this amazing breakfast of nothing but fruit. Well, I'm assuming it was fruit. It was very colorful, but we had no idea what it was. Then there was meditation until lunch, and after lunch it was more yoga."

Laura was enraptured. "Makes me want to go there."

"Just wait. You may want to rethink that. In some ways, it was like Tahiti before it got discovered. Lunch was more fruit, and salad. Or rather just lettuce. Maybe not lettuce, but it was some leafy green stuff. No dressing. Not even a piece of cashew cheese. Not even oat milk for our coffee. Dinner was a plate of raw vegetables, some of which we had never seen before. None of us has been this skinny since high school. We were free to swim or stroll the beach until seven when the drumming circle began which he claimed would induce a trancelike state."

"I must be missing something. Why did you have a problem?" Maya asked.

"I'm getting there. After the first day things changed."

"How so?"

"I'm almost embarrassed to say. . ." Bel said, holding her hands over her face.

"If you want me to investigate this, I need to know what happened."

"Yes, hurry up and tell her," the two friends coaxed

from across the room.

"Okay, his website stresses that he's all about personal attention, and he wasn't kidding. Our first clue that strange things were about to happen was when we had a group masturbation circle. Yes, yes, I know," she blushed, "I'm so embarrassed about that. It was weird, but he convinced us it would unblock our chakras, so we went along with it. After we were settled in our respective tents at night, he started coming to give us massages and one-on-one instructions – in Tantric yoga. That's when we figured out the whole retreat was about sex! We also suspected that he was micro-dosing us with psilocybin, ecstasy, or maybe LSD. The sides of the tent were rippling in waves and all the colors around us seemed to vibrate. Drugs are the only explanation. Okay, we admit it, we were bad. But he was worse. He was very adamant about not discussing our private sessions with anyone, but my two friends and I have known each other since grade school. We have no secrets. By the second week, we were comparing notes and realized he had been screwing all of us. The guy was like the Energizer Bunny, or Shiva, but with dicks instead of arms. We started referring to him as Sat Siva Tumescent. No wonder he was in such good shape. We had one more week in this sex camp, but we wanted out because of his predatory behavior."

"You couldn't just leave?"

"Ha! After forking out fifteen thousand dollars, we wanted a refund for that last week, so the three of us confronted him. That's when it got really ugly."

"Do tell," Laura chimed in. "This is fascinating."

"Unbeknownst to us, there were mini spy cameras imbedded in the tent. He'd been taping our 'yoga' sessions. He reminded us that the policy clearly stated no refunds, and then he showed us some of the footage. We were dumbstruck. That's when he cautioned us if we opened our mouths, he would send those tapes to our husbands. So, this creepy little guy is raking in twenty-five grand a week, feeding us rabbit food, and getting more sex than any one person should have in a lifetime."

Laura burst out laughing.

"You think that's funny?" Bel scolded.

"In a way, yes," Laura said. "Not that it happened to you, but that there is someone with such unmitigated gall as to lure five women to a remote spot in a third world country, charge them five grand a week, feed them plants, and then screw their brains out. Who came up with his marketing plan? It was brilliant."

"Collectively, we feel like the stupidest women on the planet right now, but thankfully, we're leaving in two days and going back to civilization. The real issue is that we will forever live with this hanging over our heads. What's to stop him from blackmailing us? As you can imagine, this wouldn't sit well with our husbands."

No, it probably wouldn't, Maya thought.

"Mine is a high-profile criminal lawyer, and Beth and Megan are both married to prominent doctors. The last thing we need is scandal, so we assured Sat Siva Sex Machine we wouldn't breathe a word of this. He insisted we leave a good review on Trip Advisor, or else. Those were the conditions, or we were screwed, and not in a Tantric way. Then he added, 'You might be leaving, but God will provide me with other angels. I have a one-year waiting list.' The name of his raw, vegan sex camp is Nirvana by the Sea. If you look on Trip Advisor, there are over a hundred glowing reviews, and I would bet they were all left under similar threats of exposure. If you do the math, it's five hundred grand he's raked in since he opened five months ago. Basically, he stands to make a million dollars a year as an enlightened stud muffin. Maybe the tax authorities would be interested. I doubt he's new to this hustle. He's probably run this scam in other places where they have these new age retreats, like Costa Rica, Ojai, or Sedona. He's safe here because there is no extradition treaty but that won't stop him from fleeing to another untapped territory if the authorities closed in. Well, do what you want with this information. And it was so nice talking to you, but we've got to run. We're spending the last two days before our flight home in Santa Lucia, mainly because we want to check out that new Argentine restaurant. After our experience we need some real meat. Have a fabulous afternoon in Paradise."

"You, too," Maya and Laura said in unison. They waited for the nearly emaciated Hampton chicks to walk out the door, then howled with laughter.

"Oh, my God in heaven, do you believe that story?" Laura asked, her eyes wide like saucers.

"Actually, I do. When you've lived here as long as I have, nothing shocks you. Not even that."

When they finished their espresso, they walked towards the park. Maya's phone rang. "You go on ahead. I've got to take this. We'll talk later."

"Hello?"

"Maya, it's Kendall Jacobs."

"Well, hello. Are you okay? I read about what happened."

"I'm a little nicked up, but nothing too serious. Hopefully, the cuts from flying glass won't scar too badly. I wouldn't want my good looks ruined by an assassination attempt."

"No kidding. What's up?"

"I have to see you."

"Why?"

"Can't say on the phone. Can you come to the city? If not, I could come there, but we need to meet somewhere private. Not in public."

"What about my house? That's as private as any place I can think of."

"I could do that. Does tomorrow work for you? Mid-morning?"

"That would be fine. Should I send you the directions on WhatsApp?"

"No need. I know where you are."

Chapter 39

The morning was uncharacteristically cool for this time of year, and by tropical standards could even be considered cold. A refreshing breeze drove a thick bank of mist along the distant ridge which then hung precipitously over the tops of the two volcanoes. As quickly as it appeared it dissipated as the air temperature increased. There was nothing boring about the weather here, that was for sure. It changed daily, sometimes hourly, and the locals made jokes like they used to in Colorado: If you don't like the weather, wait five minutes.

Preparing for Kendall's arrival, Maya made a batch of lemon madeleines and a pot of coffee. If their meeting lasted longer, she had all the makings for a simple lunch. Her anxiety ratcheted up a few notches when she wondered what could be so dire that Kendall would drive all the way from the capital to meet with her in the *campo*. She was equally worried if him coming here posed a risk to her.

By the time he pulled into her long driveway, it was a balmy eighty degrees. She rushed to the gate to greet him and was unable to conceal her shock when she saw his face. The cuts on his forehead had been stitched but were still inflamed. The gash on his cheek looked superficial but the laceration near his nose needed five or six stitches, prompting the beginning of two black eyes.

"My God," she blurted reflexively, her eyes welling with tears, "you're so lucky it wasn't worse, but it still looks very painful. Come in, sit down on the sofa. We can hang out on the terrace, or we can go inside. Whatever is more comfortable for you."

"Terrace is fine with me," he said, settling into the soft cushions. "What a fabulous view you have. Seeing those two volcanoes from this perspective, I understand why you titled your last book *Between Volcanoes*. There is something sublime about that space." Kendall inhaled deeply, dabbed at his forehead with a handkerchief, and looked directly at Maya. "I sincerely apologize for the intrusion, but I felt it was only safe to meet somewhere we wouldn't be seen."

"I'm curious, how did you know where I live?"

"You have to ask? I'm an investigative journalist. I know all kinds of shit I ought not to know," he grinned, gently touching the gash on his cheek. "Your location is one of them."

"It's fine, Kendall. Relax. Tell me what's going on. Do you think this was related to the Charlotte Wilson case?"

He winced. "I wish. Having my appearance forever altered over a rich socialite murdering her husband, or the government absconding with their assets, would make things easier."

"What's the update on that case?"

"They are going to retry her for murder. And they will keep trying her until they get a verdict that is satisfactory. To the state. There is no double jeopardy here, so she can be tried as many times as they want, the goal of which is to make sure she has no recourse to force the government to return her property. It's an arcane form of legal theft."

"That seems to be a common occurrence here."

"Yes, it is. Now, she's playing mental patient. She hasn't a toucan to her name, so she has a pro bono legal team, and they are strategizing to forestall any additional proceedings. As for my current situation, it's far more precarious."

"How so?"

"Just so you know, I wasn't shadowed, and my car was checked for devices that could track my movements, if you're worried about that. Nobody knows I'm here. Do you mind if I sit quietly for a moment and take in this view? It's the most peaceful panorama I've laid eyes on in months. Santa Lucia is like any other city – too much concrete, traffic, noise, and pollution. Plus, I need to gather my thoughts about how I am going to tell you what I know. Otherwise, it might go to the grave with me, and that would be unfortunate."

"You chill out. I'll get the coffee and cookies and then you can fill me in." Maya returned a few seconds later. "Okay, let's hear it," Maya said as she poured Kendall a cup of coffee and handed it to him. "I have fresh cream and sugar if you want."

"Black is fine. Thank you. Let's start with your husband's death. Unfortunate as that was, and I'm sorry for your loss, he got mixed up with the wrong people. The Lobos Locos cartel are brutal; one misstep and you wind up just as your husband did – in pieces and fed to crocodiles."

"I've worried about that." She didn't dare mention that they threatened to kill her, too, when they came for her husband.

"They behave just like the Sinaloa cartel, or the Juarez boys and kill everyone in any way connected to their target. And then there's Miguel Espinoza."

"Is he who was recently found murdered?" Maya interrupted, her voice rising to a near shrill.

"Yes, that's him. He has several nicknames: The Right Hand because that's the one he uses to wield a machete, or The Executioner – and either one pretty much describes his position in the cartel. Why do you look so stunned?"

"I was sitting in the park one day when he walked up and sat on the bench across from me. He asked if I was Maya Warwick. I said yes, and then he got up and sat down next to me and gave me a couple of grainy photos. We met again a few days later. Then I heard nothing more from him. A few days ago, I saw that sketch asking for leads to his identity. Ever since I've had this gnawing fear about why he approached me."

"That's interesting. What were the photos of?"

"One was two guys standing on a beach and the other was a photo of a runway with a mound of debris at one end."

"That's interesting. To be honest, I wasn't surprised when he was found butchered in a field, but the official story isn't credible. As for my situation, I'm quite sure the *sicarios* were sent by the cartel if not to kill me outright then to send a powerful message. You see, I've been investigating this enterprise for the last three years, off the record." Kendall tenderly touched the stitches on his forehead and flinched. "Let me show you something." He lifted his briefcase onto his lap, removed a file folder, and flipped through some 8 x 10 photos, setting two aside and putting the rest back in the envelope. "Here. Does this look familiar? That's a makeshift airstrip carved out of the jungle, wide enough and long enough to land large jets packed with tons of cocaine. Sometimes up to one hundred tons. Local villagers tell me they hear planes rumbling overhead at night making their approach to the darkened airstrip, flying low over the Mayan ruins. With no runway lights or navigation lights on the planes, landings are guided by drones. It takes an expert pilot to not crash into the jungle, which seems to be a common occurrence judging by the wreckage in this photo."

"Yep, Miguel gave me a similar photograph."

"As soon as the plane hits the tarmac, thirty or forty people rush from the surrounding jungle to offload drugs onto trucks that will cross the border to Mexico and then continue to the U.S. Countries like Panama and Costa Rica put a dent in the cartel's submarine delivery system, but the cartels outsmarted them, yet again. That part of the northern triangle in Guatemala, once the cradle of Mayan civilization, is now a cocaine playground. Ninety percent of the cocaine consumed in the U.S. comes through that area, and even though fifty plus abandoned planes have been discovered, many more landed, dumped their cargo, and took off again. Most of the flights originate in Venezuela. Lobos Locos have the Mexican and Guatemalan security forces outnumbered in manpower and weapons. Not to mention their ability to navigate the dense jungle. Look at this photo. These are some of the players. You might recognize Miguel in this group since you met with him briefly, and then. . . there are these two goons."

Maya's eyes opened wide in recognition. "Yes, that's Miguel although when I met him, he was well dressed and looked like an ordinary businessman, and these two," Maya said, poking at the photo, "they followed me and Lucien after having dinner downtown. I'll never get this guy's face out of my head – he looks like a Damascus goat. He was also a former member of the *Kaibiles*."

"Mr. Goat Head is Emanuel "Chucho" Ak and the other one is Bautista "Gordo" Mendez. They are the capos of the Lobos Locos cartel. And you are quite correct about them being former *Kaibiles*. In fact, every drug cartel on the isthmus and Mexico has members who were once part of that elite group, including the Zetas and the Gulf cartel. The cartels recruit these aging warriors because they are adept at evading capture and can navigate the almost impenetrable jungle."

"Who took these photos?"

"I did. I have friends in the Peten region of Guatemala where the airstrips are. In fact, one of them goes right through my friend's cattle ranch. He's been an invaluable source of information since I embarked on this project and keeps a log of the flights that land there. Every two or three days a plane rumbles over his tiny hut and descends into the jungle. If the plane doesn't hit the landing strip at the right spot, it careens into the jungle and explodes, sending a fireball into the sky that can be seen for miles. Local farmers often find hundreds of bricks of cocaine scattered through the dense undergrowth."

"How do you get there?"

Kendell smiled for the first time since he arrived. "Believe me, it's no easy task. From here it's two days on back roads and unmarked trails. First in a cargo truck, then on horseback, and the last thirty or forty miles on foot to avoid detection from drones surveilling the area. Without a local guide, I would never be able to do it. The locals are powerless when it comes to dealing with this menace because the authorities facilitate this drug operation. They are rewarded handsomely for doing nothing. The poor ranchers and peasant farmers are terrorized into quiescent silence, even when the few cattle they have are rustled to feed the throng of cartel soldiers. It's an extremely ugly and dangerous situation for those people who are already struggling to survive. There doesn't seem to be any way to stop it. I'm trying, but you see what I got for my efforts."

"Being a journalist in Latin America is the most dangerous job. Last I checked, nearly a hundred have been murdered in the last two years, along with activists who oppose multinationals raping local resources. Writing about expats is a lot safer, plus it's entertaining."

"They're an amusing bunch, I'll say that for them," Kendell chuckled. Leaning back into the cushions, he suddenly looked very serious. "I have a favor to ask of you."

"What?"

He reached into his briefcase, pulled out a bulging plastic envelope, and cradled it in his lap. "These are notes on my six trips to the Northern Triangle. I have documented every government official in Malpaís and

Guatemala who turns a blind eye to this cartel business, along with the names of the lieutenants who take their orders from Goat Boy and Fatso. I also have the names of judges, lawyers, and politicians who are on the take as well every business establishment that has laundered money for this crime syndicate through prostitution, human trafficking, and weapons. There are names of bankers who facilitate this operation, including that wannabe thug from Banco Nacional de Malpaís, Esteban Lopez, who made off with five million dollars of cartel money."

"He was my banker. I didn't find out about what he did until I went to the bank right after my return."

"I'll bet he regrets doing that. He was remanded to the worst prison in the country. A few months later, there was a riot and when it was over, he was the only one unaccounted for. Most likely, the whole thing was staged by the cartel so they could get their hands on him and exact their own punishment. I suspect he was croc dinner. Not a word made it to the press. That's not surprising either since most of the journalists in this region fear for their lives if they print one word the cartel doesn't like. That includes me. The bottom line is that Malpaís is a narco state. It is run by narcos for the benefit of narcos. I don't know who else I dare leave this information with."

"What about a safe deposit box?"

"Are you kidding? That's probably the least safe place since the bankers are all in on this. Leaving my research with you is my insurance policy that it won't be confiscated and destroyed should I meet an unfortunate end."

"And what if something does happen to you. What do I do with this material then?"

"I guess you write the book I would've written, and then get the hell out of here to a safe place."

Maya fretted for a few seconds trying to process what Kendall had just told her. He stared at her pleadingly, which only made her feel more pressured.

"I don't know, Kendall. I'd be lying if I said it didn't worry me having this in my possession."

"I get it. But nobody knows I'm here, so there's no way to connect you to me. I've come to you because you have great respect for the truth, even when it's inconvenient and painful. Your books deal with those truths, and if something were to happen to me, I hope you would use this information to your benefit. It probably also needs to be shared with some appropriate agency, although I'm hard-pressed to know which one. Maybe CIA?"

Maya said nothing. And with good reason. Was she obligated to tell Will about this? And if she didn't? What then? After a few awkward seconds of contemplating what Kendall just told her, she said, "To be honest, my automatic reflex is to balk at making any decision, even if it's the right one. So, let me suggest this: Why don't I fix us some lunch, and that will give me some time to mull this over. My gut instinct tells me it's the right thing to do, but my over-active brain is sending warning signals."

"I'll go for that. Do you mind if I lie down here? My head feels like a wrecking ball."

Kendall Jacobs wasn't the only one whose head felt like a wrecking ball. Will laid back and gently put his head on the mound of pillows before taking a photo of himself to see if the swelling had gone down. The guy he'd cornered in an alleyway in Istanbul threw a powerful punch to the left side of Will's head and knocked him unconscious for a few minutes allowing the traitorous asset to escape. Will tracked him down once and he would do it again, but it wouldn't be until he could walk across the room without his legs buckling and the room tilting and spinning. The emergency room doctor suspected a concussion and suggested bed rest for a few days. About the only thing Will could do that didn't produce waves of nausea was watch the live video stream from the security cameras in Maya's house.

The black bag team had been thorough in planting those cameras and microphones. With a push of a button Will could observe her actions and listen to everything that was said anywhere in or outside the house. Yes, he felt a twinge of guilt, but it was all in the name of keeping her safe, not from the annoying expats she thought were her assignment, but from those skulking in the shadows that Will was trying to flush out at the behest of the Agency. His team had successfully eliminated Miguel Espinoza, who, if one believed all the reports, was responsible for the deaths of at least three hundred people, most of whom wound up at the El Pozolero, the chemical vat into which the cartel's victims were ceremoniously tossed. They would probably never have an accurate body count of those disposed of in the chemical soup kitchen behind his modest house in a remote location fifty miles from Guatemala City. Even with all the inside information, they were never able to get a fix on "Chucho" and "Gordo," the two ruthless architects of so much violence in the pursuit of moving massive amounts of cocaine through the isthmus and eventually onto the streets of major U.S. cities.

Will watched as Maya prepared sauce for pasta, along with a salad, and walked to the terrace to ask Kendall if he wanted to eat inside or outside.

"The terrace, if that's okay," he replied, standing up and following her into the kitchen. "Can I help with something?"

"Take the plates and silverware, and I'll bring the food and wine."

It didn't matter that it was totally unprofessional, Will had a twinge of jealousy. He wished he was there having lunch with her, and worse yet, he wished there was some other place in her life for him besides being her handler. Even with the nausea and dizziness, there was no way to quell his libidinous feelings. He wasn't proud of the fact that he had formed an unhealthy attachment – a fixation, really -- to his asset. His conflicted feelings about her and their relationship as it pertained to Operation LUCIÉRNAGA made him vulnerable and he knew it. How could he ever tell her what he had been doing? He doubted she'd be surprised if she knew; after all, she was the one who gave him the lecture about the CIA being masters at stealth, deception, and betrayal. As much as he tried to dispel that notion, there would be no denying how devious and manipulative they really were if she knew she was under surveillance.

He watched them eat lunch and talk of trivial things relating to Malpaís, while he anxiously waited for her to acquiesce accepting his research file, which would be crucial to this operation. He wanted to text her three simple words – "take the file" – but that would not end well. All he could bank on was her journalistic integrity to drive her decision to ensure Kendall's research was protected. He was also willing to bet she wouldn't volunteer she had this information, so accessing it was a whole other issue, but that's what his team was for. They'd gotten into her house before, and they'd do it again. With any luck, Will would be able to see where she hid it and that would make their task easier. All they needed was twenty minutes to photograph the documents and they'd be gone. Getting her out of the house for at least two hours wouldn't be a challenge because surely there was some frivolous gringo get together coming up in the next week.

Maya cleared the table, and asked Kendall if he'd like an espresso.

"That would be great. Then I need to get on the road. The doctor told me to rest, but I defied him and now I'm regretting it. A shot of rocket fuel will help a lot."

Five minutes later, Maya returned with a tray bearing two cups of espresso and some chocolate covered coffee beans. "Eat a few of those things; they're like mainlining caffeine," she laughed. After she sat down, she looked sternly at Kendall. "Even though I have some valid reservations, I know how important this is to you. So, yes, I will safekeep your research and I vow to tell no one that it's in my possession. Hopefully, that's enough to ensure my safety."

"Good girl. My life just got easier," Will said out loud, bolting upright from the bed, causing the room and everything in it to spin. Before resuming his horizontal position, he pressed a number on his speed dial and when the party answered, said, "Standby for search and acquisition," and hung up.

Chapter 40

Magdalena's melodic singing could be heard as she strolled down the long driveway. There was the familiar clang of the terrace gate, then an ear-piercing shriek that sent Maya flying down the hallway from the bedroom to the terrace. Magda was riveted to a spot to the right of the door, pointing. "There! *Mire*! *CULEBRA*!" she screamed.

"What?" Maya asked, turning her head towards where she was pointing. "Oh, NO! Don't move, I'll get something." Poised in a coil was a snake. The first thing Maya did was quickly call up Google on her phone and type in the words "coral snake." The little jingle 'red on yellow, kill a fellow; red on black, friend of Jack' appeared. She darted outside and saw that the snake was now climbing vertically up the frame of the sliding glass door. "It's the venomous one!" Maya grabbed a broom, and poked at the snake, getting it to wrap itself around the wooden handle. In one swift movement, she rushed to the open terrace gate and dropped the snake onto the grate that was covering the cement drain box where the run-off from the roof was re-directed to the far side of the property. It slithered into the one-foot-deep containment.

"Not there," Magda shouted. "It's going to try and go into that pipe," she pointed, "and that pipe connects to your drains. Then it could get into the house."

"What am I going to do?"

"You have to kill it."

With adrenaline coursing through her body, Maya used the broom handle to lift the grate, moved closer to see the snake, and began beating it. It made a dash for the drainpipe, but Maya was persistent, continuing her assault, as Magda cheered her on.

"Don't stop! There is no anti-venom for this snake. If it bites us, we will be in the glory of God."

With a final whack to its head, the coral snake succumbed. "Now what am I going to do with it?"

"Get the *manguera*. Turn on the water very strong and wash it away. The pipe goes all the way to the end of your property and the snake will be deposited in the thick brush where it will harm no living thing."

Maya walked to the side of the house, turned on the water, and aimed the hose into the cement box. A few seconds later, the mangled snake was gone but Magda was wailing loudly.

"What's the matter?" Maya asked, looking triumphant.

"I was so scared. Those snakes – they are very bad. We could be dead right now and on our way to our celestial home to be wrapped in the arms of our Lord."

"But we're okay," Maya said, putting her arm around the sobbing woman. "Come in, sit down, let me make you some tea. We're safe now."

Will laughed as he watched this entire situation, although he didn't know why. His own pathological fear of snakes exceeded any terror poor Magdalena was experiencing. Had he been there, he probably would have passed out from fear, and that certainly wouldn't be good for his image.

Chapter 41

The afternoon was sweltering, which was unusual at this altitude. With both ceiling fans on high speed, there was still little relief from the oppressive humidity. Maya switched off her phone and headed for the hammock to take a break after writing a lengthy report to Will. She made no mention of her meeting with Kendall Jacobs or the research he left with her, which was now safely hidden in a false-bottom drawer of her armoire with a back-up copy on a thumb drive hidden in the most unlikely spot. She didn't need to. Will's team was already positioned for entry at the next opportunity. Will watched as she removed the front part of the drawer and slid out the bottom half, laid the folder on top of the others, and replaced the façade of the drawer. He studied the video so he would be able to give the team leader explicit instructions. All that was needed now was an opportunity, and that came as soon as she turned her phone on.

"Maya, my dear, how are you on this miserably hot

afternoon? I swear, I am drenched in sweat with the slightest movement."

"Hi, Maybelle. It's the same here. I was just having a quick lie-down in the hammock. What's up?"

"I have some bad, bad news. Charlie died about an hour ago."

"Who?"

"Linda Franklin's husband. I know you've met her. Tall, thin, sinewy blonde, and very nervous. I'm sure she's been at one of our morning get-togethers."

"Of course. I know who you mean. That's too bad about her husband. Are you helping her with arrangements?"

"Oh, dear God, yes! And the funeral is tomorrow morning. You have to come."

"Isn't that awfully soon?"

"Little did I know, but you're buried the next day if not sooner. If he had died this morning, the funeral would have been at five p.m. today. But since it was after noon, it's tomorrow at eight a.m. in the main cathedral. They don't embalm the dead here, so burial has to be quick because of the heat and humidity."

"But I didn't know him at all, and I barely know her."

"Doesn't matter. It's a show of support from the expat community. You must be there. It will look very bad otherwise. Like you didn't care."

"If you say so. Is there anything I need to know about the protocols?"

"It's a Catholic funeral, so there will be a lot of ceremony, but it shouldn't last more than an hour."

The next day dawned cool and foggy, which was a relief after the oppressive heat of the previous day. Maya dressed in a plain black short-sleeve top, and a pair of black silk slacks. She had no idea if a head covering was required so she wrapped a wide silk scarf around her neck which she could quickly undo and use as a *mantilla*. Funerals were Maya's least favorite activity and having to attend one for someone she didn't even know annoyed her, but she already knew how fast gossip and negative comments would spread in the expat community and the last thing she wanted was to be the recipient of their viciousness.

San Pedro was bustling and the only place to park was on the west side of the park opposite the cathedral. As she approached, a clutch of women stood near the entrance. They appeared to be in a group hug, perhaps with the woman whose husband was about to be laid to rest. The women then walked single file into the church. Maya didn't want to intrude, so she held back for a few seconds before ascending the stairs to the main entrance and followed them to the alter. She scooted into an empty pew several rows behind what appeared to be close friends of the widow and the departed. An ornate bronze casket covered in tropical flowers was on a bier right below the pulpit. Maya spotted Maybelle in the second pew, patting her eyes with a handkerchief. There was a buzz of hushed chatter in the room and suddenly the fifty or so attendees stood and turned to face the main entrance as the Mariachi band, led by the trumpet player, entered the cathedral. Followed by three other musicians playing an acoustic guitar, a *vihuela*, and a *guitarrón*, the large fretless, six-string bass, they played a very somber, melodic tune. Even though Maya didn't understand all the lyrics, it was still very moving as they slowly made their way to a riser next to the casket. After three more tunes, they sat down when the priest approached the pulpit. As if on cue, people stood up, sat down, genuflected, stood up again, sat down, and listened intently to the words of Father Horacio. When the mass ended the grieving widow walked to the casket, leaned down, and kissed the glass pane that was over his face. Then she placed a white, long-stemmed rose on top and accepted condolence hugs from everyone. Maya stood in line and when it was her turn, she said quietly, "I'm so sorry for your loss. Please accept my condolences."

Linda collapsed into Maya's embrace and began to sob. Thankfully, Maybelle came to her rescue, disentangled Linda, and offered her a clean tissue to wipe her face. "Please come to the cemetery," Linda pleaded. "It would mean so much to me."

Maybelle escorted Linda down the aisle as the casket was removed and placed in the back of the hearse to make its way to the cemetery on the other side of town.

"Do we drive behind the hearse?" Maya asked the person standing next to her.

"Oh, no. We walk. It's only a mile, maybe less."

Maya looked down at her shoes, a pair of black slingbacks with a two-inch heel. No way she was walking a mile in those. She'd have to do it barefoot if she did it at all. Without a reasonable excuse to not join the throng of mourners and the Mariachi band, she decided to wait until the procession started and then quietly slip away, cross the street, and cut through the park to her car. As soon as the group gathered behind the hearse and started moving forward, she made her escape.

In the meantime, Will was monitoring her location remotely. She put her phone on airplane mode when she entered the cathedral and turned it back on when she got in the car. His team entered the house ten minutes after she left, extracted the voluminous file from its clever hiding place, photographed the documents, and had just finished the task when Will sent a text urging them to get out now. After a quick sweep of the room to make sure nothing was disturbed, they left the same way they entered, through the sliding glass door facing the walled garden off the dining room. Their car was parked a hundred meters down the road on a dirt path, and in two or three minutes they would be nowhere near the development. Will sighed with relief when they texted him that all was safe. They were one step closer to eliminating their targets and sending an important message to other drug traffickers.

Chapter 42

Maya was relieved to be home again and after changing into more comfortable clothing, she logged onto her AOL account to see several new emails from people she didn't know. The one with the subject "Are there kangaroos in Malpaís?" sparked her interest. Oh, this ought to be good, she mused.

"Hello, Maya. Since you seem to be the expert on all things relating to living in Paradise, I'm asking this question because we really, really want to move there, but we have a dog with severe food allergies. The only protein he can eat is kangaroo. Are there kangaroos there? Are they free range? And do you know how much the meat costs? Right now, I spend $700 a month on kangaroo burger. If it's not available there, I don't know what we will do, except maybe raise our own? Thank you for any insight you might have. Sincerely, Meghan Farnsworth."

Maya laughed. She was quite sure there were no kangaroos hopping around the rain forest anywhere in the country. Was this woman serious? Would it even be possible to import them? Maya suggested she contact the Ministerio de Agricultura and go from there. She had neither the time nor the patience to research this, but getting a good laugh relieved the stress of the last couple of days.

The next email was from someone named Colton Harris and the subject line read "The gringo had a gun." Could this top the woman looking for kangaroo meat?

"Dear Ms. Warwick: Your magazine is intriguing and that is why I am contacting you. You see, I have one of those cautionary tales to share about investing in a place called Paradise. It's quite a long story, but I will tell you the salient parts to get your interest. I invested a LOT of money to build a hotel on the beach. Several hundred thousand dollars were deposited in the local bank to be paid out incrementally for construction and permits, etc. However, it seems that someone at the bank embezzled most of that money, thereby putting an end to construction, and an end to my dream of having a small, elegant hotel. When I demanded an explanation from the bank as to where the funds had gone, the bank manager suggested that we have a sit-down meeting in his office with other bank employees who had access to my accounts. I agreed. During the meeting, one of the employees was acting very strange. Nervous. Sweating. Looking like he was going to pass out. Then suddenly, he bolted for the door where an armed guard was positioned, and yelled, 'The gringo has a gun!' The employee fled the bank and hasn't been seen or heard from since. I was arrested but of course they found no weapon and eventually I was let go, but now I have been barred from entering the bank and have no idea what has happened to my money. I tried to find a lawyer to represent me, but so far, they have all declined, probably because they are related in some way to people who work at the bank. That's why I am coming to you. Maybe some adverse publicity would spark a proper investigation into this travesty. Is there a good time when we could meet to discuss this further? Thank you in advance for your assistance. Sincerely, Colton aka Colt .45."

As ridiculous as those two emails were, nothing prepared for the next one:

"Hola Maya: I was told you were the person to contact because you know so much about life in Malpaís. My wife, my ten-year-old daughter, and I want to move to Paradise, but we want to know what the process would be for bringing our six one-hundred-fifty-pound St. Bernards. Do you think this will be a problem?"

"Oh, for God's sake," she groaned. Her reply was the shortest email she had ever written, and it consisted of two words: STAY HOME.

Maya thought she'd heard it all until she read the final email which bested the kangaroo farm and six St. Bernards for batshit crazy. The subject line read "URGENT." It came from someone with the email handle of loveisavibration and it was a plea for Maya to publish a missing person's poster in the next issue of *Neotrópica*. In the center of the poster was a photo of a bearded man, late twenties probably, a man bun on the top of his bleached blond hair, and a dazed, or rather stoned-out-of-his-mind-on-acid, look in his eyes. The poster read: "Please help. Our Awakened Bro Sat Siva Precious is missing. If you have seen him, please tell him his parents in Paris, Texas want him to come home. Description: Often shirtless, usually asks everyone if they are into micro dosing, quotes Ram Dass and Joe Rogan, always talks about archetypes and biohacking, claims to be a Bitcoin coach, wears several rings and necklaces, has pierced nipples, and was last seen in the Sacred Valley teaching breathwork. Your vibrational family is worried about you. Please communicate telepathically and let us know you are somewhere in a circle of light."

But the very last email was the icing on the crazy expat cake. The anxiety of the person writing it was so palpable it made Maya concerned for the mental health of this poor, despairing person.

"Dear Maya: I am writing to you in the hopes that you can give me some information that would be useful in convincing my wife to move to Malpaís. We were there for a week last year and I absolutely loved it and we had a wonderful time. With all the political turmoil, racism, corruption, and violence in the US, I suggested that we sell everything and move there. My wife said it was a nice place to visit but she doesn't want to live there. To be honest, I am desperate to get out of the U.S. and be somewhere peaceful, quiet, with a little house, and room for a garden. That would be nirvana to me, but no matter how much I pressure her, she will not budge. What can I do? Somedays I think I will lose my mind if I don't get out of this country. Thank you for reading this and I hope you have some constructive advice to give my stubborn wife. Thank you so much. Kevin O'Reilly"

Maya read the email a second time. It dredged up a lot of painful memories from when Lucien dug in his heels and flat-out refused to move here. Because her primary objective to was protect her assets, she was willing to embark on this adventure with or without him. Eventually he capitulated and things were wonderful until he delved into the illegal activity that got him killed. What kind of advice should she give stressed out, overwrought Kevin O'Reilly? She thought about it for a good long minute, then hammered out this response:

"Dear Kevin: Thank you for your email. I am sorry you are in such a state of distress. It appears you have two choices: Divorce your wife, follow your bliss, and move to Malpaís; or get some psychological counseling. There are a lot of reasons to move to this country but thinking you will escape the conditions you describe in the U.S. is totally unrealistic. Obviously, you do not read our local news because if you did, you would not be pressuring your wife to do something so boldly stupid. But who am I to dissuade you with facts and reality? Wishing you the best, Maya."

Slamming the laptop closed, Maya buried her head in her hands. A few minutes later, Will watched as she walked to the kitchen and poured herself a drink. It was only three in the afternoon, but after the snake incident, the funeral, a kangaroo ranch, a herd of gigantic dogs, poor missing Sat Siva Precious, and some anxiety-ridden gringo, she probably needed to knock back that shot of vodka. After adding a short refill in her glass, she walked onto the terrace and stared at the fog rolling in from the north. She stood motionless for five minutes. Something was weighing heavily on her mind. And he was right. She walked into the house, put her glass in the sink, and picked up the iPhone.

When Will answered on the third ring, she blurted, "I need a mongoose."

"Why?" *As if I didn't know.*

She began with how upsetting it was that she had to

kill the snake, how surreal the funeral was, and how the emails asking for advice about the most ridiculous things were enough to make her head spin. "It's all too much," she moaned. "I've tried to be as cordial as possible, but it's just not me to engage on this level with perfect strangers who seem to be completely out of touch with reality. It's very stressful. I'm not a psychiatrist but it seems to me that some of these people need professional help."

Will had been waiting for this moment after sensing her frustration with each report she wrote. Most of the time, her presentations were laced with humor bordering on the absurd, but he knew instinctively that the situation was wearing on her. He wished he could tell her that her part in this situation was far greater than what she was told. Betraying her trust bothered him and he gritted his teeth every time he lied to her or encouraged her to participate in activities about which she had no interest for the purpose of observing people she didn't care about. Now that he had access to Kendall Jacobs' research, zeroing in on "Chucho" and "Gordo" wouldn't take long. He had to encourage her to continue to participate in this ridiculous scenario until that event occurred, then she was free. Free to return to France to resume her hermitic lifestyle, which seemed to suit her.

There was an awkward pause, and then she asked, "Are you still in Istanbul?"

"Yes," he replied, watching her fidget with a strand of hair.

"Oh."

"Is there something you want to ask me?"

"Now that you mention it, I'd like to talk to you about

how much longer I have to participate in this ridiculous charade?"

"What do you mean?"

"Don't play dumb; it's unbecoming. I am pretty good at connecting dots. If you don't believe me, I'd bet there is a notation or three in my file about those capabilities. So let me be frank here."

The tone in her voice told him he was going to get a glimpse of what Martin meant when he said it would be easier to wrangle cats than deal with this broad. He also feared his balls might be in danger. "I'm listening."

"I don't know what your real agenda is, but I am quite sure it has little or nothing to do with a bunch of pensioners living in a third world backwater. After a year, I have not met anyone that could even remotely be on the CIA's radar, or anyone else's radar for that matter. Apart from a few scoundrels, most of these people are normal, ordinary citizens without any remarkable characteristics. On the other hand, thanks to this ruse, a couple of key players in Narcoland are dead, and I'd bet money that flushing these people out is the agenda. At my expense, of course."

Will took a couple of deep breaths before saying, "That was purely coincidental."

"Oh, right. My guess is that you're on the hunt for the monsters who sold cocaine to my husband, then kidnapped and murdered him. Am I getting close?"

"Let's not forget your role in his untimely demise."

"Must you bring that up again?"

"It didn't happen in a vacuum, so let's just say that these other disclosures were a fortuitous but welcome revelation and ridding the planet of people like Miguel Espinoza is not necessarily a bad thing. As for your husband's killers, they'll be apprehended eventually, if not by some alphabet agency, then by their rivals."

"Now back to my original question: how much longer do I have to do this?"

"I can't tell you that exactly, but another three or four months is a good guesstimate."

"Well, alrighty then. That doesn't make me happy but if there is an end in sight, I can live with that."

"Has it really been all that bad? Your reports indicate that you've been amused by some of this."

"I could never make up some of these characters or the silly things they do when they leave their home country, and despite all our differences, I've grown quite fond of a few of them. For the most part, they are good and kind although a bit naïve, but that's not their fault."

"I've got to get ready for my flight home. We'll be in touch. Stay the course, and soldier on."

"Okay, Skippy."

Chapter 43

As usual Maya was the last to arrive to the Monday get together. It was a smaller group than normal, so they were congregated at a round table instead of the long one. A chair had to be squeezed in between Diane and Margo.

"So did everyone have a good Fourth of July weekend?" Maybelle queried.

"We had a typical gringo barbeque," Karen volunteered.

"Us, too," the others said in unison.

"That's great! What about fireworks? Did any of you participate in those? I heard a lot of noise in and around San Pedro after it got dark," Maybelle declared.

"We had fireworks all right, but not that kind," Karen said.

"Oh, do tell," Maybelle ordered, gleefully clapping her hands together.

"Ted really wanted a typical Fourth of July feast. Hot dogs, hamburgers, corn on the cob, the works."

"And?" Maya said.

"I'm getting there. Ted found hotdogs in the local market. My goodness was he excited. To be honest, he had just about had it with the local fare. All he wanted was a good old fashioned American hot dog with mustard and relish. Our next-door neighbors – a local couple who speak a tiny bit of English – were outside, so Ted invited them to enjoy a typical gringo celebration. He fired up the grill, opened some beers, and got his apron on to be the official barbeque chef. He wanted to impress our neighbors with some good ol' gringo hospitality. So, he tosses the burgers and the corn on the grill, then took the wieners out of the packaging. You should have seen the smile on his face. He was so happy. He puts the dogs on the fire, waits a few minutes, turns them over, and then looks at me with this quizzical expression and asks, 'Why aren't they plumping up?' 'Did you take them out of the plastic?' our neighbor asked in cryptic English. 'Of course,' Ted replied. Well, after about ten minutes, he slapped those dogs into the buns I made, slathered two of them with relish and a gob of mustard, and chowed down. I looked over at him and he was chewing. . . and chewing. . . and chewing. Finally, I asked him what was wrong, and he said that the outside skin of the hot dog was kinda tough. But that didn't stop him from eating three more. Our neighbors ate the hamburgers. So, we hang out in the backyard and around eight p.m. the neighbors went home, and Ted started complaining."

"Oh, dear, of what?" Maybelle said in a concerned tone.

"Let's just say he had a bad case of indigestion. I gave him some Pepto Bismol but that didn't help. By ten p.m. he was writhing with stomach cramps. I figured it was food poisoning or something, so we jump in the car and go to the emergency room. We lucked out because there was an ER doctor who spoke some English, so he asked all the usual questions about what Ted had eaten, was he constipated, did he have diarrhea. Ted tells him about eating five hot dogs. The ER doctor's eyes got really wide, and he said it was probably a good idea to do an x-ray."

"You must have been worried sick!" Diana squealed.

"Oh, dear God, yes, I was. They strapped him to a gurney and wheeled him off. Twenty minutes later, the doctor came out and summoned me to the exam room where Ted is now sitting up, white as a ghost, and holding his stomach." Karen let out a muffled giggle.

"Come on, tell us what happened." Maybelle was wringing her hands in anticipation.

"Have you all eaten these local hot dogs?"

Everyone shook their head no.

"Then let this be a warning to you. The ER doctor puts the x-ray up against the light box and there was this clump of something lodged in Ted's gut. And it wasn't going anywhere. What was digestible was already on its way south. Meanwhile, Ted is groaning and asking repeatedly if he's going to die. I was totally flummoxed so I asked the doctor the obvious question: how do you plan to get the lump moving?"

The entire table snickered. "Oh, dear, I hope he didn't need surgery," Maybelle said, wide-eyed like a toad.

"Nope. Not surgery. A nurse came in and gave him a glass of pink liquid. Stood there with her hands on her hips until he drank every drop."

"Then what?" Maya asked.

"Then we waited. Didn't take long. Fifteen minutes later, he was ushered into a cubicle and given a thing that looked like an old-fashioned chamber pot. And then the fireworks started. I was sitting in the hallway, and I heard the explosion with poor Ted swearing up a storm. Whole process took about ten minutes and then a nurse dressed in full PPE went into the room, retrieved the pot, and went down the hall. Presumably to examine the contents. Ted comes out of that little cubicle, looking pale and shaken and sits down next to me. And we wait. Neither of us said a damn word. Five minutes later, the ER doctor approaches, and he has one of those metal kidney-shaped dishes in his hands. 'You're going to be okay, Señor Ted. Here's what was causing your pain.' There in that metal dish was a baseball-sized wad of clear plastic wrapping. Ted and I looked at it in disbelief. It was almost midnight when we got home but we pulled the packaging for those damn wieners out of the trash."

"Why?" Diane asked.

"We wanted to see if there was a warning about removing the plastic on each individual hot dog. Nope. Not a word. So let this be a warning. Don't eat those things, and if you do, for the love of God, make sure you've removed all the wrapping."

"Oh, my word," Maya said, shaking her head. "That is the craziest thing I have ever heard."

"Not as crazy as the verbal lashing I gave Ted," Karen added.

"That's quite a funny incident, although I'm sure Ted had a different view of it. What about everyone else? How are you transitioning to living here?" That was all Maybelle had to ask and the flood of complaints erupted.

"Why does it rain so much here?"

"It's the tropics," Maya replied.

"I don't like the bugs. They are everywhere. In everything. And big, too."

"It's the tropics," Maya repeated.

"I hate that we don't have the long days of summer like we did in Kansas."

"We're only a few degrees above the equator," Maya said calmly.

"Why are all the signs in Spanish? Especially road signs. Geez. That could be dangerous."

"It's a Spanish-speaking country. The real question is why don't *you* speak Spanish?" Maya's agitation was building.

"I didn't know we would have so much wind. It blows like a hurricane sometimes."

"Malpaís is on the Isthmus of Panama. There is an ocean on either side, and it's only a hundred miles coast to coast. What did you expect?" Maya's annoyance was obvious by now.

"I expected better weather. If it's not raining, it's hot and humid. I thought Paradise would be, well, perfect."

Maya threw her hands up in the air, got up from her chair, and stomped to the far corner of the patio and faced the wall with her back to the disgruntled gringas. Mumbling to herself about what a bunch of idiots they were, she took several deep breaths, told herself to calm down, and returned to the table where the complaining was still in high gear. If it wasn't the weather, it was the food, the exchange rate, the poorly maintained roads, the mudslides in the rainy season, the unavailability of the drugs they were taking, and the escalating costs of essentials.

Maya sat there, hands folded in her lap (to keep from strangling some of them), and said in the coolest voice she could muster, "Did any of you do any research before you moved here? How did you not know that this was a foreign country, with a different language, a different culture, different values, different sense of humor and priorities? What image comes to mind when you hear the word tropics?"

Nobody said word. A few hung their head and refused to look at her. Finally, one of them spoke in a voice barely above a whisper, "I thought it would be different. That's all. And I flunked geography in high school."

"Aha! Well, that explains a *lot*. When someone describes a location as being in the tropics, it usually conjures up images of lush greenery, fertile valleys, beautiful tropical flowers, and dare I mention it – heat and humidity."

Not a peep out of any of them.

Maya rolled her eyes. "And why do you think those things exist in the tropics?" She waited ten seconds and when there was no response, she bellowed, "Because it's hot and it rains a lot! Good God almighty. Didn't any of you come here to investigate where you would be living?"

"We bought our house on the internet, sight unseen," Karen volunteered.

"Why would you do that?" Maya asked, totally in shock.

"Because we saw all the promo ads, and it looked like heaven. The house was being sold by other expats who had to move back to the States because of family problems. We didn't see how we could go wrong. Boy, were we in for a surprise."

"So, the sellers told you they were leaving because of family problems?" Maya chuckled. "They all say that, but I'd bet money it wasn't true," Maya said, shaking her head.

"We fell in love with the place from watching the ads, too. However, we came for five days, checked it out, and said why not? We weren't getting any younger, and the winters on the East Coast were getting to be too much. How bad could it be, we asked ourselves."

"And?" Maya asked.

"To be honest, we were shocked. Those ads were nothing but lies. Now we're here and too broke to leave," Margo said wistfully. "We're trying to make the best of it, but it's not what we thought it would be. Not being able to buy certain foods is driving my husband insane. He has his favorite things and none of them are available here."

"You do realize that their basic diet is still very Mesoamerican, right? Corn, squash, beans, sweet potatoes, rice. Small amounts of fish or poultry, and if they can afford it beef, or pork. It's a lot healthier than the Standard American Diet. Ditching those packaged foods that you miss so much might actually prolong your life, so you don't have to take all those medications you say are unavailable." Maya was beyond exasperated.

"Maya's right in so many ways," Maybelle chimed in. "Most of us were ill prepared to move here and now we are just trying to make the best of it. That's why these get togethers are so important. We can bitch about the things that are driving us loco and we have others to sympathize with us. I admit it, I knew very little about any place besides Texas. In fact, I had never been outside Texas until we came here. Shameful, I know, but true," Maybelle sighed.

"Okay, ladies, I've got work to do, so I'm going to leave you to complain to one another. Have a pleasant afternoon."

Maya grumbled to herself all the way to her car. How could all these people pack up and move to a place they knew little or nothing about? And she'd bet more than one of them flunked geography. They were wedded to the only customs and culture they knew and everything else was challenging for them. She wanted to feel sorry for them, but she didn't. The sad reality was that most of them should never have left the United States and if she had a magic wand, she would wave it and send them all back. For *good*. And then close the borders.

Chapter 44

Derek hobbled into Café Roma leaning on a cane. From the expression on his face, it was either his hips or knees giving him pain. He was a hulk of a man, and a good fifty pounds overweight even for his six-foot-three-inch frame. He stood at the entrance to the patio tugging on his scraggly beard until he spotted the table where Maybelle was holding court. It hadn't filled up yet for the regular Monday morning gabfest, so Derek took a dozen painful steps and dropped his corpulent body into the chair at the end of the table.

"Derek! It's soooooo good to see you," Maybelle cooed. "I'm glad you decided to come."

"We'll see about that," he groused, adjusting his body on the wooden chair. "I came because I wanted to present an idea to the group."

"Great, Derek. That's why we have these little get-togethers every week. We're all trying to figure out the best ways to navigate Paradise. When everyone gets here, you can present your ideas."

Fifteen minutes later, every seat at the table was filled. Maya was the last to arrive as usual and took the chair next to Derek and introduced herself when she sat down, eyeing toast crumbs sprinkled in his beard.

"Now that we're all here, I want to wish everyone a very happy Monday and I hope you all had a good weekend. Derek, whom most of you know, has an idea he wants to present to the group. Go ahead, Derek. Tell us what's on your mind."

Derek cleared his throat and coughed a few times into his clenched fist. "Almost everyone has had an issue with the screwy addresses in this country. But if you look at San Pedro on Google Maps it shows the names of the streets. Typically blocks are a hundred meters long. So, if you wanted to tell someone where the supermarket was located, you would say, it's seventy meters west of the intersection of Calle 10 and Avenida 7. Simple and accurate. If we all started doing this, we would learn that the San Pedro Hospital is on Avenida 11. Or that the main road into San Pedro is Calle 1. And that the next street to the East is Calle 3, an odd number. And the next street west of Calle 1 is Calle 0, and the next street west is an even number, Calle 2. So, the intersection of Calle 0 and Avenida 0 is the southeast corner of the downtown park. The Avenidas are even numbers as you go South. I know, it's little confusing at first, but if we start using the street names found on Google maps to describe locations, we will have less confusion."

In all the months that Maya had attended these kaffeeklatsches, she had never experienced such a weighty silence. It was as if everyone had been struck mute. Nobody moved, nobody said a word. They all gazed at Derek, like cows staring at a passing train. When the silence became awkward, Maybelle spoke.

"I don't know, Derek," she said, shaking her head. "That seems even more confusing than the ridiculous system we have already, using landmarks that often are not there."

Nancy, a relative newcomer to the San Pedro expat scene, cleared her throat and said, half-laughing, "With your system, I'd be lost the minute I left the house. Why change it? I was just getting used to the concept that a legal address is fifty meters north and fifty meters south of some place whether it's there or not. Now you want me to learn a whole new system. I barely mastered this one."

Maybelle added, "In other words you want us to look at Google maps every time we're going somewhere?"

"It's not that difficult," Derek grunted.

"It is for me," Karen said. "I'm a complete luddite and dunderhead when it comes to those navigation devices or apps or whatever you call them. I much prefer getting lost and driving around in circles. At least I get to explore new neighborhoods."

"I'm with Karen and Nancy on this one," Maya chimed in. "There's a certain charm about these convoluted addresses and directions. The next thing people will want house numbers, and eventually it will be just like the places we all left."

"Why are you all so resistant to progress? This old, ridiculous way of doing things is obsolete. It's time to change with the rest of the world."

"Why do people feel the need to change the way things are done in a country they chose to move to?" Maya asked, unable to mask her exasperation. "Nobody invited us here, and I doubt they want our input on how to make their country just like gringolandia."

"Technology and progress are what allowed you all to come here. You didn't walk. And you all use electronic toys, and Facebook, and the telephone, and the internet. What would be wrong with updating a totally antiquated system of directions?" Derek snorted derisively.

"Because the squirrelly addresses are a tradition here. Personally, I think we should respect those traditions even if we don't agree with them. We came here of our own volition. It wasn't by invitation. Now you want to change the way things have been done for a few hundred years. It's the hubris I don't get. Not to mention the typical gringo attitude of superiority and entitlement." Maya slammed her espresso cup down on the table and folded her hands in her lap.

"You're a stubborn lot, that's for sure," Derek bellowed. "I was trying to find a way to make things easier. Why are you all so thick-headed and defensive? Too real for you? If it weren't for progress, we wouldn't be having this conversation and you wouldn't be in Malpaís. San Pedro needs street addresses. The oxcart days are history. Move on. Ridiculous directions aren't charming, only confusing. Nothing practical about it and it's confusing to visitors. Tradition can be just another way of ignoring progress. A friend owns some land here and has come up against rules that denote ancient oxcart paths as 'roads' but which are no more than paths. Those rules determine how he can develop the land for a small residential community. And he can't get the municipality to change it. That's just dumb. But my all-time favorite is the green church that is now blue, but it is still called the green church. Then there are the business cards without addresses, distances in meters from this place or that, which may or may not still exist. That's so practical. Not!" Derek shifted his carcass on the chair and defiantly crossed his arms over his barrel chest.

"Derek," Maya said soothingly, "San Pedro is a town that is twelve blocks in any direction. We don't need no stinkin' addresses. Get out of your car and walk the streets. Soon you will know every nook and cranny of this place. Talk to the shopkeepers, they will tell you tales about where this or that place used to be. This charming little town is full of kind and generous people. Is it too much to ask to appreciate those things without always wanting to inject our exceptionalism into everything? Besides, this screwy address system is a cultural identity, frustrating a lot of the time, unless you are well grounded in the ins and outs of every small town. It's probably even dangerous, in the case of an ambulance getting lost trying to follow bad directions from someone who doesn't know all the landmarks. The locals love this old system. Those crazy directions might be annoying to you, but for them it's an insider's code."

"Fine! If that's how you want it. I don't really care what you think anyway." Derek hoisted his body off the chair and shuffled toward the exit. "Stupid old cows," he muttered under his breath.

There was a good fifteen seconds of silence as the women watched him lumber through the main dining room and exit the restaurant. Then everyone burst into uproarious laughter.

"I guess he won't be a regular at our Monday get-togethers," Maybelle snorted.

Chapter 45

It started out as any normal Wednesday. Magdalena arrived at her usual time, bouncing into the house while softly singing to herself. She started by sweeping the kitchen and living room before moving to the terrace. Maya was about to pour herself another cup of coffee when the phone rang. It was Laura Huxley, her neighbor up the hill. Maya could only imagine what terrible fix this clueless woman had gotten herself into this time.

"Maya, are you busy?"

"I was just having a cup of coffee before I started writing."

"Got enough for me? Can I come down for a few minutes? It won't take long."

"Sure. Come on down."

Five minutes later, Laura walked onto the terrace, grunted a greeting to Magda, and walked into the house where Maya was seated on the sofa. "Nice to see you," Maya said, jumping up and walking toward the kitchen.

"Let me get you a cup of coffee. What's on your mind?"

"I'm so frustrated, I don't know what to do."

"Tell me," Maya said, handing her a cup.

"To be honest, I don't know how these people have managed to survive this long," she said, nodding her head toward the terrace.

"What do you mean?"

Laura sighed, pushed a strand of honey blonde hair off her forehead, and took a big gulp of coffee. "I gave my gardener specific instructions about how I wanted something done and he did the exact opposite."

"Did you ask him why?"

"It's a little difficult when you don't speak the language," she replied in a huff.

"Maybe he misunderstood you then?"

"I don't know. I told him to use the hedge trimmers to cut the hibiscus and when I looked, he was out there butchering them with a machete."

"In his defense, a hedge trimmer is not likely something he knows how to use. He probably didn't feel comfortable using that when his machete works just as well."

"Yes, but I am paying him by the hour. A job he could have done in fifteen minutes took him more than two hours to do."

"Laura," Maya said, rolling her eyes, "be reasonable. How much are you paying him an hour? Three dollars? Surely, it isn't a big deal to you, and he was doing what he knew how to do and how it's always been done here in the *campo*."

"That's just one example. Then the other day, he started cutting branches off one of my trees. By the time he was done, that lemon tree was nothing but a stump. It's going to take years for it to grow back."

"Did you ask him why he did that?"

"I tried but there's that damn language barrier. All he could do was point to some leafy plant that was on one of the branches."

"Oh, that. Well, that's a parasitic plant that will eventually kill your tree. It's a good thing he removed it."

"Seriously? Oh. Okay, I guess I over-reacted, but sometimes I think these people are dumber than rocks."

There was a loud crash on the terrace and suddenly Magdalena appeared in the doorway with her hands on her hips and a murderous scowl on her face. She was panting from rage and said, "*Disculpe*, Doña Maya, I do not mean to disturb you, but I couldn't help overhearing this woman's horrible comments," she said, jutting her chin in Laura's direction. "I beg you to please let me have some words. It is my Tio Francisco who works for you. He has told me many things about the '*gringa estupida*' – how you like things done the way they are done in gringolandia, but you are not in gringolandia anymore. And to refer to my people as dumb rocks, you should be ashamed of yourself."

Maya stood up and walked towards Magda intending to lead her to a chair so she could sit down. Magda brushed Maya's hand away. "Please, let me have my say to this woman who insulted my uncle and all of my people. So, you think *campesinos* are stupid, eh? Let me tell you about the things my uncle and almost every *campesino* knows how to do. He smokes, drinks, knows how to tell stories, smells bad, fights, supports seven or more children, sows beans, potatoes, cassava, corn, bananas, cocoa, sugarcane, milks fifty cows from four in the morning, knows how to whistle, talks to the dogs and they even bark back at him. He never retires; he does not have Social Security. He is not affected by the altitude, he goes without sunscreen, he recognizes a ripe avocado without squeezing it. He has one long nail to peel tangerines, he knows by eye how much a sack weighs; and by looking and turning it, he knows how much a pig and a cow weigh. He can handle up to eight horses or mules at the same time, and he carries a machete ready to strike.

"He does not need his front teeth to laugh. He knows the names of all the grandchildren, he has the recipe for donkey's milk, he does not know how to dance but he dances. He does not get depressed. He knows one hundred and forty-two rude words, has seen the devil, knows who is a witch, does not get burned by boiling coffee, wakes up before the alarm goes off, is not knocked down by a flu, and walks out of adjustment. His pants are two sizes too big, but they never fall off. He knows trails to get there faster, knows when it is going to rain and fails less than any meteorologist. He knows how to scare the rain and stop the thunder, is not affected by gluten or lactose in unpasteurized milk, and caffeine does not bother him. He recognizes bad boys, and knows which boys are bad for women. He knows how to call chickens, get oranges by shaking the branches, enjoys a fresh papaya and a mango for dessert, or lemonade and cashews, watermelon, or melon. He listens to the radio in AM, he does not give 'likes,' he does not come out pretty in the photos but there is a painting where he is so handsome with his wife." Magda wiped a tear from her cheek. "He knows two jokes and repeats them, and he is trusted by everyone. He knows how to change the tire of a car, he knows how to fish, he does not like soft beds, he takes contraband especially at Christmas, Coca Cola only on very special occasions, beer always and if it is warm, it does not matter. The mosquitoes do not bite him, he has eaten tartúzas, iguana, armadillo, deer, badger and snake and it all tastes like chicken, he does not know when it is a holiday and he does not know who to vote for, because everyone is bad. So, there, Doña Hookslee or whatever your name is, if we did not have *campesinos*, you would have no food to eat, and life would be practically impossible." Magda took a deep breath.

"There is no one more beautiful than Malpaís peasants. And because of *fufurufas* like you, I love my *tio* and the other *campesinos* even more because they are not the stupid ones." Magda whirled around and stomped back to the terrace and resumed whatever task she had been doing.

Maya looked at Laura as the color drained from her face. Her jaw slacked, and her eyes opened wide with disbelief. Secretly, Maya laughed to herself because Magda had done a brilliant job of putting this woman in her place. "Well, that was an interesting encounter."

Laura set her coffee cup on the counter and stood there with an expression of disbelief. "Nobody has ever spoken to me like that before. I don't even know what to say except that I am totally ashamed of myself."

"As well you should be," Maya said *sotto voce*.

"I'm so sorry. Please forgive me and please tell Magda I am humbled by what she said. I am too embarrassed to do anything but go to my house and hang my head. I don't know what I can do to redeem myself at this point," she sniffled.

"GO BACK TO YOUR COUNTRY," Magda hollered from

the terrace.

Before Maya could soothe her, Laura bolted out the door. Maya walked to the terrace and silently approached Magdalena folding her arms around her quivering shoulders. Maya realized that the things she had learned about the culture and the traditions of this little country had given Maya a perspective she didn't have before. There was a profound wisdom amongst the locals who were descendants of the original shipwrecked settlers. They knew how nature worked and they knew how to survive with very little. Ingenious and intelligent in ways not appreciated or even perceived by most outsiders, it was at that precise moment that Maya realized she loved Malpaís and was honored that Magda shared *campesino* wisdom and history with her, expanding her worldview and creating a bond.

Five days later, Maya heard a large truck rumble over the narrow dirt road. When she looked out the window, she saw the moving van trying to negotiate the sharp turn that led to Laura Huxley's McMansion at the top of the hill. Maya giggled. "That didn't take long."

Chapter 46

As she sipped her cup of coffee, she booted her laptop and went to the Facebook page for the local news in English. The headline made her gasp. "Prominent journalist assassinated in Santa Lucia." She held her breath and let out a mournful cry when she saw Kendall Jacobs' name. He was gunned down a block from his apartment by two men on a motorcycle. *Sicarios*, the article said, speculating that he was killed because of his ongoing investigation into the drug cartel known as Lobos Locos. Maya began to hyperventilate. Shoving her laptop aside, she raced to her bedroom and dismantled the drawer where she had stashed the research Kendall gave her for safekeeping. A wave of relief engulfed her when she saw it there, but then she hesitated. Something was not right. The other plastic envelopes, like the one Kendall gave her, were all neatly stacked with their flaps pointing in the same direction. She would have placed the one containing Kendall's research the same way. Instead, the flap of that envelope was facing the other direction. Never would she have done that, as obsessed with order and symmetry as she was. Nobody knew she had this, not even Will. Opening the gallery file on her phone, she clicked on the photo she took of the documents in the drawer. It was an odd habit leftover from when Lucien was alive and always rifling through her personal things. The photographs were a reference point in case he gaslighted her when she asked him if he'd been snooping. Lucien was very dead, but old habits were hard to kill. And then it hit her. Why hadn't she thought about this before? What made her think doing the bidding of this infamous intelligence agency would be any different than the last time? The time they installed listening devices and cameras in her house and recorded her and Harry's every move, including their lovemaking. That had to be it. There was no other explanation. Nobody other than Magda had spent any time in her house and how this complicated hidden drawer worked was not something anyone could figure out on their own. Now what? She looked around the room wondering where they had hidden the surveillance equipment. Nothing seemed out of the ordinary but then they were clever, weren't they? Clever but sloppy if they didn't put the folder back exactly as they found it. She replaced the components of the drawer, hoisted herself from the tile floor, and went to the living room. Stifling her urge to pick up the phone and scream at Will, she sank onto the sofa and sat motionless for a good five minutes.

To gather her senses and think things through, she wandered down to the lower part of her property and meandered through the citrus trees. She remembered Kendall remarking how their scent was intoxicating and soothing. Trying to find comfort in that memory, she sat on the ground leaning against the banana plant. After an hour of peaceful silence, she calmed down enough to think about this situation methodically. If they had gotten into that drawer, did they also find her back-up copy? Thank God she had the foresight to make that detour into the laundry room where her old fax machine/scanner was stashed in a cupboard. It had taken exactly twelve minutes to set it up and transfer all the documents to a thumb drive before placing the folder in the secret drawer. Now she needed to check the hiding place to make sure the thumb drive was still there.

Back at the house, she opened her email, hoping to see something more about Kendall. Instead, there was an email from her best friend's husband informing her that Liz died peacefully early this morning. She didn't even read the rest of the message, just slammed the laptop closed and tried to get her emotions under control. Liz and Kendall on the same day? What kind of cruel joke was the universe playing?

Will replayed the footage several times. An expression of awareness fell like a curtain across her tensed face when she saw the envelope, picked it up, turned it around, then looked at something on her phone. No doubt she had figured it out and was madder than a puffed toad. He would have to talk with his team and castigate them for being so untidy. Now the whole thing was blown. She knew. And his job was to figure out how to assuage her fury. He was unprepared when his phone rang an hour later, and it was Maya.

Chapter 47

"I'm done."

"Done with what?"

"This. I've reached the end of my tether. My best friend died this morning after a battle with cancer, and Kendall Jacobs was assassinated a block from his apartment. Two in one day, Will. That's too much. The article said Kendall was assassinated because of his investigation into Lobos Locos. You wouldn't happen to know anything about that, would you?" she said, her voice tinged with annoyance.

"I'm sorry about your friend. Is there a funeral? Maybe getting out of Malpaís for a little while would do you good."

"There won't be a funeral per her wishes. As upset as I am about Liz, I am more upset about Kendall because I might be in the crosshairs."

"Why do you think that?"

"Stop playing games, Will. I would bet my favorite

Louboutin shoes you spooks bugged my house. You see, I photographed the contents of that drawer so I would know if things were tampered with."

He was busted. There was a long silence before he spoke. "What if I came to your house?"

"Why would you do that? Aren't you in Langley, or Istanbul, or wherever people like you hang out?"

"Actually, I'm in Santa Lucia."

"What?"

"It's complicated. But if I left now, I could be at your house in two hours. I would rather explain everything in person. And it sounds as though you need some support right now."

Maya looked at her watch. "It's three p.m., so I guess I'll see you around five."

She was ambivalent about Will's arrival and worried what it was he had to tell her. More importantly, would she be able to keep it together and not go ballistic on him? Liz's death was no surprise. She knew it was coming. Kendall's murder hit her harder because it underscored the risk all journalists take when they investigate the underbelly of society.

The gray sedan pulled into Maya's driveway at five-thirty. Maya watched through the kitchen window as he exited the car carrying a leather satchel and a small shopping bag. She greeted him at the terrace gate.

"Sorry I'm late. Who knew there was bad traffic between the capital and here? I brought a bottle of wine," he said, handing her the shopping bag as she ushered him into the house.

"Thank you. Have a seat and I'll get a corkscrew and some glasses. We can sit here or go out to the terrace and watch the light change. It's the magic hour."

"Whatever you desire," he said, looking around the room and admiring the paintings and Mayan artifacts arranged neatly on a long sideboard.

"Then let's go outside. It's my favorite time of day."

While the clouds scuttled across the horizon, she talked of life and loss. Will listened intently as she expressed her profound grief about losing her friend, and the tragedy of Kendall's assassination. He gave her his full attention, reaching over several times to squeeze her hand in a show of support, otherwise he said very little as she worked through these complicated emotions. When darkness fell, she heaved a sigh of resignation and suggested that dinner would be a good idea.

"I can whip up something simple, and we can eat outside until the weather changes. It looks like we may get a storm later."

"Fine by me," Will said, following her into the kitchen.

She made balsamic lamb chops, orzo with Italian parsley, green beans, and a salad. They ate dinner at the round glass table then moved to the seagrass sofa to finish the bottle of wine Will brought. The storm began right after dinner and when the wind blew rain onto the terrace, they moved inside. Maya lit the fireplace. There was a certain magic about a tropical rainstorm drubbing on the roof with a roaring fire offsetting the sudden drop in temperature. After laughing about some of the exploits of the expats she'd been monitoring, she realized that he wasn't the officious and snobbish handler she originally thought. With a gift for funny one-liners, and an interesting view of the world, he revealed a sensitive and introspective side when they waded into personal territory. And he was ever so gentle as he comforted her about Liz's death. All he had to say about Kendall's assassination was that it was an unfortunate risk of the trade and that his journalistic skills would be a tremendous loss. But they were still skirting the real issues. Neither mentioned Kendall's file and she sure wasn't going to disclose that she had a complete copy of everything saved to a thumb drive and hidden in a place no one would think to look. Not even the wily spooks. So, what was it he was going to tell her? Because so far, they only talked about her loss and grief. She suspected all this camaraderie was a diversionary tactic to disarm her and that he had nothing of any importance to share with her about this operation.

And then it happened. Multiple bolts of lightning illuminated the valley followed by a massive thunderclap directly over the house. Everything shook violently. With the first crack of thunder, Maya spontaneously jumped six inches in the air and right into his arms. The woodsy scent of his cologne ignited her senses and with their faces so close, she impulsively leaned in so he could kiss her. It was over in a second as she pulled back and stared at him. And there he was with that smug expression on his face. What was she thinking? Why did she do that? It seemed the natural thing to do at that exact moment. Then her fling with Harry Langdon flashed through her mind. She didn't want to go through that heartache again, but intense working relationships caused boundaries to be breached when normal human emotions got in the way. And here they were. There was no way to deny the magnetism between them. It was as electrically charged as the weather outside. She broke from his embrace and walked to the terrace doors, opening them slightly, and gazing at the torrential downpour and the lightning show in the valley.

"No way you can drive in this. You'd be washed off the road. Literally." She turned to face him.

He shrugged his shoulders innocently, got up, and walked to where she was standing. "Well, if that's the case, it looks like you're stuck with me as a houseguest," he murmured into her neck.

"I've had worse. Believe me," she laughed.

"Then what do you say we go to bed and listen to the rain?"

"I'll lead the way," Maya murmured. *Oh, what the hell? Why not*?

Their lovemaking was tender, slow, and passionate. Maya felt clumsy and awkward at first mostly because it had been years since she was intimate with anyone. Will allowed her to set the pace but as soon as their naked bodies touched, it was the most natural thing in the world. "Kind of like riding a bike," she giggled when it was over, and they lay entwined in the dim light from the salt lamps. The storm subsided to a gentle tropical rain. Its freshness wafted through the open bedroom window creating a romantic and cozy atmosphere.

Will's index finger stroked her back.

"I'm not used to such affection and tenderness," she confided.

"It's what you deserve, you know," he whispered.

"I had almost given up, to be honest. My solitary life suits me, but I admit that I've missed this kind of intimacy. But isn't this going to complicate matters?"

"Why should it?"

"Oh, shucks, I don't know. You're my handler. You're not supposed to get involved. And I've been there, done that, and it didn't end so well. I try not to repeat my mistakes. But here I am."

"It's a little late for that now, don't you think?" he teased. "This operation won't go on forever. In fact, I would guess that in a few short weeks, your indebtedness to the agency will be fulfilled."

"Getting tired of reading about those expat shenanigans, are you? Assuming that was even the point of all of this," she said, poking him in the sternum. "Come on, you and I both know my cover is totally absurd. I'd put money on you using me as a lure for a bigger agenda. You came all the way here on the pretense of telling me something important, but you haven't said a word and you're not going to. Right?"

"We need you to be patient a while longer and continue the routine you've already established. But seriously, *chica*, this is not the time to be discussing work," he said, leaning in to kiss her on the forehead.

"You're right. Why don't I bail on that expat gossip session tomorrow and let's do something fun?"

"Hmm, I do have two days before I have to be back in Langley."

"We could go to the hot springs. It's an hour from here. I haven't been in ages, and it's a real paradisaical setting – right in the middle of a rainforest. You'll love it."

"As much as I love you?"

"Did you just say that?"

"I did. Now, let's hold hands and go to sleep."

"You're a real mystery, William Balthazar Hastings."

He was gazing into her eyes when he noticed a subtle

change in her expression. "Why the furrowed brow?"

"It's nothing." But it *was* something. It was Lucien's demise. How he died, where he died, when he died. She never really dealt with her role in any of it. It became the secret she hid and shared with no one. Now, she felt compelled to unburden herself of this guilt she harbored, or she would never be able to have a relationship with anyone.

"I see. Then let's say good night, and when we awake, it will be a brand-new day."

Chapter 48

"How much farther?" Will grumbled. "This had better be worth it."

Maya walked along the riverbank another fifty meters with Will trailing behind, swearing under his breath and his shoes squishing on the rainforest floor with each tentative step. "I didn't realize the river would be so swollen," she yelled over her shoulder. The roar of rushing water drowned out her voice. "Don't worry, you're going to love it." When they reached a cluster of palm trees, Maya pointed. There, nestled in the dense, soggy, entangled jungle undergrowth, was a stone-lined pool, with clouds of steam rising into the humid air. "Look," she said, pointing, "isn't this divine?"

Will stood next to her and gaped at the pool and the foliage surrounding it. There were gigantic ginger lilies perfuming the air, elephant ears, and another plant referred to as a poor man's umbrella because the leaves are so huge, they can be used to shield a person from a tropical downpour. He was wide-eyed with wonder.

"Is this safe?" Will asked, removing his mud-caked shoes.

"As safe as anything. And it's the perfect temperature. Come on, let's get in."

"Are we alone? Because I don't have swimming trunks."

"That's the whole idea, Skippy." Maya stripped naked, folded her clothes, and placed them on a huge rock. "This side is easier to get in, and it's not deep. When you're sitting down, it's only up to your chest."

"If you say so." Will undressed, crouched down, and carefully lowered his body into the hot water. "Oh my God, this is fabulous," he exclaimed when he was fully submerged in the steaming mineral water. "How did you find this spot? This is so off the beaten path, there must be a story behind how you discovered it."

"Lucien and I took a road trip and got lost. Then we got stuck in the mud. He was convinced we would run into someone at that picnic area who could help us, and when nobody was there, we just kept walking and came upon this. It's the best kept secret. There are other hot springs near here with really nice hotels and restaurants, but this spot has been ignored. I wouldn't come here by myself, but I thought you would enjoy it. Your body will thank you for this experience. The mineral water is good for your muscles and bones."

"This is like Eden," Will said, "but what is all that buzzing and humming and why is the ground rumbling?"

"That's the volcano, which feeds this pool. As for the jungle sounds, it's alive with all kinds of creatures we can't see."

After fifteen minutes of soaking in the therapeutic pool and being serenaded by jungle sounds, Will asked, "Does this river have a name?"

Maya pivoted and looked toward the raging river. She said nothing for thirty seconds. Then she faced Will with a wistful expression. "Yes, it's the Rio Dulce."

Chapter 49

Through partially opened eyes, she saw the valley was still blanketed in darkness. Distant lights along the ridge twinkled like fireflies. Several minutes later, a thin orange line shone on the horizon signaling approaching daylight and revealing the volcanoes swathed in a wisp of mist. When Will left yesterday for Santa Lucia, she felt a strange emptiness that she was still trying to understand. Their two magical days together fostered an impulse she could no longer ignore. Where did this compulsion come from directing her to embark on this mission?

She pulled an overnight bag from the closet and packed a few articles of clothing. Then after coffee and a piece of toast, she showered and dressed, grabbed the overnight bag, and headed for her car. Not for one second was she ever curious about that dreadful location even after Lucien was officially declared dead. Now she felt bound to see it. Even if she didn't know why. Yet.

The morning was splendid, as tropical mornings usually are, with dazzling sunshine and a scattering of clouds in the distance. Rain would arrive later. San Pedro had not yet come alive. Businesses were shuttered with only an occasional person outside sweeping the sidewalk in front of their house. It was the most peaceful time of the day, before the chaos began, before the traffic snarled, and before the world was apprised of some calamity in a far-off place.

The highway to the coast was deserted. It would be a different story in an hour, when workday traffic began, but for now she drove miles before passing another car. Roadside fruit stands prepared to open in anticipation of future customers. One that displayed hundreds of watermelons and cantaloupes artfully stacked in perfect pyramids and a dozen *racimas* of bananas hanging from hooks under the roof captured her attention. She pulled off the road and stopped. For a few toucans totaling less than fifty cents, she bought a hand of tiny bananas called monkey fingers and an ice-cold coconut water in a plastic bag before continuing her journey.

The road snaked its way through sweeping valleys with breathtaking mountains in the background. Every couple of miles a sign announced a ranch nestled in the rolling hills off the main road. Names like Finca Grande, Finca Hermosa, Finca Feliz were proudly displayed on ornate signs over the iron gates guarding the properties. Eventually, this quaint country road connected to the new IMF-funded highway that led to the beach. Maya fished in her purse for coins to pay the toll. Once past the *peaje,* it was a straight stretch to the coast.

The closer she got, the faster her heart raced, and when a sign announced Rio Dulce three kilometers ahead, her hands began to sweat. She could see the bridge in the distance. Not *any* bridge. *The* bridge. She guided the car into an open area on the side of the road and parked in the shade of a mango tree. The heat was oppressive at sea level. With a straw inserted into the plastic bag of *agua de pipa*, she gulped the cold liquid and sat quietly for a few minutes before exiting the car.

With measured steps, she approached the one-lane bridge, amazed that it could support any type of vehicle given its precarious condition. The rusted suspension girders and the horizontal wooden planks across its width looked unstable. A cargo truck approached and stopped. The driver got out and stood stoically for a minute assessing the probability of this relic collapsing, plummeting him and his payload to a certain death. Swearing under his breath, he got back in the truck. Gripping the steering wheel, he inched his way across, while the structure faltered left and right. Maya waited for the truck to reach the other side before venturing across. There were gaps in the planks and a misstep could result in serious injury. Hugging the right side of the wobbly bridge, she glided her hand along the uneven railing for support. When she reached the center, she stopped and stared at the Rio Dulce fifty meters below. There, sunbathing peacefully on the muddy banks, were a dozen crocodiles, each between fifteen and twenty feet in length. She whimpered and clutched the railing as her knees buckled. *So, this is where my husband ended up?* "Pay up or we're tossing you into the Rio Dulce," the message said.

Farther down the bridge, a young couple giggled as they flung a raw chicken into the air, following its trajectory as it spiraled downward into the river with a resounding splash. What happened next was a scene from a horror movie. The instant the chicken hit the water those sun-bathing crocodiles slithered into the river with wavelike motions of their formidable tails determined to get their share. Maya gasped as she pictured Lucien in those same waters. Gruesome as it was, she couldn't look away, and thankfully, it was over in a few seconds. With the carcass now consumed, the crocs slinked back to their lazy idle on the shore as the river churned its way to the ocean.

Overcome by revulsion, she returned to the car. Leaning her head against the steering wheel she cursed the impulse that had brought her here. But this was only the first step.

All she knew about the location where Lucien's femur was found was that it was two kilometers south of where the Rio Dulce emptied into the Pacific Ocean. Could she even find this exact location? Miguel had given her a photo of a crescent-shaped cove with a white sand beach ringed by towering palm trees tilting towards the ocean, but that was almost every beach along this stretch of coastline.

After crossing the bridge, she tootled along keeping her eyes peeled for any kind of beach access. A piece of splintered driftwood with faded lettering, hanging lopsided on the trunk of a palm tree, announced Playa Cielito in one hundred meters. More of a cow path than a road, and deeply rutted from the recent rains, it would be a disaster if she got stuck in the viscous mud. She parked the car in a grassy area and turned off the engine. A gush of humid breeze enveloped her when she opened the car door, bathing her in sticky sweat. White-faced capuchin monkeys screeched and hooted in the canopy while eyeballing her to determine if she was a predator or if she had something worth stealing. A crescendo of cicadas with their shrill, persistent whine, provided the jungle soundtrack while a kaleidoscope of blue morpho butterflies fluttered in total silence through the trees reflecting sunlight off their shimmering wings. A huititi tree draped in tiny cascading orchids called Rain of Gold buzzed with thousands of stingless bees and a susurrus of unseen things slithered in the tall grass. Lofty coconut palms, strangled by vines as twisted and tangled as her emotions, cast shade on the path. Batting at insects that flew at her face, she was relieved to see they were dragon flies. A pandemonium of sapphire blue parrots, glittering like feathered jewels, glided from one tree to another. The crashing of waves in the distance told her the ocean was nearby. Fifty meters later, she was standing on the most pristine beach she had ever seen. It was appropriately named because this certainly was a little piece of heaven. A perfect crescent, two hundred meters long, with not a soul in sight. Stuffing her shoes in her bag, the sizzling sand forced her to sprint toward the waterline where gentle waves caressed her ankles. Wading out twenty feet, she turned to get a full view of the beach. Yes, it was the same beach in the photo. But what exactly was she doing here? Purging the guilt that consumed her soul? After all, wasn't it her fault that Lucien wound up like that chicken? She had intercepted those warning messages, then scrubbed them, destroying any evidence of the incoming calls. Or so she thought, until she met William Balthazar Hastings. Now here she was, coming to terms with what she had done. For the last five years, she had suppressed the guilt. Tamped it down so deeply into her subconscious, it was as if it never happened. If she didn't think about, didn't speak the words, didn't acknowledge her crime, she could deny her complicity. All that changed when Will informed her that Lucien's cell phone had been recovered and those messages retrieved, resurrecting her wicked deed. And when he told her it had been determined that Lucien was not in possession of his phone when those calls came in, the appalling reality set in. It was that information the CIA used as leverage to coerce her into doing their bidding. The justification for her treachery was the relentless emotional and financial abuse she had endured throughout her ten-year marriage. By the time those messages were received, she was already past the breaking point. A way out presented itself and she would have been a fool not to take it. That had assuaged her guilt back then. To be fair, she didn't kill him; her hands were clean, but as Will reminded her, she facilitated his kidnapping and saved her own skin by going to Guatemala in advance of the kidnappers' arrival. And to ensure that Lucien would be the perfect quarry, she pocketed the only car key and took it with her. Maybe she didn't kill him, but could she be anymore guilty?

Now knee-deep in turquoise water, waves drowned out her feral scream. She pivoted and looked at the vast ocean fighting the impulse to wade into its infinite and eternal vastness. Not because of guilt, but because the memories that surfaced were too painful to deal with. Liz warned her about this possibility. She brushed it off then but standing where what was left of her husband was found put an entirely different spin on things. The extremes to which she went to save her own life, at his expense, horrified her now. That flight to Guatemala

City ensured his death sentence. She had to make peace with the monster she became when her life was threatened.

With torturous steps, she approached the spot where "Chucho" and "Gordo" stood in the photo and looked down at the shimmering sand. Was this where his femur was found? She fell to her knees, weeping. For Lucien; for herself. For the pain he had caused her; for the years she had trusted and loved him; for believing she had no other way to extricate herself from his tenacious grip. If there was any chance at all for a relationship with Will, she had to put the ghost of her marriage to Lucien and her part in his gruesome death to rest and relegate this sorrow, this guilt, to the cemetery of regrets and move on. She had lived in the shadows long enough.

Chapter 50

When the heat radiating up from the sand became unbearable, she donned her sandals and walked back to the car. But she wasn't ready to go home and was glad she had the foresight to pack an overnight bag. Up the road a few miles from here, she remembered seeing a quaint beachside hotel with brightly colored cabinas dotting the shoreline. A day at the ocean would enable her to get her thoughts sorted out and think about what lay ahead, with or without Will in her life. This new element was so unexpected, yet it seemed like the most natural progression of the relationship they had established over the last year and a half. How could she not have reservations though? The biggest one being the fact that he knew her secret; the one she had guarded and kept neatly hidden for so many years. The secrets in her marriage to Lucien were the glue that held them together, creating a diabolical intimacy. Why would this be any different? Maya looked up and saw the skies turning ominous.

Her goal now was to get to the hotel before the tropical downpour.

Playa Azul was an isolated stretch of pristine beach with four quaint *cabinas* to rent. She was given a complimentary rum cocktail and shown to the *cabina* on the farthest end which was painted hot pink and trimmed in teal green and lavender. Consisting of one big room with a queen-sized bed, a small bathroom, and an outdoor shower with lush ferns and orchids on the walls, it was bright and cheerful while outside a dozen scarlet macaws squawked relentlessly as they perched in the almond trees on either side of the structure. The ocean, with calm and limpid water, was a mere fifty meters away. But was it safe here? Wasn't there an incident just last week where tourists on another remote beach were assaulted, tied up, and robbed? It was a chance she was willing to take as she indulged herself in this beautiful setting.

Maya threw herself on the bed and stared at the sugar cane ceiling. The rain started but it lasted only a few minutes and then the skies cleared. She hadn't packed a swimsuit, but with a bath towel wrapped around her body, she walked the short distance to the water's edge, and let it fall to the sand. She paddled around in the warm, therapeutic water, dove under the waves, and for the first time in countless years, felt unburdened. A half-hour later, she emerged prepared to think about tomorrow instead of struggling to survive day to day.

Chapter 51

When she heard the car turn into the long driveway, Magdalena snatched the ringing iPhone from the counter and dashed outside to greet Maya. "*Aqui! Tómalo*!" she insisted, thrusting the phone into the open window on the driver's side. "*Dios mío*, it been ringing every fifteen minutes for three hours."

"Where have you been?" Will shouted angrily when she answered.

"There was something I had to do. What's going on? Why are you so agitated?" she asked, grabbing her purse and overnight bag and walking towards the terrace.

"I've been trying to reach you. Log onto your laptop and go to the local news page. Call me back when you've seen the news."

In the sixty seconds it took for her laptop to boot up, Magda scolded her. "Doña Maya, why didn't you tell me you would be away for *una noche*? *Mi corazón* cannot take such worry."

"I'm sorry, but I had a very personal thing to do."

"*Claro que sí. Mis ojitos* have been observing you, and I see a positive change."

"What do you mean?"

"Forgive me for saying this, but you were like the snake that slithers across the jagged edge of a saw and injures himself. Instead of getting away from the source of the pain, the snake wraps itself tightly around the saw and squeezes with all its might. *Ay*, no, that snake is not going to let the saw get away with this and continues to punish the saw by squeezing the life out of it. *Pero, tristamente*, the snake, now severely injured, dies. It didn't know that it needed to let go of the initial pain to move forward. Storing pain in our hearts only hurts you in the end, causing your life to slip away when you could have been embracing the future without pain."

Maya stared at her housekeeper and realized that the woman knew her better than she knew herself. "You are right, Magda. It will be very different from now on."

Logging on to Facebook, Maya quickly navigated to the *Santa Lucia News Network* home page and saw that it was inundated with various accounts of the latest bust in a wealthy area outside of the capital.

"Yesterday, in a wealthy suburb of Santa Lucia, officers of the Judicial Division of the Financial Crimes Office, the Agency for Drug Enforcement, and the CIA orchestrated the largest cocaine bust in Malpaís history. Along with fifteen tons of cocaine seized in one of the luxury mansions, they also confiscated fourteen luxury cars, one luxury hotel, three hilltop mansions, and seized close to four hundred million dollars in U.S. and local currency. Twenty-five people were arrested and charged with international drug trafficking and money laundering including six officials of the Office of Investigative Crimes, four members of the Legislative Assembly, five deputies, three medical doctors, five accountants, several lawyers, and notaries. All are being held without bail in the Santa Lucia Penitentiary. Killed at a remote location in a separate raid were Emanuel "Chucho" Ak and Bautista "Gordo" Mendez, reputed leaders of the Lobos Locos cartel. All suspects currently in custody are believed to be part of the same cartel. This is a developing story and there will be periodic briefings throughout the day as the investigation continues and more suspects are apprehended."

Maya picked up the iPhone and hit redial. "What the hell? How did this happen?"

"You know I can't possibly divulge anything that would compromise the operation. Let's just say, this has been in the works for a long time."

"Is that the real reason you were here?"

"You might say that."

"And what does this mean for me?"

"Basically, that the role you played, unbeknownst to you, was successful."

"What did I really do? How did my reporting about expats in any way influence a bust such as this or the killing of the leaders of the cartel?" She had a sneaking suspicion, but she kept it to herself. Maya paused and then in a soft voice asked, "So is this the end?"

"For now," he said.

How could Will possibly tell her that the information they retrieved from her bottom dresser drawer was everything they needed to close in on the cartel; that Kendall Jacobs' information was the key, and that it was unfortunate that he was killed for his efforts. No matter how much Will told Maya; she would always have a hundred other questions he wouldn't be able to answer.

"Now what happens?" she asked.

He thought hard to come up with a plausible answer and the only thing that came to mind was, "If I tell you, I'll have to kill you."

"You're not the least bit funny, Mr. Hastings. Does this mean my services are no longer needed? That I can go back to my anonymous life and pick up where I left off?"

"Is that what you want to do?"

"I don't know, to be honest."

"Do you want to tell me where you disappeared to for twenty-four hours?"

"Let's just say I was purging my life of ghosts."

"That's an interesting way to put it."

"I don't want to talk about it. Not on the phone. Am I going to see you anytime soon?"

"Do you want to see me?"

"I wouldn't have asked otherwise."

"It's going to be hectic for at least the next week, maybe two, so I am stuck in Santa Lucia. But after that, I will come to see you."

"Okay. Let me know."

Chapter 52

She had only been out of the loop for a little more than twenty-four hours and her email was flooded with messages. Maybelle was desperate to get together to give her an update on which ex-pats were packing it in and high tailing it back to the U.S., which ones had been burgled, robbed, swindled, assaulted, or held hostage. Bentley Beresford had an update on his long-running legal battle to get his property back and after more than five years of navigating the labyrinthine legal system, a trial date was finally set only to be cancelled an hour before the start time because the judge had been swept up in the big drug bust and was sitting in the pokey on preventive detention. As a result, the case was thrown out and had to be refiled, starting the entire ridiculous process all over again. But he would like to have lunch if Maya had an afternoon free as there was much more to the story than he dared to put in writing. Lastly, there was an email from someone named Marilyn at East Hampton

Hospice advising her that Andrew Chase, with whom she once had a relationship and who was an integral part of her adventure with the leader of the Nazi party many years ago, had died peacefully in his sleep after a lengthy battle with liver cancer. Maya gasped for breath. She slammed her laptop closed and sat there staring into the middle distance.

She was hard-pressed to know why news of Andrew's death was such a shock. They hadn't been in touch for several years. Maybe it was because he had been part of her life during a completely different time. They had shared so many precious moments and her heart still ached from him telling her that he was staying in East Hampton after his father passed away. He didn't have to tell her why; she knew. He was trying to figure out his place in a world he felt he never belonged. With Andrew and Liz both gone, and her part in Lucien's death resolved, that chapter of her life was officially closed.

Thunder rumbled in the distance and a low bank of fog blew through the valley below. It would rain in a few minutes and the air would be redolent of wet earth, lemon and orange blossoms, and the scent of green. Sitting on the terrace and watching nature's slideshow filled her with a sense of peace and longing. Longing for that which she could not name. It was a hollow deep inside her that needed to be filled with something meaningful and real. When the clouds broke and the rain poured down, she went inside and lay on the sofa, thinking. Thinking about Kendall Jacobs and the envelope he entrusted with her. His explicit instructions were to not read what he gave her, and she hadn't, not even when she frantically scanned every page to a thumb drive. But Kendall was dead. And what good was all that research which cost him his life if it was hidden in her bottom dresser drawer?

Maya poured herself a glass of hibiscus tea and retreated to her bedroom. Crouching down on her hands and knees, she pulled open the bottom drawer of her dresser, slid the front part of the drawer to the left, and placed it on the floor. She stared at the bottom section for a few seconds before pulling it towards her to remove the envelope. With the packet of documents, she climbed on the bed and leaned against the headboard. Why was she so hesitant to look at his research? Was she afraid of what she would learn? Surely none of what he was investigating related in any way to her, so why were her hands trembling? She sat quietly for a few minutes, sipped the garnet tea, and then began to sift through his reports.

Kendall was nothing if not thorough. He listed players in the grand money-laundering machine that had risen to power in the last five years. He named drug lords, specifically Emanuel "Chucho" Ak, and Bautista "Gordo" Mendez, their minions, politicians, police officers, judges, lawyers, doctors, hotel owners, and a long list of minor players who were actively involved in the drug trade. He had evidence of bribes with bank statements showing large cash deposits, photos of a small-time lawyer posing against his brand-new Mercedes, which cost more than his reported earnings in a year. Maya couldn't help but wonder if these were the same people who were recently arrested in the huge drug bust? The last document was only two pages long. It revealed the identities of two CIA officers and a DEA agent who had been monitoring these activities. Why did it not surprise her that William Balthazar Hastings's name was on that list. An hour later, she set the papers aside, laid down on the bed, and wondered what to do next. Her eyes scanned every square inch of her bedroom. The walls, the corners, the *tablia* on the ceiling, the light fixture. And then something glinted in the beam of waning sunlight pouring in through the side window near her bed. She went to the kitchen, got a screwdriver and the step stool, and came back to her room. It took her less than ten seconds to pry that tiny camera from the wooden molding around the ceiling. Smaller than a baby pea, she rolled it around in her hand several times trying to decide what to do with it. She walked ten steps to her bathroom, lifted the lid of the toilet, and tossed it in. *Let's see what kind of intelligence gathering it can do from the inside of my septic tank*!

Her phone rang. She walked to the kitchen to answer it.

"Hello."

"Hi, Maya, I don't know if you remember meeting me and my wife at the fundraiser a few months back. My name is Lou and my wife's name is Shirley. Maybelle suggested that I call you because she said you might be looking for some material to write about in your magazine."

"Hmm, well, that depends. What kind of material?"

"You probably know by now that there is an exodus amongst the expat community. My wife and I are included in that group."

"What happened?"

"There is no justice here for Americans. No equality even though they say we have the same rights as the locals. It's a lie. After five years here, packing it in is best thing we could do. Our lawyer stole fifty thousand dollars out of our account. We took him to court and of course we won but then he moved all his assets including his seven properties, his Hummer, his son's Mercedes, and put them in an offshore account in Costa Rica. If you saw the recent developments in the drug bust, you would know that Malpaís is number one for criminal injustice."

"I'm so sorry that happened to you. But there really isn't any way I can help you."

"You could write about it and warn others."

"To be honest, I think the magazine has run its course. I won't be generating any more content, at least not for quite a while. I don't mean to cut you off, but I'm late for an appointment. Please stay safe."

Maya hung up and blocked his number.

Chapter 53

Maya spent the next few days processing the copious amount of information she read online about the drug bust and the killing of the leaders of the Lobos Locos cartel. She had so many mixed emotions about this, but the predominant one was relief. The death of "Chucho" and "Gordo" provided her a new level of safety and security. It would take a few days for her to adjust to the new reality, and she hoped when Will was here over the weekend, he could provide her with details she desperately needed to reconcile all of this. Her thoughts were interrupted by the phone ringing. The only sound Maya heard on the other end of the line was a gasp followed by a few rhythmic sobs. "Hello," she repeated. "Who is this?"

"It's me," Maybelle said.

"What's wrong?"

She blubbered, then blew her nose loudly. "It was James and Monica."

"Do I know them?"

"You met them. He was that nice older gent, a retired judge, and she was that beautiful young woman from Santa Lucia." There was another round of sobs and nose-blowing.

"It must be something awful for you to be so upset."

"Their bodies were found in the mango grove behind their house."

"Oh, that's ghastly," Maya said, her voice cracking. "What happened?"

"Give me a minute to collect my thoughts." Maybelle sighed, sniffled some more, then said, "When his family in the U.S. couldn't reach him by phone, they called the authorities. The police came to the house and talked to the housekeeper and her teenage son. Apparently, the son was acting all squirrelly, so the cops took him to aside for questioning. He cracked under pressure and admitted that he and his mother killed them, wrapped their bodies in sheets, and stayed in the house for three days trying to decide what to do. They finally dragged them out to the mango grove and doused them with gasoline. A neighbor called the fire department and when the *bomberos* came they discovered the charred remains."

"What was the motive?"

"Nobody knows yet, but it seems that the maid who was once Monica's friend was jealous that she had landed this rich gringo and now she was reduced to working for her friend. There was a disagreement, a brawl broke out and the son bludgeoned the old man while the maid strangled Monica."

"I don't even know what to say. It's beyond horrible. What's going to happen now?"

"Mother and son are in custody and the remains have

been sent to Santa Lucia for examination, although from what I heard from the neighbors who live across the field, there wasn't much left of either of them."

Maya thought for a minute, then said, "They were the couple with the big age disparity, right?"

"You could say that. He was eighty-two, and she was twenty-nine. Monica thought she was doing something nice by hiring her friend as their housekeeper. We see how well that worked out. No good deed goes unpunished."

"Maybelle, I don't mean to cut you short, but my housekeeper just arrived, and she's visibly upset. I'll call you later." Without waiting for a response, Maya ended the call and jumped up from the sofa to approach Magdalena.

"Magda, what's wrong?" she asked, ushering the distraught woman to a chair near the sofa. Magda was sobbing and shaking. This was so out of character for the otherwise stoic and wise woman that Maya knew it had to be something terrible. "Sit down. Let me get you a glass of water." This was way more *Sturm und Drang* than Maya could handle after all the distressing news of late.

Magda sank her quivering body in the chair and buried her head in her hands and began to wail. "What is the matter with your people? Are they all *loco*?"

"Huh? What are you talking about? Here, have a sip of water and take a deep breath."

"I cannot tell you." She handed her cell phone to Maya. "You have to see it with your own *ojitos* to believe it."

Maya took the phone and hit the play button on the cued video. First, there was a blurred image and some distant shouting before it all came into focus. A disheveled man in his late twenties with matted blond hair to his shoulders, wearing a dirty tank top, ripped cargo shorts, and a pair of flipflops, raised his fists triumphantly before lunging toward the person recording his actions.

"CIA, American military, we're filming this. I will make adrenochrome out of your children," he shrieked. Then he lunged forward, spat at the person filming, screwed up his face and shouted, "Translate *that*!"

"I call the police, I call the police," Magda shouted in the background as she continued to film him. He turned, yelled something unintelligible, then walked away.

Meanwhile, Magda gasped for breath.

"When did this happen?"

"A few minutes ago, on my way to your house. I stopped at the *pulperia* to pay my phone bill. This gringo was there, standing outside as I went in. Ana, the owner of the *pulpe*, told me he had been there for the last hour talking *paja* to other customers and taking out his, you know, his, his. . ."

"Penis?"

"Yes, that one," Magda said, her face reddening. "Ana said he waved it at some children passing by on their way to *escuela*. That's when I started filming him and when he saw me, he got even angrier and began shouting at me. I got very afraid because as you can see *él es loco en la cabeza*."

"This is very upsetting, but please Magda, take a deep breath and let's figure out how we can deal with this. Does anyone know his name or where he comes from?"

"Nobody knows. According to Ana he was in another village *cerca* the beach, then he came up to the *mesa central* but nobody knows where he's from or what is wrong with him. Ana said he threatened other people about torturing their children, then killing them to drink their blood." Magda began to howl loudly. "Why are all you gringos so crazy? You come to my country, you buy up our land, you make things more expensive for us and our only choice to survive is to work for you. Then you – well, not you, Doña Maya because you treat me very well and you are like my family – but the others – they treat us as though we are not deserving of respect or even a decent *salario* for cutting your grass or cleaning your toilets. My country was so much happier before the gringos came. The gringos make fun of us because we have gardens for our vegetables, a cow for our milk and to make cheese, chickens for our eggs, and yet we laugh at these *burros* because they are buying their food in the super wrapped in *plástico* and full of *quimicos*. They sneer at us because we do not wear fancy clothes or dress like *fufurufas*, so they think we are stupid and poor. They believe because we smile at them that we are impressed with their *dólares*, but behind our smiles we are laughing because they don't speak Spanish, and yet act like they are better than we are. They don't honor our customs or our culture and think we are lowly peasants who don't deserve dignity or respect. Like that *pinche gringa* who left," Magda said, pointing towards the hillside.

"Are you talking about Laura Huxley?"

"*Sí*, Laura. *Una estupida*. My *prima* cleaned her house, but she did not know that Lidi understood *inglés*, and Laura was laughing about our clothes and how we buy things that are not new. Yes, that is true, because we do not care to impress the *campesino* who lives next door, or the *muchacho* at the *ferreteria*, or the bus driver. If we are neat and clean, we are happy, and it's not because we are too poor to buy new things. We would rather save that money, and I tell you, Doña Maya, we all have a mattress full of toucans because we do not use credit cards or buy things we do not need. We are cautious and we are frugal, but we are not stupid. We do not want people like that *pinche gringo* in the video to be in our country. We have plenty of *maldito pendejos* of our own."

"I'm so sorry you experienced that. I hate to admit it, but I feel the same way you do about a lot of the gringos. I told you this once before, but I am going to say it again: I have learned more about life and things that are meaningful from you. You have taught me humility and to appreciate the beauty of nature and the way it interacts with our lives. I wish it had not taken me so long to learn those things. My life would have been much better and easier if I had your wisdom twenty or thirty years ago. You're so very special to me, Magdalena, and without you, I would have never survived living here. I don't know what I can do about this guy who terrorized you, but believe me, these people always meet a dreadful end." In the meantime, Maya added "crazy, disheveled, blond hippie" to the ever-growing list of crooks, creeps, and crazies.

Chapter 54

The news about *Neotrópica* shutting down spread like a virus through the expat community. Maya received several messages from women in the weekly get together expressing their sadness at no longer having such an interesting magazine to read that addressed so many issues of concern to the expats. One message gave her a good laugh. It was from Roger Faraday, and she remembered him fondly from several big parties over the last year. He was always entertaining, full of humor and sarcasm, and no topic was off limits for his acerbic wit.

"Dear Maya: Maybelle just gave me the bad news that your magazine is in its death throes. I am so sorry because it was a fun read. You may have heard that I am joining the exodus of expats repatriating to the U.S. Living here the last four years has totally worn me out. But I had some insights about this experience that you may want to put in your final issue.

"On average, I get at least one phone call a week from

someone I know who wants to come to Malpaís or they refer a friend to me who wants to come. Boy, do they have a lot of questions. You know me, I'm not one for beating around the bush so the first thing I tell them is there are two types of people in Malpaís: the ones in jail and the ones who haven't been caught yet. That usually elicits a huge gasp on their end. Then I tell them rent for two years before you even think about buying property here, and when those two years are up, don't buy anything. Ever. Not even a square foot of land. They are usually crestfallen because they had some idea that they could sell their little two and two in some ghastly suburb and come down here and buy themselves a mansion. Ha! I tell them it's like the Jules Verne novel *The Time Machine* where he goes to the future and it's like the Garden of Eden with an abundance of beautiful nature and seemingly innocent, friendly people. That is, until the siren sounds and the Morlocks are hungry and you're on the menu. Yep, I tell them they will get eaten alive here. You know, I've lived in about twenty countries and stayed in at least twenty more and I always thought Costa Ricans were the most deceiving, most passive aggressive, most child-like society with their incredible non-confrontational false personas, but this bunch here in Malpaís? They have elevated passive aggressive behavior and deceit to an artform. You can't trust anyone. Not a soul. They will tell you whatever they think you want to hear to get what they want from you. I traveled so much my whole life and I always considered myself an amateur anthropologist and it pains me to admit almost all my opinions have been gathered in hindsight. The joke is on me because these people are experts at playing the long con. And the unsuspecting suckers coming after us need to be warned. It will save a lot of heartache and financial ruin. As my *campesino* neighbor said to me one day, 'when you live in Malpaís, you are in the middle between the door to heaven and the door to hell, and it depends on which side opens each day.' I think that pretty much sums it up. Wishing you well in your next venture. Cordially, Roger"

As Maya was about to compose a reply to Roger's email, the internet stopped working. "Oh, come on," she grumbled, slapping her laptop. "I don't have time for this."

"*Cual es tu problema*, Doña Maya?"

"Internet is out. Again."

Magda giggled.

"It's not funny. I have work to do, and I need the internet. Don't you use the internet?"

"I use the one our Lalas invented."

"What do you mean? What is a Lala?"

"That is our *abuelas*, what you call grandmamas. Lala is what we call them with love."

"How did they invent the internet?"

"They did it by sitting in their eyeball chairs on the sidewalk during the warm evenings of *verano*. They didn't need a *tecla* or a mice to send a message. They had their lips to make chatter and to cut and paste information to send to everyone they knew. If someone passed by the *abuelas* in their eyeball chairs, a hand would go out and grab them. '*Ay*, Pablo, *dígame*, what is your *pápi* up to? I do not see him go to work in the morning. Is he okay? Oh, he has a new *trabajo*? That is *muy bueno*. Is he happy? Does he provide well? And *tu mamá*? She is *feliz* now? And *que esta pasando contigo, chico*, how are your studies going? Tell me everything.'

And so, it would be until the light faded into darkness when the stars appear, and the air got cool. Then the Lalas would take their eyeball chairs and go into the house. But *mañana*, it would be the same *rutina*. That is how our *abuelas* invented the first wireless. Today, if I want to know something about somebody, I ask my Lala and she can tell me, and I do not have to worry if the electricity goes out and I lose my connection."

Of course, the grandmothers invented the internet. As they did in villages all over the world where old women congregated, observed, made notes, and compared stories. With each anecdote Magda told her, Maya became more and more enamored with life on the isthmus. She remembered what Ryan McAfee told her on her very first trip here: living in Malpaís was like living in the forties - the 1840s! Life was so simple and uncomplicated back then and Magdalena's endless narratives of customs and traditions gave her a glimpse into the real Malpaís, not the one being marketed for exploitation. As the thunder rolled in and lightning cracked overhead, there wouldn't be internet for a while. The only thing Maya could do was make a cup of tea and chill out. Power outages were only temporary... usually.

Fifteen minutes later, there was a series of pings and then the phone rang

"Hey, Maybelle. What's going on in your show?"

"I was just calling to say hello."

"Is there anything going on I need to know about?" Maybelle never called for no good reason.

"Not really. Things have been quiet at my house although somebody did just send me an email asking about renting a house for a year near San Pedro. Want a good laugh? Let me read this to you. 'My wife Harmony and I are a younger couple in our thirties soon to be having our first child. We just arrived back in Malpaís after a month visiting family in the states. We are casting out a message for anyone that can point us to an affordable, cozy casa to rent that is suitable for a natural home birth. Our budget is currently less than three hundred dollars a month. We are both adept in the vegan/raw vegan chafing arena, and deeply passionate about holistic health. Harmony offers Naturopathic consultations, TCM fire cupping, and facial lymphatic drainage massage. I am a detoxification specialist (certification from International School of Detoxification), offering personalized detox plans, healing intuitive massage, infrared-heated amethyst crystal Biomet sessions, and Native American flute sound healing sessions. Muchas gracias to anyone who can help connect us to a beautiful home-birthing space. Blessings a todos.' I swear, where do these people come from? I suggested he look on the Facebook pages in that area where all the new age hippie freaks with weird made-up Hindu names live. But seriously, is the international school of detoxification a real thing?"

Maya laughed. "I have no idea."

"Well, I give these folks about six months, and then they'll be trotting back to the U.S. with their little anchor baby. Hey, how's this for an idea. Let's start a pool where we predict how long these newbies will last? We invite them to our Monday morning get together, ask them a bunch of questions, and then make predictions for when we think they'll pack it all in and get the hell out of here."

Maya chuckled. "That could be amusing. Certainly,

more interesting than Gringo Bingo. We could offer prizes too."

"This could be so much fun," Maybelle chortled. "The way this mass exodus is going, we should have started it six months ago. Soon it's only going to be you and me here." Maybelle paused before saying, "Oh, dear God, I hope you aren't thinking of leaving. Is that why the magazine has come to an auspicious end?"

"No, I'm not going anywhere. I'm not sure I'm fit to live anywhere else after this place," Maya laughed.

"I do understand. I told Bert the other night that if we went back to the U.S. after living here nonstop for these five years, I would probably be dead or in jail within twenty-four hours. Especially with my big mouth and the way the U.S has become so politically correct these days. See you at the luncheon tomorrow?"

"Definitely," Maya said, relieved that this part of her assignment would soon be coming to an end.

When she got off the phone with Maybelle, she thought about the steady exodus of people who had gone back to the U.S. As hesitant as she was to come back here, she didn't want to leave now. In the time she had been here, she changed. Her habits changed, her viewpoint changed, she was no longer fit for city life after living in the *campo* where life had its own rhythm. When Maya was a child, she had fantasies about this life. But it seemed unattainable when she was living in Los Angeles, New York, Paris, or on the outskirts of Denver. During those years, she was properly dressed in expensive designer clothes and shoes, wore make-up, and spent hours and exorbitant amounts of money on her appearance. Now, she barely wore shoes, except to drive, and her daily uniform was a bleach-stained pair of yoga pants that should have gone to the rag bag long ago, and a plain black tee-shirt. The only time she wore proper clothes was when she left the house. The few times she went to Santa Lucia, which seemed like a metropolis compared to San Pedro, she was overwhelmed by everything – the traffic, the noise, the things that were available, and the general chaos of a city. Every outing to the capital left her enervated for two days after. The times she went there for a cultural event, she barely made it past eight p.m., which was her normal bedtime in the *campo*. She didn't understand how people ate dinner so late or stayed up until midnight. Yes, those events were glamorous and interesting, but she had outgrown the need to be part of that scene, and now, the only place she felt at peace and not stressed out was Finca Azahar. Even returning to her little farm on the outskirts of Aix-en-Provence seemed like a daunting idea. And she never thought she would say that.

Chapter 55

Friday morning was cool and crisp for the middle of rainy season. The skies were clear but off in the distance a thin band of clouds would bring torrential rain in the middle of the afternoon. It was market day, the one day of the week Maya really looked forward to. The farmer's market called a *feria* was the biggest in Malpaís. One could buy every kind of vegetable and fruit along with fish, meat, and poultry, even milk and cheese. About the only thing Maya bought in the grocery store these days was olive oil, soap, and toilet paper. If she wanted to get to town and back before the rains started, she'd have to hurry.

The main road to San Pedro was blocked by an ambulance parked sideways across both lanes. Hazard lights were on as were the flashing lights on the roof of the ambulance. She was about to get out of the car to see what was going on when the driver exited and dashed into the middle of the road behind the ambulance (and just in front of her car) to rescue a tiny bird fluttering on the ground. He gently plucked it from the road, cupped it in his hands, and approached Maya's side of the car to show her the little bird.

"I could not stand to see it there lying helpless in the road where it surely would have been run over," he said in broken English. He walked to the side of the road and gently placed it in a patch of grass, hoping it would recover enough to fly off. The driver returned to the ambulance, straightened it out so it was in his lane, and drove off, waving out the window to the cars behind him.

Maya had to pull off to the side of the road to search for a tissue to wipe her tears and her nose. This kind deed performed by the muscular ambulance driver was just one more example of the humanity of this culture. It embodied a gentleness and respect for all living creatures that seemed to be totally lost on the rest of the world. As the end of her indebtedness to the Agency loomed on the horizon, she would need to decide whether to stay here or go back to Provence. Now that she had stopped running from herself and the issues she never dealt with, she would have to weigh this decision very carefully. In quiet moments when she had only her own thoughts, leaving Malpaís, its magic and its tragedies, seemed unimaginable. She couldn't even explain what it was about this little country that had captured her heart in such a way that the thought of leaving it caused her physical pain. Maybe it was the old-world traditions, the inherent gentleness of the people who were now part of her life, or because the pace of life here was even slower than in Provence.

Chapter 56

Maya started to worry. Magdalena did not arrive for work at her usual time, and now it was almost noon, and she still had not heard from her. As she was looking for her phone number, she heard the distinctive clank of the terrace gate and whirled around to see Magda walking through the front door. Her shoulders were slightly stooped, and it was obvious from her swollen eyes, she had been crying.

"Magda, I was starting to worry about you. Please, come and sit down. Let me make you a cup of tea and then you can tell me why you are so upset."

"*Ay*, Doña Maya. You are so kind to me. I am sorry to arrive so late, but this morning was the funeral of *mi abuelo*. He has been welcomed into the loving arms of our dear Señor and will now rest in everlasting peace and glory."

"I'm so sorry. I remember when my own grandparents died and the terrible effect it had on me. Would you like to tell me about your grandfather while you drink this tea?"

Maya sat opposite Magda as she sipped the tea, waiting for her to calm down.

"Do you really want to hear about how special he was?"

"Yes, of course. I always learn something new when you tell me about your family."

"My grandfather Arturo was a very unusual person. One of his odd behaviors was his fascination with death. Perhaps, it was because his mom died in childbirth, and that left a huge scar on him and his sisters. He never got over it. He was both attracted to death and at the same time he rejected it. He told me many times that death terrified him. But the paraphernalia of death fascinated him, and unbeknownst to his *familia*, he organized his funeral and burial many years before he died. He wrote down all the details of his funeral including that he wanted the musical piece *Carmina Burana* to accompany him to his heavenly home. He also made a list of the *cositas* he wanted to take with him. A lock of his mother's hair, and some dirt from his *finca*. And he did not want to be buried in an ordinary coffin. Oh no. Many years before his death, he worked in his *taller* making it to his liking. It had to be cedar to repel the *bichos*, and he didn't want a single nail. Everything was put together like a puzzle. He also did not want the typical glass on the top because he didn't want anyone to see him in that state. He also did not want the usual white satin lining. When he finished making it, he moved it to a large warehouse that he owned. It was tucked safely in the corner, out of everyone's way, but the employees were not comfortable having a coffin in their workplace. It was a bad omen they said. So, he brought it to his house and put it in the little chapel. I thought it was normal to see a coffin in their house. It was just another silly thing about my family. But one day, I came to visit *mis abuelos* and two friends from school were with me. We greeted my Lala, and she said to us, 'Go see Tata in the chapel, and have coffee with him.' That was so exciting, having a café with my beloved *abuelo*. We went to the little chapel, but it was empty. My friend said, 'I thought we were having a café with your Tata. But nobody is here.' At that moment, a voice comes from the coffin saying, *'Hola, mis chicas. Cómo están*?' And then *mi abuelo* sits up and my friends screamed in horror and had to be given sugar water to recover. One of those friends never spoke to me again after that. I asked him, 'What are you doing in your coffin?' 'I am checking to see if it is comfortable. After all, I will be resting in there for all *eternidad*.' But last night he must have had a premonition because when my Lala got up this morning, he wasn't anywhere. She looked outside, checked the garden, checked the chicken house, and just before she was going to call the police, she checked the chapel and there she found him, lying peacefully in his hand-made coffin without nails, holding a lock of his mother's hair in one hand and a clump of dirt in the other. He was even dressed in his best *traje*, looking ready to meet our heavenly father. My Lala called the undertaker and the only thing left to do was to have a service for him in the cathedral. That is why I didn't come to work this morning. The funeral was at eight a.m. and then we went to the cemetery." Magda began to cry softly. "I will miss him so much. There was no one like him on our *planeta*."

Chapter 57

Maya hadn't heard a word from Will in a week. Not a phone call, not a text, nothing. It was total crickets. Just as well. She needed downtime after all the bad news lately.

Maya gave Magdalena the rest of the week off to mourn her grandfather. So touched by the story of this idiosyncratic man, she sat down and wrote about his death. It was one more story to add to the long list of reasons why Maya was so enamored of the culture here. Not the culture that the average person sees on the surface, but the culture that was the very fabric of society and the body of beliefs. With each little anecdote Magdalena shared with her – whether it was the first air freshener (that rotting *cohombro*), or the eyeball chairs, or the spirits that came in the night if you left dishes out, and now the wacky grandfather who built his own coffin and had dress rehearsals for its final use, how could she not be captivated by this new and strange way of viewing the world?

After a much-needed break from the ills of the world and the expat crowd, Maya opened her laptop and logged onto the local English news page. The headline read "Regime Change in Malpaís." Her timing was impeccable. A live press conference was going to start in five minutes. A representative of the press stood at the podium shuffling papers, waiting to make the announcement. Next to him stood an imposing figure, with military bearing and authoritarian good looks, his hands firmly clasped in front of him, an unflinching expression on his face. He was introduced as Bob Hamm, former U.S. Army and DEA, now in charge of a financial crimes division of the U.S. government. Bob Hamm approached the podium as the media rep stepped aside.

"Thank you, Mr. Davis. It is a pleasure to be here today especially because I can announce that our combined taskforce was successful in unraveling a vast and mounting threat network that included fraudulent money laundering schemes that have affected the peace and democracy of Malpaís. Because of this work and that of others who shall remain nameless we have dismantled the most dangerous drug cartel with tentacles in every aspect of Malpaís' government, and arrests have been made of those who perpetrated and participated in this massive fraud. Like corruption, fraud is an element of deviant behavior that degrades the quality of life in society. The fraud makes me think of the character of Thrasymachus found in Plato's Dialogues. Fraud in many cases creates a justice system that 'de facto' builds on the power of the strongest. The strongest is measured by the availability of your resources. The strongest - the Thrasymachus - is the one who can pay with money, goods, or services and gets satisfaction. 'White collar' crimes in many countries are considered of little importance. This creates a relationship of social asymmetry between rich and poor. The corrupt state, the state where the amount of fraud is enormous (private and public sector in alliance) is an illegitimate state. I am happy to announce that the illegitimate state that was the government of Malpaís has been replaced with an interim government until new and fair elections can be held. Many in Malpaís prefer peace to justice. Injustice exists within regimes of terror, where the citizen lives forced into a state of peace. In Malpaís, it seems that many intellectuals confuse the word peace with a lack of armed violence ... exclusively. However, corruption and insecurity are states of violence. A form of war where the strongest triumph. Operation LUCIÉRNAGA has come to an end. Long live peace and democracy. Thank you for your time."

Bob Hamm shook the hand of the media rep and walked off stage. Meanwhile, video clips flashed across the screen showing a dozen SWAT team personnel storming the presidential palace. The voiceover explained that they are here to peacefully remove the president and his family, cabinet members, and co-conspirators. A few seconds later a stream of people are led to armored vehicles to be spirited away to the local penitentiary where they will be held in preventive detention.

Bob Hamm's speech was cleverly cloaked in vague references, euphemisms, and spook speak. His announcement explained why she hadn't heard from Will. He'd been busy doing what the CIA does best – overthrowing governments. Except in this case, it was probably justified given everything she had read about the recent scandals. But what didn't make sense – yet – is why she was recruited to come here and pose as a magazine editor while she galivanted around town with a bunch of expats, none of whom were a threat to anyone. And she certainly wasn't a honeytrap. But was she a lure of some other kind? Were they hoping that "Chucho" and "Gordo" would contact her, or do something worse? Was Miguel murdered by a rival cartel or was this the work of the CIA? It made her brain hurt trying to put all these pieces together. She wanted to call him, but she hesitated. Too many questions were on her mind, and they would all remain unanswered. He wouldn't tell her anything and even if she put all the pieces together nobody would ever acknowledge that she had been involved in any way whatsoever. Exactly like Operation SHADOWHAWK. As she sat there staring at the iPhone, it suddenly rang.

"I just saw the news," she said when she answered.

"Well, then, I don't have to tell you what happened."

"So, is this the real reason you are in Malpaís? Don't bother answering if you're going to lie to me. What I'm curious about is why all the subterfuge, the phony magazine, and the way in which you lured me back here – to do what exactly?"

"Maya, the less you know, the better."

"Ah! I see, it's the old plausible deniability routine, eh? I'm not totally dense, you know. Considering my now deceased husband got involved with the cartel, whose leaders were systematically eliminated, I suppose it makes perfect sense that you used me in some capacity that I am unaware of. Am I right?"

"Right as rain. And that's all I'm going to say.

"Can you tell me who orchestrated this *golpe de es-*

tado? I'm assuming it was various branches of the U.S. government."

"Yes."

"Was there no opposition?"

"Who would oppose it? Remember, Malpaís is the only country in Central America with no military force whatsoever."

"And no latitude or longitude."

"Do you know why there has never been a military?"

"The party line is that they appropriated any money that would be spent maintaining a military and divert it to education and healthcare."

"Doesn't that sound idyllic? There's a more sinister reason."

"What?"

"For the last one hundred fifty years, one family has basically ruled this country. Yes, it's true there was nothing to protect, really. No threat of invasion because who would invade? This country didn't even wind up on a map until twenty years ago."

"Then what's the real reason?"

"The Alvarado family, who have been in power since the 1850s, decided if there was no military force, they could basically steal everything from the people and there could be no *golpe de estado*. With no military to do the dirty work, who was going to mount the overthrow? Landless peasants? Dairy farmers? Crumbs were thrown to the people to keep them happy – free health clinics, schools, even a public transportation system. Meanwhile, everything that could be stolen was stolen. And until now, with impunity. There will be a new Malpaís when there are legitimate elections. . ."

"And the U.S. approves the candidates," Maya interjected.

"Something like that. Now, can we change the subject to something more pleasant?"

"Such as?"

"Are you free this weekend?"

"What did you have in mind?"

"I could come up. We could take a little road trip, or we could stay in and enjoy each other's company."

"Well, alrighty then, William Balthazar Hastings. When should I expect you?"

"I've got loose ends to tie up here so probably can't get out of the city before Friday. I'll be there in the late afternoon. I have a Monday morning flight back to the U.S."

"*Hasta viernes.*"

Chapter 58

When Magdalena pranced into the house, Maya was already busy cleaning the kitchen, organizing the cupboards, and making lists of food she would need to buy at the Friday morning *feria.*

"*Por qué* you are so busy doing my chores this morning, Doña Maya?"

"I'm going to have a guest this weekend and I want everything to be perfect."

"Is this your *novio*?" Magda smiled mischievously.

"Not exactly."

"*Y por qué no*?"

"Oh, Magda. You know what I went through with Lucien. It was very traumatic, and it took me years to get my balance back. My guest is a very nice man, handsome, smart, *bien educado.* But. . . I admit that I am afraid."

"Of what?" Magda asked, placing her hands on her hips.

"I don't know exactly. Afraid of loss, afraid of commitment." Maya shrugged her shoulders.

Magda set her purse on the counter then took Maya by the hand and led her to the sofa. "*Siéntate*, Doña Maya. I must tell you about my great *tia*, who is now in the heavenly presence of our Lord."

"I would love to hear this story, Magda. What if I make a *cafecito* and we sit outside in this beautiful morning?"

"I will make it, Doña Maya. You go outside."

A few minutes later, Magda appeared with a tray bearing two cups of strong black coffee and a plate of dainty *galletas* left over from the celebration of life for her grandfather.

"*Entonces*, I will tell a story why you shouldn't be afraid of love. Tia Marina died when she had ninety-three years. She was my last great-aunt on my father's side. She taught me to knit, and she taught me the trade of female confidence. She used to tell me as a child everything about her secret love, the stolen kisses, and the quarrels of lovers. Unfortunately, she was supposed to be the one to take care of her parents until they died.

"When I was nine years old, one sunny afternoon in February, I saw her behind the church with a man unknown to me. She signaled something to me, but I didn't understand her, and I passed them swift and fast on my bike. When I got home, I told my mother and she told me that man was Tia Marina's *novio*, but nobody could say anything to her mother. By then they had been dating for fourteen years. His name was Lorenzo. He promised that when her mother died, they would marry. Unfortunately for my *tia*, her *mamita* was in unshakable health. Ten years passed and, finally, Doña

Úrsula died. The year of rigorous mourning passed, and my aunt put the subject of marriage back on the table and, this time, Lorenzo told her that they should wait for her father to die, an event, which according to him, was very close. The old man seemed related to Rasputin, he survived two heart attacks, a motorcycle run over, a broken leg that sent him to a wheelchair until the end of his days, and some bronchitis; he died at the tender age of ninety-nine. By then another eight years had passed.

"My aunt kept the year of mourning with a permanent smile because she could already see herself in the church dressed in white, the party in the beautiful garden of her house, with flowers, white tablecloths, glasses of champagne, dancing the waltz, and the honeymoon in Italy. She wanted to go to Rome to see the Pope. She told Lorenzo she would love to get married on July 16, the day of the Virgen del Carmen. Lorenzo, without looking at her, told her that his brother was very ill. *Mi tia* wouldn't let him finish, she looked at him full of anger and said: 'I hope a lightning bolt will strike you, coward.' Lorenzo died twenty-four years later, sad, and single. Tia Marina did not go to his funeral, but every Friday she brought a red rose to his grave, to her only love, and told him about the latest events in the family and in the town. She had spent half her life waiting for the right time to marry. Do not be like my *tia*. We only have so many opportunities for a beautiful love in our life. You deserve to have that, but you cannot be afraid or think you must wait for the perfect time. There is no perfect time. She was buried in a white box because she was a virgin, and a martyr, I would add. At her funeral, before the coffin was closed, I left a red rose in her hands, like her passionate heart that waited for love for thirty-three years."

Chapter 59

Friday morning, Maya flew out of bed eager to start her day and plan for Will's arrival in the afternoon. In the previous two days, she sent emails to the expats on her mailing list informing them that *Neotrópica* had published its last issue and that she was so grateful to all of them for their participation in its content over the last year and a half. She wished all of them a continuing wonderful experience as expats in Paradise. To Maybelle, she wrote a more personal email and suggested that they get together for lunch the following week at her convenience. When she hit the send button, she felt unbelievably liberated and unencumbered. Her mission, whatever it really was, had ended and she could go back to being Maya Warwick, and that meant she could choose her destiny.

After making a detailed list of all the items she needed to buy, she set off for San Pedro's Friday morning farmer's market. Admittedly, she bought way too much food, but she had a plan. And it did not involve going on a road trip. On her way home, she stopped at the liquor store and bought two bottles of Montepulciano wine, a bottle of Limoncello, a few *cervezas* and when she spied a bottle of Veuve Clicquot in the store's cooler, she bought that, too. As soon as she got home and unpacked the groceries, she started prepping and cooking. There would be a rack of lamb, a good Bolognese, lots of fresh fruit and vegetables, and she even made a loaf of sourdough bread that could go into the oven just before his arrival. The new shop in town also had a fabulous selection of French and Italian cheeses, so she stocked up on gorgonzola, parmesan Reggiano, and a very ripe brie. The last thing she had to make was a chocolate flourless tort. Then she was ready.

Her biggest dilemma was what to wear. Bleach-stained yoga pants and a rag of a tee-shirt would not do. She didn't want to be too gussied up, but she wanted to look her best. After trying on a few outfits, she settled on a pair of black silk pants and a cream-colored tunic embroidered with bead work around the neck. It was simple and elegant. She wore no jewelry except her gold coin earrings. Nervous didn't begin to describe what she was feeling as she awaited Will's arrival. Pacing like a caged animal she finally plopped herself down in the hammock to enjoy the shifting clouds. A few minutes later, his car pulled into the driveway, and she rushed to the terrace gate to greet him.

"Wow, you look unbelievably gorgeous. What have you done?"

"Well, for starters, I got those pesky expats, the crooks, creeps, and crazies, and that damn magazine out of my life. Now I have something to look forward to," she giggled. "Come on in."

Will eyed the *hors d'oeuvre* tray on the counter and the open bottle of Montepulciano. Two wine glasses delicately etched with 'Finca Azahar' and an orange blossom stood ready to be filled. "You've outdone yourself, but then I would expect nothing less of you." Setting his bag on the floor, he said, "Come here." Opening his arms wide, he pleaded, "Let me wrap my arms around you. I think we both need a hug after the stress of the last couple of weeks."

Maya fell into his embrace and let his arms encircle her so tightly she felt as if she had melted into him. It was a sensation she wasn't used to, but one that she had missed terribly.

"I've missed you, my little firefly," he purred against her fragrant neck.

Pushing him back slightly, she looked at him and exclaimed, "Wait! Why'd you call me that?"

"Uh, well, because fireflies generate their own light, just as you do, and because they represent hope and inspiration imploring us to listen to our hearts."

"That guy Bob Hamm referred to the regime change as Operation LUCIÉRNAGA. That's firefly in Spanish."

"Do you always ask so many questions?" he sighed, tightening his arms around her.

"You know I do. Come on, tell me."

"Okay, if you must know, the firefly was you, and that's all I'm going to say about that," he said softly, nuzzling her hair.

And there it was. She had been an integral part of the operation, manipulated in ways she would never fully know or understand. But what did it matter now? Even though there would always be a shroud of secrecy consisting of things Will could never share with her, at this moment in time, she was content to be in his embrace. After all she had endured – the losses, the disappointments, the challenges, she had finally arrived at a place where she felt safe. Safe to feel, and safe to love again. All the traumatic events of her life were now far behind her. She had conquered all of them and emerged a stronger, more determined woman, and she was proud of that. It was no easy task, but now that she was embarking on a new period of her life, she was hopeful for the future. And that was more than she could say five years ago.

Chapter 60

It had been a beautiful weekend and all the effort Maya put into the preparation paid off. They had a wonderful two days, lounging on the terrace, sleeping late, gorging themselves on all the delicious food, and most importantly, relishing each other's company. It was uncomplicated and blissful, but Maya still had reservations. About what, she wasn't sure. Maybe because an uncomplicated relationship was the antithesis to her relationship with Lucien. She had to check herself constantly because she was looking for clues of deceit and betrayal. When she found none, she felt guilty for assigning those characteristics to a man who seemed to be without guile. However, that didn't make any sense because guile was an integral part of his job description.

Sunday morning, over a leisurely breakfast of sourdough pancakes and homemade sausage, Will suggested a drive. "I haven't had the luxury of seeing very much of this country, and I know you have some secret spots. Such as that wonderful hot springs we went to last time."

Maya thought for a minute. "We could go to Lago Azul. It's about a half hour from here, a gorgeous spot, like an alpine lake and there are nice spots for a picnic. I'll pack up some food and we can head out."

They had the lake to themselves. It was quiet, pristine, and as picturesque as any lake in Italy or Switzerland. They walked a few hundred yards around its edge and found a flat spot under the shade of an oak tree, spread the blankets, and uncorked a bottle of wine. For an hour they lay in silence, listening intently to the symphony of nature and the rustle of leaves in the gentle breeze.

Will turned on his side, propped himself up on his elbow, and stared into Maya's eyes. "Do you think you would ever want to live in Alexandria? With me? My father has a lovely cottage on his estate that was modeled after Marie Antoinette's Petit Trianon. You would love it."

Maya looked at him with surprise. "Oh, Will," she sighed, rising to give him a quick kiss. "As tempting as that sounds, I don't think I can go anywhere right now. I'm stuck with a house in Provence and the house here. Besides, I've been mulling over an idea for another book, which I'm anxious to start now that my indentured servitude to an unnamed alphabet agency has ended." *Using all the documentation Kendall left me in that secret file.*

"Would you at least think about it?"

"Of course, I will. But I need time. Let's see where this goes. Oh, no, look," she said, pointing to the horizon. "Those clouds are building. We'd best get on the road because we don't want to get caught in one of these sudden storms."

Monday morning, they were up early. Will packed his bag and set it near the door. His flight wasn't until mid-afternoon, but he had details to wrap up in Santa Lucia. For so many reasons, he was hesitant about saying goodbye. He took Maya in his arms, held her close to him for a good, long minute, and then kissed her on the lips. "I've got to go. I don't want to, but I have no choice."

"I understand. Do what you have to do," Maya said, detecting a subtle shift in Will's energy. "I'm not going anywhere, so you know where to find me." She wanted to add "if you're sincere," but she kept it to herself. "Have a safe trip home."

She stood in the driveway and watched him drive away. He didn't look back. Her emotions were all over the place and she was trying to make sense of what she felt intuitively. Something was different. Something had changed. . . over night. The way he kissed her goodbye had an air of finality. After a full weekend of tenderness and intimacy, their farewell felt so terribly ordinary, like two good friends instead of the entangled lovers that they had become. Boundaries had been blurred, emotions she hadn't felt in years had been rekindled, but now as he drove out of sight, she felt oddly untethered. *Maybe he had a lot on his mind*, she said to herself. After all, orchestrating a *golpe de estado* was a complicated matter even in this tiny pineapple republic. But it was more than that. Because of their complexity she was incapable of putting her feelings into words, but on a deep emotional level she knew things had shifted. And they would never go back to where they once were.

With little incentive to do anything, she crawled into the hammock, gazing across the valley before shifting her focus to the perfect volcanoes and the serene place between them. Her head churned with ideas for the new book and thanks to Kendall, may he rest in peace, all the research she needed was stashed in that bottom dresser drawer and, as an extra precaution, on a thumb drive. After lunch and a nap, she would get it out and think about how to organize it into something that would astound her agent and her readers.

Two hours later, as she lay between the sheets that still bore Will's scent, rather than finding it comforting, it irritated her. Leaping out of bed, she stripped off the sheets and threw them in the washer. This simple act signified the beginning of a new phase of her life. Her first task was to focus on the book, after which she could think about selling the house in Provence and staying here at Finca Azahar permanently.

She crouched down and opened the secret drawer, relishing the idea of poring over the research that Kendall had so meticulously gathered. Research that had gotten him killed, either by the Lobos Locos cartel or . . . the CIA? *Oh no*, she thought to herself, *I don't want to even entertain that scenario*. She owed it to Kendall to use his research wisely. Setting aside the facing piece, she pulled out the bottom part and was so stunned by what she saw that she let out a yelp. Kendall's research was *gone*. It was there two days ago when she added a document to her property file. Leaning back against the foot of the bed, she buried her face in her hands. Is that why he wanted to go for a drive yesterday? So someone could sneak into my house and steal that information? That had to be what happened because Will was never out of her sight long enough from Friday afternoon until Monday to have done it himself. But why? Hadn't they already accessed that file? After a few thoughtful minutes, she knew. Of course. It was to make sure she didn't have any sensitive information that may have been contained in those papers.

After the initial surprise wore off, she laughed. "*Touché*, Will. Nice try," she said, getting up from the floor, "but you underestimated me." She went into the laundry room and reached for the bag of flour stashed in the back of the cupboard. Trying not to make a mess, she stuck her hand in the bag and carefully removed a Ziploc bag, wiping the flour against her pant leg. There, wrapped with tape, was her insurance policy: the thumb drive onto which she scanned Kendall's research. Apparently, the ever-so-bright spooks had neglected to put surveillance cameras in that space. *The joke's on you, Will.* With the thumb drive in her pocket, she pranced to the living room and grabbed the iPhone. There was a thing or two she wanted to say to him. Was their weekend together nothing more than a ruse to get that file? Of course, it was. Especially when she factored in the insipid, dispassionate kiss he gave her as he was leaving. He was only doing his job. She was his asset. And his task was to do whatever was necessary to secure her cooperation, even if it meant feigning amorous interest. The funny thing was, she wasn't the least bit distraught. Or disappointed. She'd been paid handsomely for her participation in this charade, and another fringe benefit was that it had provided interesting encounters she might never have had. Meeting some of the characters who flocked to this Central American Paradise was a bonus and every single one of them would find their way into the next book.

She hit Will's name on speed dial and waited. The call didn't go through, so she tried again. This time, she got a recorded message: "The number you have reached is no longer in service." Her heart lurched. Events of the last year and a half scrolled through her head. *Yep. I was played. And now he ghosted me.* With her role now ended, she was of no use to the CIA, or to Will, whose voracious appetite for betrayal knew no bounds. More importantly, was William Balthazar Hastings even his real name? For a few fleeting seconds, she was afflicted with a sense of derealization and disconnect from the life she had lived for the last eighteen months. It suddenly felt very dreamlike but then it became brilliantly pellucid. Sighing deeply, she tossed the iPhone into a drawer, and slammed it shut, signifying a ceremonious end to her involvement with whatever-his-name-was and Operation FIREFLY. It took a few minutes to gain her equilibrium and then she smiled, thinking to herself, "I could have never dreamed up anything as intricate or insidious as this assignment, so in the end, it was a fantastic gift. And it's all going to be part of the book about the last undiscovered Paradise on an isthmus between two oceans."

Acknowledgement

You probably think this book is about you, don't you....

And it may well be. Especially if you live on the isthmus.

I owe a profound debt of gratitude to all the people who either unwittingly or willingly contributed to this work by providing me with anecdotes, historical perspective, comments, quips, or their own personal experiences or those of their friends or relatives about life on the isthmus. I forgot some names, and for that I apologize. That doesn't mean your contribution was less important, only that after eighteen years of compiling information and then weaving it into a narrative, I often couldn't discern if it was a figment of my imagination or if someone told it to me. Here are those names I do remember, and to whom I am forever grateful for your friendship which has enriched my lfe on this piece of dried bologna:

Sheldon Haseltine, who inspired the character Bentley Beresford and who over the years shared endless anecdotes about the culture of crime in Paradise; Christopher Lopez, who inspired the character William Balthazar Hastings, and who taught me about mongooses; Linda Rochford Gray, whose *ojitos* were invaluable, together with the stories about that famous valley; Hillary Avenali Cash, who provided tales about those dirty hippies; Alejandra Campos, who graciously allowed me to include her Tia Marina's love story; Daniel Ruiz T., whose article about *Campesinos* was absolutely brilliant; Robert Bacon aka Bob Hamm, who continues to provide me with information bout financial crimes and threat assessments; Grettel Barboza Herrera, whose insights and perspectives about life inspired the character Magdelena Sanchez; Victor Brown, whose humor and insights are unparalled; Roger Gonzalez Serrano, who made the observation about living between the door to Heaven or Hell; Andrew Mastrandonas, who really did have a list titled Crooks, Creeps, and Crazies; Brian Code, who knows a thing or two about emus; Stephen Duplantier, who created the real magazine *Neotropica* for which I was the senior editor, and his wife Ghislaine Yergeau, who inspired the character of Madeleine, and yes, they really do have peacocks; Mark Drolette, who has been my sounding board, emotional support, and lifeline since I first set foot on the isthmus, and who allowed me to make fun of his Viagra-blue house with balls; and John Edward Heaton, who knows better than anyone about perils of life in an undiscovered Paradise on the isthmus.

Thank you all from the bottom of my heart.

Other Books by

Roan St. John

Blind Reason

A novel of pharmaceutical intrigue

No Good Deed

A fracture fairy tale

Between Volcanoes

Love and revenge on the isthmus

If you enjoyed this book, please leave a short review on Amazon. Reviews, even a line or two, are important tools for every author.

Made in the USA
Middletown, DE
07 March 2023

26333357R00208